Rock Black

About the author

M. G. Sanchez is a Gibraltarian writer based in the UK. He attended Bayside Comprehensive School and later studied English at the University of Leeds, obtaining a doctorate in the subject in 2004. He has spoken about his writing at different university venues across Europe. For more information about his books, please visit:

www.facebook.com/mgsanchezwriter

or

www.mgsanchez.net/.

Rock Black

Ten Gibraltarian Stories

M. G. Sanchez

Rock Scorpion Books
2008

ISBN-10: 0-9552465-3-9
ISBN-13: 978-0-9552465-3-1

Other books by M. G. Sanchez:

Novels

Solitude House

Jonathan Gallardo

The Escape Artist

Short Stories

Diary of a Victorian Colonial and other Tales

Non-Fiction

Bombay Journal

Past: A Memoir

The Prostitutes of Serruya's Lane and other Hidden Gibraltarian Histories

Historical Anthologies

Georgian and Victorian Gibraltar: Incredible Eyewitness Accounts

Writing the Rock of Gibraltar: An Anthology of Literary Texts, 1720-1890

Note

I have tried to use names that sound Gibraltarian in this book. Any resemblance to actual persons, living or dead, is entirely coincidental.

The Spanish that people speak in Gibraltar is very different from that spoken in mainland Spain. I have endeavoured to reflect this on the odd occasions I have used Spanish in the text.

M.G.S.

1. Dago Droppings

By Gibraltarian standards, he was a corpulent man. About fifty-five years old, I'd have said, with a thick, bristly moustache and the stretched, tea-coloured skin of your typical Costa del Sol expat. He was dressed in a black cotton T-shirt and a pair of cargo shorts, originally khaki-coloured but now covered with innumerable smudges of grease, from the belt of which hung an electronic measuring tape and an old FM transceiver with the initials S. K. written across it in cuneiform streaks of Tippex. Probably a building surveyor, I thought from the other side of the bar. Or maybe a civil engineer. Not the quiet, office-bound type, that was pretty clear — but the kind who likes to rough it out with the rest of the crew. Your disgruntled English white-collar type, in other words. Equally dexterous with mallet or laptop computer. You know: the sort that wears his half-moon spectacles on a chain around his neck, but likes the smell of sweat wafting from his standard-issue flannel shirt.

'Excuse me, luv,' our moustachioed friend suddenly said to the barmaid. 'What am I supposed to do with them lot?'

He opened his hand to reveal a small heap of loose change. From the holes punctured in one or two of the coins, I could tell that they were pesetas.

'You want your change in sterling?' the barmaid muttered as she noisily chewed some gum.

'If you please, luv. Can't do much in Gib with these dago droppings, can I?'

Dago droppings. Quite a striking phrase, you'll have to admit. Racism, scatology and hints of comedy all rolled in one. Wrapped up in a conveniently alliterative package too. Sheer linguistic wonder.

'Can I ask you a question?' I suddenly said from across the room. 'Do you have any idea where the word 'dago' comes from?'

'What?' the surveyor asked, turning around. 'What was that?'

'A dago,' I repeated, swallowing hard. 'Do you know where the word comes from?'

The surveyor shook his head slowly, meditatively — like a provoked gunslinger in a cowboy saloon. 'A dago?' he finally spat out the words, obviously unsure what it was I had asked him. 'That's a spic, innit, mate? A wop, a greaser, a filthy, backstabbing, lazy little Spaniard, that's what a dago is.'

'You may be shocked to hear this,' I said, swallowing even harder, 'but the word "dago" traces its origins to the reign of Mary I — when a Spaniard by the name of Diego (or "Dago", as his name came to be mispronounced) allegedly defecated on the high altar at Saint Paul's Cathedral. The incident is mentioned in a play by Thomas Dekker and also in one written collaboratively by Dekker and John Webster. Although, if you ask me, I believe that the story in question is ... well ... sort of a bit ... well ... apocryphal ... if you know what I mean ... you know what I mean, don't you?'

Clearly the surveyor wasn't amused. You could tell from the way his eyes had widened and his nostrils had dilated. If that wasn't enough, his right fist had suddenly clenched itself by his side — rather like a mechanical claw retracting into the closed position.

'Are you trying to be funny, mate?' the surveyor said, standing up from his stool. 'Cos if you are, you picked the wrong man to be funny with.'

I looked at him across the smoky, ill-lit space that separated us and guessed he was about six feet. Maybe six foot two. At least half a foot taller than myself, to put things into their proper perspective.

'I'm not trying to be funny,' I quickly mumbled back, by now sorely regretting my attempt to broaden the guy's etymological knowledge. 'I'm just ... well ... you know ... curious about these kinds of things ... you know what I mean.'

'Curious, are you now?' the surveyor replied, exposing a row of fledgling stalactites under his hirsute upper lip. 'Well, you know what they say about curiosity, don't you, mate?'

I looked at him and then looked down at the half-drunk beer in front of me. Just my luck, I thought. Betrayed by my big mouth again. What could be more typical? Peter Rodriguez comes down to the Packhorse to anaesthetise his romantic and academic failings and there he is about to get socked by a racist boor. If that was the case — and I was pretty damn sure that it was — I decided that I might as well let him know what I thought about his dago droppings. Go tell the idiot to shove some Anglo-Saxon suppositories up his ass or something equally retaliatory and stupid!

'Listen, matey,' I finally said, puffing out my chest in the wonderfully reckless manner of someone who knows he's going to get clobbered one way or the other. 'I don't give a shit about what happened to the cat or what you think about my bleeding curiosity — right? I just didn't like the phrase you used before — *dago droppings*! Who the hell do you English think you are? What makes you so superior to the rest of us? What's your goddamned bloody problem?'

I closed my eyes real tight and waited for the bastard to hit me. I waited and waited and waited — with my eardrums on the verge of exploding and the fear of God about to plop out into my pants — but nothing happened. Nothing. Not even a mild expletive or a grunt of disapproval. Instead — silence. Pure, unremitting silence — prescribed by professional torturers the world over as the best tool for dislocating common fantasies of immortality. Finally, after what seemed like an eternity's worth of silence, I began to hear a soft, hissing sound — kind of like air escaping out of a battered old tyre. Realising that something wasn't quite right, I slowly opened one eye and saw the surveyor clutching his stomach, his features swollen and purple, victim to one of those silent attacks of laughter that leave you desperately floundering for breath.

'What's ... what's wrong?' I eventually asked in a puzzled whisper.

'Did you hear that by any chance, Tommy-Boy?' the surveyor muttered between gasps to the person behind him. 'Did you hear what our friend here just said?'

I leaned to one side and saw that Tommy-Boy was a prematurely aged man of sixty or sixty-five. Most definitely English. You could tell from the whisky-bags under his eyes and the crumpled orange tan that stretched like an ill-fitting pair of nylon tights around his head. Walk into any Main Street pub and you'll see plenty of the same type — swapping dirty jokes, smoking rollies, talking about lorry driving on the M1 or playing darts with their mates back in Blighty. English to the core of their beer-fuelled souls.

'Jesus H. Christ,' the surveyor finally said, still extremely purple in the face, 'you really are a funny guy. I mean real funny, like. Most Gibraltarians I know, hell, they consider themselves so British you'd think they were related to the Queen or something. Mention one good word about the Spanish and the little fuckers go ape-shit on you. Know what I'm getting at, Tommy-Boy? Like Pepe down at Coaling Island. Jesus, have you heard that guy harp on about the Spanish royal family and the Spanish Prime Minister and the rest of that twaddle. And yet this kid here takes offence because I said something about them dago droppings. What's wrong with you, boyo? Aren't you a *British Gibraltarian* like the rest of them? Or do you by any chance regard yourself as a piece of filthy dago scum?'

'If your question is whether I consider myself Spanish,' I replied in a much more fierce and determined tone than before, 'my answer is: No, I don't consider myself Spanish at all.'

'There you go, then,' he said, winking in Tommy-Boy's direction. 'Nothing to worry about. If you consider yourself British like the rest of them, then you're all right, aren't you?'

This was clearly too much of a provocation to be left unchallenged. 'So what you're, in effect, implying,' I said, 'is that, even though Gibraltarians *consider* themselves British, they are about as close to true Britishness as Morris dancing is to bullfighting or paella-making?'

'That's not what I said, mate.'

'Let me ask you something,' I continued in spite of the uncomfortably defensive look on his face. 'What do *you* yourself consider Gibraltarians to be? Be honest now. Do you see them as proper British citizens ... or as English-speaking, slightly upmarket versions of your average ordinary everyday dago?'

The surveyor cocked back his head for a moment and then turned to the old man. 'Do you hear that, Tommy-Boy? Do you consider Gibraltarians dagos?'

Tommy-Boy carried on smiling blankly without answering.

'No, my friend,' the surveyor all of a sudden said, 'I wouldn't say Gibbos are dagos. If they was, I wouldn't have married meself a Gibbo girl in the first place, would I?'

'You're married to a local girl?' I asked, almost reeling at the revelation.

'Still, Swankie,' Tommy-Boy suddenly croaked, 'you must admit that they are *quite Spanish* in a lot of ways.'

'Fifteen years, mate,' the surveyor carried on in spite of the interruption. 'There's me kid over the road to prove it. That little fella playing football with the other little 'uns over there.'

I looked out of the window and saw three kids playing football with a squashed Coke can. Two of them wore Manchester United shirts and the third had an Aston Villa top tied around his neck. They were all very tanned and scrawny, with masses of curly black hair bouncing upon their shoulders and little golden studs gleaming in their ears. Typical Gibraltarian kids, I thought to myself. Seeing them made me remember what I had come to the Packhorse to forget: my ex-girlfriend back in the UK and her recent cleaving of my colonial heart. If I had still been a student at the University of Manchester, I now sadly reflected, we would have been like this guy and his wife in reverse — an Englishwoman with a Gibraltarian man. Pathetic though the thought was, it almost brought tears to my eyes.

'*For starters, they all like olives ...*'

'Which one's him?'

'*... and octopus ...*'

'The one who's kicking the can now.'

'*... and dancing seviyanas or whatever you call that horrible fucked-up flamenco shit ...*'

'How old is he?'

'*... and going to Il Cortay Inglay store in Marbella ...*'

'He'll be ten in a couple of weeks.'

'*... not to mention that every single Gibbo speaks Spanish exactly like they do in La Línea across the border.*'

'Leave it out, Tommy-Boy, will you?' the surveyor suddenly said, turning with some irritation towards the old man. 'I'm trying to have a conversation with me friend here, aren't I?'

'No, no, no,' I pleaded on Tommy-Boy's behalf. 'Don't shut him up. He's right about most of the things he's said, after all, aren't you, Tommy-Boy? Although I wouldn't go as far as to compare Gibraltarian Spanish to the kind spoken in La Línea. That's a bit too much. To someone from Madrid, for example, it may sound similar — that's true enough. But ask anyone from Andalusia and they'll tell you it's totally different. "*Joder*," they'd say, "that's not like Spanish at all." The truth — and I am sure that anyone in La Línea could tell you this — is that Gibraltarian Spanish is even less formal than anything they're accustomed to in Southern Spain. Gibraltarians, you see, don't just remove one or two letters from their endings like the Andalusians do; we lop whole syllables off. Reduce words to their barest essence, if you like. It is similar to the sort of Spanish spoken in some parts of Latin America, I've been told. Especially to Uruguayan Spanish.'

'Gibbo Spanish similar to Uruguayan?' the surveyor said, winking at the old man. 'You learn something new every day, don't you, Tommy-Boy?'

'I don't know what he's on about, Swankie,' Tommy-Boy said to the surveyor without even looking at me. 'But even if he's right — and Gibraltarian is nearer to bloody Uruguayan than to bloody Spanish — he won't deny that most *British Gibraltarians* can't even speak proper English, like. That's pretty bloody obvious, wouldn't you say, Swanks?'

I took a quick sip of my beer and belched under my breath. Putting my pint glass on a San Miguel beer mat, I turned to face the old man:

'First, let me make one thing clear. I haven't said Gibraltarian Spanish is closer to Uruguayan Spanish than Spanish Spanish; I've only said it *sounds closer* to it. Is that clear? Secondly, if you don't mind me saying so, I think that what you've just said about Gibraltarians not being able to speak proper English is a load of rubbish. Okay, I accept that unless you're some rich, stuck-up snob who lives in Sotogrande and plays polo every weekend, you will, if you're local, have an accent. That I do agree with. But that doesn't mean to say that those of us who speak English in this way have no command of the damn language. That's just ridiculous! Look at yourself, for example, Tommy-Boy. You have quite a strong West Country accent, haven't you? Where are you from — Plymouth, Exeter, Bristol? Let me ask you this: how would you feel if someone turned around and said you weren't speaking proper English because you spoke with a strong Plymouthian accent? Pretty pissed off, I bet.'

'What about all those locals who get interviewed on GBC or whatever they call that poxy little TV channel of theirs?' Tommy-Boy addressed me directly now for the first time. 'You must have seen them before. Policemen, firemen, shop managers. Can't speak a bloody word of English, the lot of them. "Because, you know, we cannot do that, you know, it would not be right, you know, it would be very bad, you know what I mean." Are you going to tell me that all those fine fellows have been to Oxford and speak the Queen's bloody English as well, like?'

'Okay, okay — so maybe there is a percentage of people here who have trouble *speaking* English. I won't deny that. But that doesn't mean to say that they are as thick or incompetent as you seem to imply. You see, Tommy-Boy, in bilingual societies people sometimes undergo what is known as a process of linguistic compartmentalisation. In other words, they use language in a ...'

'Did you hear that Swankie, my man?' Tommy-Boy interrupted me with a quiet chuckle. 'A process of linguistic compartmentalisation! This kid could give the Chief Minister a right run for his money, couldn't he? Next thing you know, he'll start arguing that tobacco smugglers are the most important pillar of the Gibraltarian economy or something!'

I raised my pint glass to my lips and held it there for some seconds. Through the concave windows in the interior of the glass, a dozen Tommy-Boys smirked at me in mocking unison, elongated and bloated, grotesquely out of focus.

'Take it easy, kid,' the surveyor suddenly said, perhaps sensing my growing resentment towards the old man. 'Tommy-Boy doesn't mean no offence, do you, Tommy-Boy?'

'Sure, kid,' Tommy-Boy said. 'Carry on. Tell us about this process of linguistic competition or whatever you call it. We're all dying to hear you, like.'

'It's very simple,' I resumed after a short pause. 'All it means is that people in bilingual cultures will sometimes use one language for speaking, and another for writing or thinking. That is what happens in Gibraltar, more or less. Many of those who have trouble speaking in English probably write better than most Englishmen.'

I picked up my drink again and took another long swig, closing my eyes for a moment as the acrid taste of cheap lager gushed down my throat. Out of the corner of my eye, I saw Tommy-Boy shake his head and look away.

'That was quite a lecture,' the surveyor said moments later. 'You're very much into this sort of thing, aren't you?'

'Into what?' I asked.

'Bilingualism and all that palaver.'

'No, not really,' I replied with an awkward effort at a self-effacing grin. 'I'm just curious about things.'

'You should talk to our kid,' he said, nodding over to where his son was playing across the road. 'He's always chatting in *Llanito* at home — or whatever you call that crazy mixture of Spanish and English you guys speak. I've told him to speak more in English, but he just doesn't listen.'

I thought there was a hint of regret in his voice. I don't think it was regret in its purest and truest form — that is to say, the kind that claws daily at your conscience and continually consumes your insides — but a softer, less intense type of regret, the sort that creeps up on you every now and then, that intrudes upon the happiness of the current moment with the thought of what could have been had things turned out slightly different. It reminded me of a story I had once read by Robert Louis Stevenson. It was about a hardened old sea-dog who settled down with a mulatto woman somewhere in the tropics. Wiltshire or Wilson, I think his name was. Left to bring up his daughter on his own after the premature death of his mulatto wife, he comes to the conclusion that he does not really like half-castes that much

— but at the same time realises that the girl is all he has left in the world and loves her accordingly. In other words, he decides to readjust his priorities — even though he still wonders from time to time how things would have shaped up had he never married a mulatto woman in the first place....

'He'll be all right,' I finally said, trying hard not to sound patronising. 'I'm sure he will.'

The surveyor looked at me in silence for some moments and then smiled rather wistfully. Meanwhile, Tommy-Boy got up from his stool and began to stagger in my direction. He came with a drunken leer on his face, obviously not quite done yet for the night.

'Excuse me, you,' he bellowed out just yards from where I was sitting. 'What's your name? I didn't quite catch it before.'

'My name's Peter. What's yours?'

'I don't mean your first name,' he rasped out irately. 'I mean your surname. What's your surname?'

'Rodriguez. My surname's Rodriguez.'

'Rodriguez?' he said, his eyes widening with glee. 'That sure is a nice name you got there, partner. *A real nice name.* What is it you do for a living, Mr. Peter Rodriguez?'

'I'm sort of ... well ... I'm kind of looking for a job.'

Tommy-Boy turned back to his younger mate. 'Did you hear that, Swanks? The kid here don't have no job. Awful shame, innit? Real awful shame. Why don't you offer him a job at the welders' hut? We could do with a few more Gibbos down at the yard, don't you think? Them Moroccans know bugger-all about making a decent cup of char.'

'What do you want from me?' I asked.

'I just wanted to ask you a question, my lad,' he said. 'Nothing complex, like — just a small matter that needs a little clarification, if you know what I'm saying. You see, while you was talking before, I couldn't help noticing you spoke real good English. I mean, *for a local boy at least,* it was real good. You still have an accent when you speak, of course. That's part and parcel of the way you guys talk, like. But it was so small, well, that it was almost not noticeable.'

'And?'

'Well, it made me wonder whether you've been studying in the UK or something. You know, been to college and all that shite.'

'Yes, Tommy-Boy. I went to college for a while.'

'And what degree did you take while there, if I may ask?'

'I didn't take a degree,' I responded with my hand wrapped firmly around my glass. 'I quit my course after a year.'

'*Did you now?*'

'Yes.'

'And was that recently by any chance?'

I nodded.

'And was it during that year that they taught you all them things?' he said as he walked back to his seat, by now almost panting with malicious excitement. 'You know, how Gibraltarian Spanish is closer to Uruguayan Spanish than Spanish Spanish and how everyone in Gibraltar speaks real good English, like? I mean, is that where you got all them ideas from?'

I shook my head and put my glass down. 'Let me tell you something about my time in England, Tommy-Boy,' I said. 'Before I travelled there, I was your typical pro-British, anti-Spanish Gibraltarian. You know — the kind you regularly see on GBC and whom you obviously find so endearing. That was the way I had been brought up, you see. From the age of four I supported Liverpool football club and the England national football team, and I had a scrapbook in which I kept newspaper cuttings of all their triumphs in Europe. I was simply obsessed by them. But if there was one thing which matched my passion for Liverpool and England, that was my hatred of Real Madrid and the Spanish national football team. That was much stronger. And I mean *much, much* stronger. When Spain lost the European Nations Cup final to France in 1984, I didn't sleep for two nights out of sheer happiness. And when Real Madrid lost five-nil to AC Milan in the European Cup in 1986 I literally cried tears of joy. That's how *British Gibraltarian* I was during those days, Tommy-Boy.'

'Then you went to England to study,' the old man butted in, 'and discovered that no one gave a flying fuck about little Gibraltar? Is that what you're trying to tell us here?'

'Not exactly,' I replied in a much calmer voice. 'You see, Tommy-Boy, in a funny kind of way I *already knew that*. When I was a kid I spent six months in England while my father was doing a mechanic's course. I got bullied there really badly by the other English kids. Dago, spic, wop, greaser — I was called every term of abuse you could possibly think of to describe a southern European. I guess I had every reason to be 'anti-English' by the time I returned to Gibraltar. I mean, I had been insulted, humiliated, regularly beaten-up. But for some reason I didn't feel like that. I can't really say why. Maybe it was because I loved English football so much. Or maybe it was because I was just an eleven-year-old kid and kids have this wonderful ability to move on without continuously poking their doubts and uncertainties into the events of the past — I don't know. Anyway, the years passed and I got a scholarship from the Gibraltar government to go and study in England. It was a big day for me, that — one of the great 'milestones' in my life. Some people, I'm sure, would have had second thoughts about going back to the place where they had been badly bullied as children — but I certainly didn't. I was genuinely excited, really keyed up. I had heard so much from some of my older mates who were already there — how easy it was to pull English girls, how they and their mates were always going out drinking and clubbing together. The thought of me being unable to settle down just didn't cross my mind. Why shouldn't I, after all? I mean, I felt British. Maybe not British English like you are, Tommy-Boy, but certainly *British Gibraltarian*. I watched *Match of the Day* every Saturday, my father bought the *Daily Mail* most mornings, my mother did her shopping at Marks and Sparks. Never for one minute did I doubt my status as a British Gibraltarian. And I really mean that. A few little incidents had happened here and there, of course — but nothing that could remotely be described as disrupting. Once, when I was sixteen, for example, this drunken Royal Navy sailor came up to me in what used to be the old Buccaneers down by the Naval Ground and told me that *I was a Spanish shit and I would remain a Spanish shit for the rest of my life.* That sort of thing. Nothing too greatly upsetting, I'm sure you'll agree — considering that, almost without exception, all these provocations came from English squaddies and sailors who were pissed up to their eyeballs.'

'Is that when it all kicked in?' Tommy-Boy said without any trace of sarcasm. 'When you went back to England a second time?'

I looked down into my pint glass and nodded. 'Yeah, that's when it happened. Right from the day I got asked where I was from. "Gibraltar?" they'd all say, staring at me blankly. "Where's that?" Or, if not, the other typical response: "Oh, yeah. Gibraltar. That's somewhere near Benidorm, innit? Great part of Spain, that. One of my mates went down there last year and had a real laugh...." Funny, isn't it? Absolutely bloody hilarious. You spend all your schooldays being told to be proud of your *British Gibraltarian* identity and then you go to the UK and find out that everyone takes you for a flamenco-dancing bullfighting aficionado who's also a dab hand at playing the castanets. In a way, I guess that I should have been half-expecting it. Especially after my experience in Pontefract nine years earlier. Still, it is one thing to be told that you're "a dirty little greaser" when you're eleven and another to be laughed at as an adult for simply stating the nationality stamped on your passport, don't you think? Unfortunately, though, the matter didn't end there. You see, Tommy-Boy, when I tried to "get in" with my "fellow Britons" I found that they didn't want to know. As simple as that — they just didn't want to know. I was snubbed, ignored, ostracised — call it what you will. It was almost a case of history repeating itself. Apart from a certain member of the female species — who only a few days back, I should perhaps add, broke my heart via a long-distance telephone call — no one cared who I was or where I came from. That's how it went. In their eyes I was a Spaniard and that was that.... Two things happened then. First, something broke inside me that should have broken all those years before but somehow didn't. I can't explain what it was exactly, but I could feel it snap inside me. You know, like a spring snaps in a watch or something. Second, I realised that the term "British Gibraltarian" is the biggest bloody joke going.'

I stopped talking and looked at Tommy-Boy. He was sitting there with his hands interlaced, his whisky glass nestled in the hollow space between them. He seemed to be mulling things over.

'Well, what can I say?' he said at last, shrugging his shoulders in an expression that was not exactly devoid of sympathy. 'Life's a bitch, innit?'

I shook my head and picked up my pint glass, this time smiling at the thought that the old boy was finally on my side. Just then the surveyor's kid burst in through the pub's entrance. He weaved in and out of the tables and chairs and ran up to his father. It was patently obvious to anyone watching that the kid was the surveyor's son. He was big-boned and substantially less athletic than the gangly prepubescent that I had first taken him for, a smaller, duskier version of his stocky North European progenitor. Also, in spite of the shiny olive colour of his tan, I noticed that he had the same pale, wispy, curling eyebrows as his dad. A living, breathing miracle of Anglo-Gibraltarian miscegenation.

'Dad, Dad, Dad, Dad,' the kid shouted out excitedly in a very pronounced London accent. 'Can I have a packet of Wotsits, Dad? Can I?'

The scene amused me considerably. 'I thought you said he always spoke *Llanito*,' I said.

'I was lying, wasn't I?' the surveyor answered me with a devilish wink. 'He speaks a bit of the old Cockney just like his Dad, don't you, Gav?'

'Yes, Dad,' the kid said wearily. 'Whatever you say, Dad. Can I have a packet of Wotsits, Dad?'

'Another one?' the surveyor replied with a pained expression on his face. 'But you've already had three today!'

'But I'm *hungry*, Dad! You know that I am, Dad!'

The surveyor turned towards the old man. 'What do you say, Tommy-Boy? Do you think we should buy the little ruffian another packet of Wotsits or not?'

'Why not?' Tommy-Boy replied. 'He's a growing lad, in't he?'

'You're a lucky little rascal,' the surveyor said, playfully ruffling his son's hair. 'If your mum knew how badly I spoil you, she'd murder me!'

He tweaked his son's cheek and bought him a packet of Wotsits. The boy immediately took a large handful of crisps and began to force them into his mouth, scattering little orange crumbs on the bright red polyester of his football top and the thick brown carpet underfoot.

'Easy, Tiger,' the surveyor barked affectionately from his stool. 'Make sure you don't choke on them!'

'Don't worry, Dad,' the kid replied, holding the empty packet between his thumb and forefinger as if it were a dead mouse. 'I've already finished them!'

With these words the surveyor's son dropped the empty packet into an ashtray and ran out of the bar. All eyes in the Packhorse watched him as he dashed away, laughing and singing to himself as he hurtled through the swinging louvre doors. 'That's a fine boy you got there,' Tommy-Boy said while the doors continued rattling. Someone else in the room agreed. For a second the surveyor gazed at his son through one of the windows — his brow contracted in thought, the tips of his moustache quivering ever so slightly. Then he turned around with a grin and said, 'Gentlemen, allow me to buy you both a drink.'

2. Harry Pozo and the Brazilian Prostitute

Harry Pozo was nineteen years old when he discovered he was seriously ill. He was sitting in a small room in Saint Benedict's hospital, staring at a middle-aged doctor reading his notes beside a window. Through the window a rather unusual view of Gibraltar town could be seen: a crumbling collection of Victorian rooftops and terraces, stretching all the way from *Los Espinillos* down to the eighteenth-century sea ramparts.

'I'm sorry, Mr. Pozo,' the doctor suddenly said, looking up from the papers spread on his desk, 'but from what this is saying it looks like bad news.'

'Bad news?' Harry said.

'Yes, I'm afraid so, Mr. Pozo. The blood tests indicate that you have a high number of white blood cells. You also have an abnormally low amount of platelets in your blood.'

'I don't understand you, doctor. What are you trying to say?'

The doctor coughed and looked down. 'What I'm trying to say, Mr. Pozo, is that we will have to conduct some more tests over the next few days. Essentially, to determine whether you're suffering from the first stages of leukaemia. I will be making a recommendation later on this afternoon so that they admit you to hospital as a priority case. You should report to Admissions on Monday at eight o'clock in the morning, Mr. Pozo. Your ward and bed number will be allocated to you then.'

Now, if anyone else had been sitting in that doctor's room, this news would have come as quite a shock. More than that: it would have been the sort of thing that puts the fear of God in you. But for the nineteen-year-old Harry Pozo, PWD worker and Airfix model enthusiast, things weren't quite that dramatic. He knew that leukaemia was *a bad thing*. He knew that it was like cancer and that people eventually died from it. But instead of being scared or worried that he would die and never see his family or friends again, Harry found himself thinking about something other than his own mortality: he found himself thinking about sex. Or perhaps not so much about sex itself, but about the fact that he was still a virgin and that it'd be a shame if he died without screwing first. It'd be a real, real shame.

**

Harry went straight back to work after he left the hospital. It had just gone twelve-thirty on a Friday afternoon and the refuse incineration plant where he worked closed at three on Fridays. If he cut through Casemates and then walked along the back of Laguna Estate, he could still, with a bit of luck, get back in time to put down another two hours on his clock card for the day. That would suit Harry just fine — even if it meant not phoning his parents straight away after hospital like he was supposed to....

Harry had got a job at the plant just after leaving school at the age of sixteen. It was not the best of jobs — pushing skips laden with refuse from the dumping ground outside to the actual incineration hall — but it wasn't that bad either. Two men were required to push the fully loaded skips down the track that led to the incinerator, and, unless you got a real bastard on your shift, you could end up having as much of a laugh as you would have expected from a job that went unsupervised ninety per cent of the time. You could joke, you could race the other skips, you could climb into your own skip and lie down for a short nap, you could even smoke the occasional joint provided you did not wave it about too much. There was just one aspect of the job that Harry did not like. It was not work-related in a strict sense, but it still cropped up enough during his time at the yard for it to become an issue: the fact that Harry did not have a girlfriend. Because of this — and also, no doubt, because he was the youngest of all the skip-pushers — one or two of his workmates would sometimes feel obliged to crack a joke at his expense. 'Hey, Pozo,' they would shout, winking at each other as Harry's skip creaked past. 'When are you going to lose your cherry? Don't you think it's about bloody time, *hermano?*' As a result of this, Harry always preferred working on the same shift as Mario Bonello — or *el Viejo*, as he was known by everyone else in the yard. Mario was an ageing man of sixty-four who had been married twice and had only been divorced from his second wife a couple of years ago. He had arrived from Malta forty years earlier on the promise of a contract at the local dockyard — and had stayed in Gibraltar ever since. He led a grandly dissipated lifestyle for someone who was a grandfather eight times over, getting drunk at the weekends and regularly visiting brothels across the border in La Línea. He was also a real 'positive thinking' freak — continually harping on about how life was 'like a box of chocolates' and 'an unwritten film script' and other shit like that. More important than any of this, though, he never brought up the matter of Harry's sexual inexperience — something that suited the self-conscious nineteen-year-old quite nicely. Come eight o'clock on a Monday morning, Mario would roll back into the plant with a weary smile and dark bags under his eyes, telling everyone within earshot about his weekend excesses. Although Harry always felt slightly disgusted by his stories, he still enjoyed listening to the old man all the same. At sixty-four years of age and with the kind of ego that never lets anyone get a word in edgeways, it was clear that Mario had a master storyteller's eye for detail, interspersing his narratives of drunken debauchery with little poetic flourishes that always caught his listeners by surprise. Thus, you would get descriptive rhapsodies about the way *la Paula's* hair smelt as you held its strands in your hands — *tan dulce y fragante como si la palma de tu mano hubiera sido empolvada en canela* — or the milky-white softness of *la Manola's* arse — *blanco y suave, como la luna misma.* Not that *el Viejo* was always so poetic in his proclamations, mind you. That has also to be said. Still smarting from his recent divorce, he had a habit of ending half of his phrases with an insulting remark about his ex-wife — not exactly one couched in lyrical terms either. 'I just wish that the old bitch had been there to see me in *la Paula's* arms,' he would typically say, shaking his head and spitting on the ground. 'May God curse *la puerca puta guarra* and send the fucking bitch to hell one day!' It was not meant to be funny, but Harry would always smile whenever he heard the old guy speak like this.

As soon as he arrived at the yard that day, Harry could see that *el Viejo* was not in a good mood. He could tell from the way the old man talked to himself as he pushed a skip together with one of the other labourers. *El Viejo*, the nineteen-year-old knew, had a habit of doing this: he would constantly be telling all and sundry what a sexagenarian rebel he was, but would only talk about his own problems in a low, indecipherable monologue while pushing a skip. Only while pushing a skip, what's more — never while sitting in the canteen or idling around in the yard. It was his way, Harry figured, of getting people to ask what was wrong with him.

'Hey, *Viejo*,' Harry shouted at the Maltese divorcee as they crossed each other down the centre of the yard. 'What's up with you, mate?'

'What's up with me?' Mario Bonello hollered back. 'I'll tell you what's up. My fucking wallet got stolen. That's what's up. Some no-good, *hijo de la gran perra puta* swiped it from me while I was pissed at *La Mamma Negra* in La Línea. Do you know how much money there was inside?'

'How much?'

'Three hundred pounds, brother. *Trescientas jodidas libras.* Almost my whole bastard monthly salary. *Me cago en la leche*, how am I going to afford going to Marbella tomorrow for George's stag night?... By the way, what did the doctor tell you?'

'They think I might have leukaemia.'

'Yeah, yeah. Whatever. What did the doctor really say?'

'I've told you — they think I might have leukaemia.'

El Viejo started to get angry. 'Listen, kid, I'm not in the mood to piss about today. Just be straight with me, for Christ's sake. *Qué te dijo el puñetero mierda medico?*'

'I've told you, *Viejo*. They think I might have leukaemia.'

For a second *el Viejo* looked at Harry without saying anything. In the silence that enfolded them only the drone of the incinerator could be heard — a low, interminable rumble, shaking the ground slightly and jarring your insides almost without you realising it. Finally, *el Viejo* reached forward and put his hand on the adolescent's shoulder:

'And to think you only went to the Health Centre because of that bruise-thing on your throat and shoulders! How fucking fucked up is that!'

**

Harry did not do any work that afternoon at the yard. Acting on *el Viejo's* advice, he went straight to the corrugated iron shack that served as his boss's office and asked to see the gaffer. 'Sure, Pozo,' a rough, *testosteroned* voice echoed from inside, 'just give me a sec, will you?' For the next twenty minutes Harry sat on an old armchair outside the shack, reading a magazine and occasionally waving away some of the ashen flakes that kept wafting around the yard. The magazine's name was *Motorcycle Dreams* and the piece he was reading was entitled 'Rocking and Rolling all over the world.' Although there were many words in the article that he could not understand, Harry could make out that it was about some bloke called Andrew who was travelling around the world on a Harley 'Fat Boy' with his wife. Scattered through the article were photographs of this Andrew dude doing different things — riding along a deserted beach, crossing a knee-deep river, holding his arms up on top of a mountain, eating something that looked like a rat or a guinea pig. In one of the pictures you could see his wife sitting in the vehicle's sidecar. She was wearing a pair of aviator's goggles and a helmet spray-painted with a Welsh dragon. She was also bra-less, judging from the clearly observable form of two medium-sized nipples under her thin white vest. As he tried to determine whether her left nipple was adorned with a piercing, Harry suddenly heard his name called from inside: 'Pozo, where the hell are you? Come inside, *coño!*'

It smelled of farts and take-aways inside, the way it always smelled in the gaffer's office. The foreman, a fat, unshaven man who always wore the same dirt-encrusted brown T-shirt and whom everyone knew as *el Máquina*, nodded at a chair next to his desk and asked him to sit down. 'Well,' *el Máquina* growled, taking a bite from the Mars bar in his hand, 'what the hell do you want, Pozo? You're not going to tell me you're getting really tired again, are you?' Swallowing hard, Harry moved to the edge of his seat and began to relate what had happened that morning. He did so nervously and in a quiet voice, unable to stop himself stuttering the occasional word. For a while the foreman listened without looking at him. He twirled the tips of his greasy *bandolero's* moustache, he took regular bites of his chocolate bar. He seemed calm, genuinely relaxed, quite unlike the short-tempered old sod that everyone knew him for. Then, all of a sudden, as Harry was finishing his story, something snapped inside the man and *el*

Máquina became *el Máquina* again. 'Are you fucking crazy, kid?' he shouted abruptly and in an aggressive tone that almost made the nineteen-year-old cry. 'What the fuck are you doing here? Go back home and spend some time with your family, for the love of the crucified Christ!'

A short time later Harry and *el Viejo* stood outside the incineration hall smoking one last cigarette together. Once again an awkward silence had fallen between them, broken only by the sound of humming machinery in the background. It was odd seeing *el Viejo* so quiet, Harry thought. Kind of unsettling. In the end the adolescent could not stand it any longer:

'Do you know what's the worst thing about all this, *Viejo?*'

'What's that?' *el Viejo* muttered back with his cigarette dangling from his mouth.

'I'm still a virgin, *Viejo.*'

The old man shook his head and sighed. 'I know, Harry, I know. Why do you think I'm always trying to convince you to come with me to La Línea?'

'I don't want to die without shagging at least once, *Viejo,*' Harry continued. 'I don't mind if I have to kick the bucket, but not without shagging first, *sabes lo que te digo?*'

El Viejo forced himself to smile. 'Take it easy, kid. Your time will come. It comes for everyone, trust me.'

'Are you sure?' Harry asked in an even quieter and more subdued voice.

'Why, of course I am, kiddo!' he said. 'My name's not Mario 'the whoremonger' Bonello for nothing, is it? Just try to be positive and everything will be all right! That's the most important thing: be positive and things will happen! I've told you that time and time again, haven't I?'

**

That night Harry Pozo could not stop thinking about what his friend Mario had said. 'Will my time come?' he wondered, staring at the plastic DC-10s and 737s hanging from his bedroom ceiling. 'Or will I die without screwing at least once?' It was a thought that had never left him during the course of that day, not even while telling his parents a few hours earlier about what the doctor had said. *Nineteen years old and still a virgin*, he had silently reflected as he stood there locked in his mother's weepy embrace, *still untouched, still pure, still praying for the day when I can finally start doing it like everybody else*. It was just not on. More than that: it was an absolute disgrace. Yet what could Harry do? What could he possibly do? He was not rich or good-looking, nor was he gifted with a smooth tongue like all those slick bastards out there who were permanently surrounded by women. He was also shy. Very, very shy. Whenever he was introduced to a woman — even to a woman he did not fancy — he would always blush and become extremely self-conscious, having to think hard about what to say next and consequently coming up with the most mundane and idiotic of remarks. 'Nice weather we're having, don't you think? Looks like the Levanter will be gone now for the next few days.' Even worse, Harry could not tell anyone how much he hated himself for being like this. Each time the other skip-pushers talked about sex and women, for example, he would sit there quietly in the background, trying to look as inconspicuous as possible and in this way avoid being asked any questions. And, of course, whenever they asked him anything, he would always blush and bluff his way through some purely imaginary amorous episode he was supposed to have had while on holiday with his parents in Tenerife some years earlier. Lying like this was not something that Harry was proud of, but what else could he have done? Tell his workmates that he had never been with a girl before? That his knowledge of female anatomy was derived solely from the Spanish porn mags that everybody else left lying around in the yard?

Harry finally fell asleep at four o'clock and did not wake up until half past nine in the morning. Just before coming around, he had been dreaming he was kissing a girl's breasts while *el Viejo* stood behind him. The girl's nipples were pierced with small golden rings and a tattoo of a red-winged butterfly could be seen on her midriff. She was making elaborate, high-pitched noises as he kissed her — just like *el Viejo* claimed that women do when they are about to climax. Harry could not actually see his friend in the room (being fully immersed in what he was doing), but he still knew he was there somewhere. 'I just want the kid to be happy,' the old man was saying in that famously husky voice of his. 'It's the least I can do for a mate.' Two remarkable things happened then. First, the butterfly-girl's breasts metamorphosed into the saliva-moistened contours of Harry's pillow. Second, the teenager realised that he had not been imagining everything — Mario was actually somewhere in the flat!

'Harry!' his mother bellowed moments later from the corridor outside. 'It's your friend Mario from work. He wants to speak to you. Try to wake up, *anda?*'

He found *el Viejo* standing next to the front door. A tattered old rucksack was slung over his left shoulder, while the usually spiky tuft of grey hair on the old boy's head (his nine-to-fiver's crest, as *el Viejo* called it) had been carefully and lovingly gelled back. He was smiling like his numbers had been called out on the Gibraltar government lottery.

'Pack your bags, *niño*,' *el Viejo* immediately grinned. 'You're coming to the Costa del Sol with us, kiddo.'

Harry wearily shook his head. 'I'm not going to a brothel with you, if that's what you're trying to get at.'

'We're not going to a brothel, jackass,' *el Viejo* quickly replied. 'It's my grandson George's stag night tonight and you're going to come and have a laugh with me and the boys.'

'How many times have I already told you, *Viejo?* Just walking down to the bus stop really takes it out of me. How do you expect me to go partying up the coast?'

'*Venga ya*, Harry,' *el Viejo* said, nervously drumming his fingers against the wooden door frame. 'We're going to drive down to the beach and then go for a few drinks later in the evening, not run a bloody marathon. *No me seas tan pelma, niño, anda!*'

'Anyway, what's all this about? Didn't you say yesterday you had no money to go anywhere?'

'Money, kiddo, is no object to Mario Bonello when it comes to having fun. How many times have I told you that already?'

'Besides,' Harry said, stifling a yawn, 'I don't know George or his mates. How am I supposed to mix with them?'

'Oh, come on. Didn't you once say you were in the same class as George at school?'

'Yes, but I hardly ever spoke to him. I said that *también*.'

El Viejo tightened his grip on his rucksack strap. 'George is cool. You know that as well as I do.'

Harry, stroking his chin and yawning a second time, remained unconvinced.

'Listen, kid,' *el Viejo* finally said, 'in two days' time you're going to check into that hospital and God knows when you'll get out — if you'll ever get out at all. Just pack your bags and come with us, *por el amor de Dios*. We'll go down to the beach, check out some topless Scandinavian totty and then go to a couple of bars. What's so bad about that? None of the lads even know that you're ill, so none of them will treat you any different to how they would treat anyone else. Come on, Harry — stop playing the goddamned martyr and have some fun for once. I've told you time and time again that life is about taking risks, haven't I, it is about moving forwards and never looking back. Just because some no-good *matasanos de mierda* has told you that there may be something wrong with you doesn't mean you have to give up on everything and stop living!'

**

About two hours later, Harry sat squeezed into a Honda Civic with four blokes he did not know. They were stuck in four lanes of traffic on the Gibraltarian side of the border, waiting to cross over into Spain. They were not in the best of moods. They had already been stationary in the Civic for the last forty minutes, with all four windows rolled down to combat the oppressive August heat, reading and re-reading the *Gibraltar Chronicle* they had bought from the gnarled Danish guy who earned his living selling newspapers to those stuck in the border queue. Meanwhile, some twenty or thirty yards away, behind the six-foot wire fence that separated the Rock from its much larger Iberian neighbour, Spanish *guardias civiles* were searching every single Gibraltarian vehicle that drove past them. You could see them rummaging in car boots, inspecting sunroofs, tapping tyres to check if there was anything concealed inside them, crouching on all fours to look at undercarriages.

Closing the *Gibraltar Chronicle*, Harry cursed the bastards under his breath and then remembered how happy and excited his companions had been just before arriving at the frontier. He remembered how they had laughed and fooled about, clapping and shouting and stamping their feet, constantly turning around to wave at the car with *el Viejo* and the others behind them.... All that, alas, was gone now. It had evaporated into the summer heat almost as suddenly as Harry now regretted that he had ever listened to *el Viejo's* words that morning. Instead the radio was tuned to some Spanish pop station and no one spoke. No one even moved. A numbing sense of inertia had descended upon them — broken only when someone roused himself enough to wave off a passing fly. 'Is it always like this?' an English guy everyone knew as Ticker finally sighed with exasperation. 'Always,' George, *el Viejo's* grandson and the driver of the vehicle, responded. 'As soon as the British government does something which they don't like, this is how the Spanish dipshits respond.'

What George said was more or less true. A week earlier the British foreign secretary had made some unguarded remark about Britain never handing Gibraltar back to Spain against the democratically expressed wishes of the Gibraltarians, and Madrid had responded in the only way it knew — by slowing down traffic and harassing Gibraltarians on their way into Spain. It was the same old rubbish as usual. If you wore glasses and didn't have a spare pair with you — a mandatory requirement, it suddenly transpired, according to some obscure, half-forgotten Spanish law — they'd drag you out of your vehicle and fine you 25,000 pesetas. Similarly, if an 'essential item' like a pair of scissors was missing from your first-aid kit, they'd turn you around and send you promptly back into Gibraltar. *Lo siento, caballero, pero usted se va a tener que dar la vuelta y regresar a Gibraltar si no lleva unas tijeras en el botiquín de primeros auxilios.* ('I'm sorry, sir, but you're going to have to turn around and drive back to Gibraltar if you're not carrying a pair of scissors in your first aid-kit.') Not the best way to go about promoting friendly relations between two neighbouring peoples, that's for sure.

Considering all these factors, it was something of a minor miracle that they finally got into Spain after two hours and twenty-five minutes in the queue with no more than a cursory check of the car boot. '*Algo que declarar?*' the Spanish *guardia* had asked George after he opened the boot. '*No, nada,*' George replied. '*Okey,*' the man responded. '*Sigan adelante.*' And that was it — they were in Spain. An almighty anti-climax — but all the more so when you took into account the motley crew sitting in the silver Civic that Saturday morning. Even the greenest of Customs officers, you'd have imagined, would have felt suspicious of such a strange mix of men.... First of all, there was George, Harry's classmate from the age of thirteen to fifteen and the guy who was having the stag party. George was one of those cocky, self-assured Gibraltarian kids who seem larger than life — a long-haired, heavily tattooed musclehead who had both eyebrows pierced and loved to get the crowd going down at the Victoria Stadium: *Cómo están los llanitos? Bien, coño, bien!* He worked as a welder in the Royal Navy side of the dockyard and was about to marry some posh-talking bit-of-skirt he had met at an all-night charity disco. Harry remembered how shocked he had been a few weeks earlier when hearing from *el Viejo* about his grandson's forthcoming wedding. Georgie Bonello — *casándose con una tía del pish?* Next thing he knew, the Rock apes would be giving lunchtime concert recitals down at the Piazza or the Spanish government would drop its claim to the sovereignty of Gibraltar! The news just didn't make sense. George had always seemed such a brute of a guy, the sort of bloke who drinks beer for breakfast and treats girls as if they were lampposts to be pissed upon. His nickname at school had been 'Georgie Polli' — a bilingual pun that celebrated his famously oversized and overworked privates. Not that George was a complete bastard either, mind you. To be fair to him, Harry could not remember the guy ever getting cocky or confrontational during their two years together at school. Rather, he was the kind of bloke that everyone liked, always approachable despite having loads of girlfriends, never using his physique to intimidate anyone like some of the other muscleheads in class. Harry supposed that he was one of those men who can be good friends with other men, but whom women have to beware of. Your stereotypical lad's lad, in other words.

It was a description that could easily have applied to Sammy, Ticker, and Manolo, George's mates at the yard and the other passengers in the car together with Harry. Three big blokes with equally big paunches, all of them heavily suntanned and doused with lashings of expensive designer cologne, totally interchangeable except for the fact that one of them was a Scouser (Sammy), the other a Geordie (Ticker) and the last a Gibraltarian (Manolo). All that Sammy would talk about, for instance, was the tattoo of a red devil he had recently got on his arse. 'You see this little rogue down here,' he would say, pulling down his shorts and revealing a discoloured little imp etched on his left buttock. 'Some lady's gonna be engaged in deep and meaningful conversation with this little fella tonight, I promise you, lads.' Meanwhile, Ticker would be scowling disgustedly beside him. 'If you ask me, only queers get tattoos on their asses,' he'd growl under his breath, 'and only raving arse bandits like yourself end up showing them all day to those around them.' It was rather funny listening to this half-jesting, half-serious dialogue between them. But it also proved a little repetitive after a while. The impression that one got (at least that's what Harry thought after a couple of hours in their company) was that they both liked each other more than they were prepared to admit.

The remainder of the party travelled in the trailing car and was composed entirely of George's relatives — his cousins Joe and Willy, their father Mickey, and, of course, his grandad Mario. The most interesting of the first three was Mickey, George's uncle-in-law and the organiser of the expedition. Mickey was a short, stocky bloke of forty-eight — twenty or twenty-five pounds overweight and totally bald except for a thread of greasy black hair that ran like a felt pen line down his scalp. He worked as a police sergeant on one of Gibraltar's housing estates, ushering school kids at street crossings and giving information to lost day-trippers from over the border. The living, breathing incarnation of a respectable, happily married police sergeant, you'd have thought.... Until he opened his mouth, that is. For all his seeming normality, you see,

Mickey had one distinguishing feature that quickly became apparent when you spent more than five minutes in his company — he was absolutely sex-mad. Couldn't spend ten seconds without thinking, talking or fantasizing about the insidious charms of the opposite sex. In a sense, he was quite similar to *el Viejo*. Like the old man, he was an assiduous visitor of Spanish brothels and would even bump into the Maltese Lothario on his trips there.... There was just one slight difference between the two, what could be termed 'a minor legal discrepancy': Mickey, unlike Mario, was married. He had been married for the last twenty-three years now. It was this last fact — together with the added encumbrance that the girl he was married to was none other than *el Viejo's* eldest daughter — that ensured that Mario lived with a perpetual longing 'to smash the tip of his nose right through into the cunt's skull' (as he himself confided to Harry shortly after having introduced the nineteen-year-old to his son-in-law). But, as Mickey was a policeman and everyone else in the family adored his smooth-talking ways, there was little that the ageing skip-pusher could do — except hope that one day his poor daughter would take his advice and file for a divorce. 'Be careful with that one,' *el Viejo* duly said to Harry, nodding in the direction of his son-in-law. 'He'll use anyone or anything to get what he wants.'

Mickey's sons were a different proposition altogether. Almost in every way you could think of, both of them had turned out to be the antithesis of their womanising policeman father. Joe was a short, overweight nobody, very red in the face and with ginger freckles all over his body, who worked as a petrol pump attendant at the Shell Station on Devil's Tower Road. He lived with an equally dumpy Englishwoman called Sheila whom he had met while filling up her Mini Cooper with unleaded gasoline. He did not speak much, his conversational contributions being limited to the occasional lifting of the eyebrows in assent to whatever was being said around him. His brother Willy, meanwhile, was even quieter and weirder. A pale-skinned guy with receding black hair who never said much apart from 'please' and 'thank you,' he spoke in a hushed and deferential tone of voice and, if that wasn't bad enough, had this habit of never looking people in the eye. He also had a very pronounced stutter. *Tha-tha-thank you, but I've alre-re-ready read the Chro-chro-chronicle this morning, thanks.* Not what you would have expected with a father like his. Or perhaps exactly what you would have come to expect, who knows? Before introducing him to Willy, *el Viejo* took Harry by the arm and told him not to mention anything about hospitals or operations in front of Mickey's younger son. 'Willy is receiving dialysis treatment at the moment, you see,' he said. 'He's been waiting nine months for a new kidney, the poor bugger.'

The drive to Marbella took just under an hour. It was an impossibly hot August afternoon, one of those oppressive, cheerless days when the sirocco blows like a blast of bad breath from the North African mainland. Pockets of warm air could be seen floating over the motorway tarmac, enfolding the road ahead in a swirling, gaseous haze that blurred everything on the horizon. For the first part of the journey, they drank cans of Fosters that Ticker had brought with him in a chiller bag and listened to some old Led Zeppelin and Whitesnake tapes that Manolo insisted on playing. Then, just as they were driving past the town of San Roque, Manolo leaned forward and turned the stereo's volume down.

'You boys want to know why we Gibraltarians dislike the Spanish so much?' he said, wrapping a tattooed arm around his headrest and turning towards the two Englishmen.

'You what?' Ticker and Sammy replied almost in unison.

'Look at that large sign over there. The one carved in stone. *Bienvenidos a la ciudad de San Roque, donde reside la de Gibraltar.*'

'What about it?' Ticker asked.

'*Welcome to the city of San Roque*, it says, *where the real Gibraltar resides.*'

'I still don't get you, Manolo.'

'Every time people ask me why we hate the Spanish so much, I says to them, "just drive a few miles up north, mate, and look at the sign just outside San Roque. See for yourself what the friendly fucking Spanish think of us." '

'I still don't understand.'

'It's to do with what the Spanish think of us, innit?' Manolo continued brusquely. 'That's what we're talking about here. Ever since Franco's day, the Spaniards have been saying there is no such thing as a Gibraltarian because the "real Gibraltarians" left the Rock in 1704 (or whenever it was that the British took over the place) and came to settle here, in bleeding fucking San Roque. The "real Gibraltarians," they believe, are these fuckers here — the *San Roqueños*. We, the *Llanitos*, on the other hand, we, who live on the Rock and have been there since God knows when, we're just foreigners to them, innit, scumbags, piece of trash without any real identity, *nada más que rateros y chorizos* like they're always saying, just a bunch of Maltese and Genoese immigrants with no claim to anything except the shit that comes out of our own asses. That's why the fuckers put up that sign over there, in case you're still wondering. *We are the real Gibraltarians*, they're telling the world, *not those bastards across the border.'*

**

They reached Marbella at half past three. Leaving both cars at an underground car park, they walked down to the seafront and then shuffled their way through the beach to the nearest *chiringuito. Beach Bar El Rosario* was its name — an ugly, ramshackle affair built out of palms and bamboo canes and topped with a strand of red and yellow lights. A polyurethane statue of a Red Indian stood guard by the entrance, looking faintly ridiculous thanks to the *'jódete yanqui'* that someone had graffitied on its forehead. A hand-scrawled sign beside it announced that *'sardinas al espeto'* were available inside. Going through the door, they discovered that the *chiringuito* had an attached *terraza* which overlooked the beach. Not only that: a group of topless young women could be observed some ten or twelve yards away. Real brazen ladies they were too — constantly standing up and fidgeting with their sunglasses and applying suncream to their breasts.... There was just one small problem: the three tables on the *terraza* were currently occupied by a group of middle-aged Spanish couples.

'*Ven pacá*, Manolo,' Mickey immediately said, grabbing hold of the Gibraltarian carpenter by his shirt. 'Stand here next to me and start talking really loud filthy shit to me.'

'You what?'

'Stand here and start talking *porquerías* with me, *coño*. I want these oldies here to scram so that we can get hold of their tables.'

'What sort of shit do you want me to talk about?'

'I don't know. Sucking tits, licking ass, fingering clits, having someone fisting you up the ass. *Use your imagination, man.*'

It took them about five and a half minutes to carry out the deed. Once the old couples had gone, Mickey brought all the tables together and arranged them in a semi-circle facing the beach. The guys then took off their vests and sat down, making sure that Georgie occupied pride of place in the centre between *el Viejo* and Mickey. That done, there was nothing left for them to do — expect order drinks and watch the array of topless Scandinavians that seemed to pop up wherever they looked:

'Look, look, look — look at that one over there, the one sitting down just now. Jesus, has she got big *melones* or what?'

'That's nothing, Ticker. Next time you go in for a dip, check out the floozy by the Larios umbrella, the one sat next to the little bald guy with the white Speedos. Now that's what we in Gibraltar call *un buen par de tetas.*'

Probably the highlight of the afternoon came when George was picked up by the others and thrown into the sea. At Mickey's instigation (who else could have been behind such drunken tomfoolery?) they all pounced upon the unsuspecting stag and then lifted him between them. George's reaction was predictable enough: he kicked and cursed all the way down to the shoreline and did not shut up until he was dropped with a loud and unceremonious splash into the sea. 'You fucking bastards!' he gasped, spitting out seawater. 'Wait till I get you! Wait till I fucking get you!' Let's be honest: it was probably not the wisest thing to say to a posse of half-drunk guys at your own stag party. Led by Mickey the hairless once again, the shoreline party immediately charged into the water and proceeded to launch a full-scale attack upon the rapidly retreating George. A frantic aquatic mêlée ensued — 'You bastards, what do you think you're doing? Let go of my fucking legs!'— that only came to an end when the groom's swimming trunks were removed and brandished like a trophy in the air. Loud screams of laughter followed, a cascade of ear-piercing wolf-whistles. 'Come and get your shorts, Georgie-boy,' Sammy the Scouser finally shouted, waving the oversized trunks like a mock flag of truce from the shoreline. 'They're waiting for you, baby.'

Some ten or fifteen yards offshore, Georgie Polli was not amused. He coughed up seawater and spit; he swore under his breath; he threatened the guys with thunderous curses one moment and then pleaded tearfully the next, quite unsure how to get his trunks back without leaving the protection of the shoulder-high waters. In the meantime a crowd of holidaymakers began to gather nearby. You could see their numbers swelling on the shoreline, a mixture of Spaniards and foreigners, suncreamed brats and bemused lifeguards, topless Scandinavians and towel-wrapped matrons, *Speedoman* posers and lobster-pink Englishmen. *Vaya por Dios, valiente poca vergüenza que tienen!* — *Mein Gott, das ist mega geil!* — *My God, how embarrassing for him!* Finally, after yet another round of taunting and wolf-whistling came to an end, the red-haired Scouser took pity on the stag and cast the trunks into the sea. 'There you go, you Gibbo meathead!' he shouted as the green and gold shorts unfurled into a soggy Brazilian flag on the water. 'Get your dirty kecks back on!'

It was not until quarter past seven that things got serious again. This time they were in a place called *Casa Pepito,* one of those rundown motorway cafés that dot the N-340 out of Marbella and which always seem to be full of either working-class Spanish families or expatriate Moroccan workers on their way back to their homeland. You know the kind: medieval-style bogs and a massive plate of fried fish all for just under five hundred pesetas. They had driven there a couple of hours earlier on Mickey's recommendation. He claimed to have visited the place recently with his wife and really enjoyed their *merluza frita.* Plus, of course — typically from Mickey — the young waitress who worked there was supposed to have the largest set of knockers this side of Málaga. As it happened, this last fact did not prove to be strictly true: the acne-ridden waitress was as flat-chested as they come. But this did not stop them from messing about every time she came near their table:

> *Get your tits out, get your tits out! Get your tits out for the lads! Get your tits out for the lads!*

Boys will always be boys.

'All right, lads,' Mickey shouted as the final set of dishes was being cleared from the table. 'Time to go and have some fun.'

George, however, did not share his uncle-in-law's desire to get going. 'Give over, Uncle Mickey,' he said with a baby squid stuffed in his mouth. 'There's still time for a few brandies and coffee.'

Mickey shook his head. 'If you want your women as soggy as that *calamar* you're chewing on, Georgie, that's your problem. But, as for me, I don't exactly like to dip my wick after twenty others have done so before me. *Me entiendes lo que te digo?* I like my tuna fresh and clean, straight from the sea to the dining table, as they say. So either you get your fat arse off that chair — or I take a taxi and make my own way to the place.'

It was only as Mickey spat out these last words that Harry realised that Mario's son-in-law was planning on going to a brothel. The teenager had heard about these Costa bordellos from *el Viejo*. He knew that most of them were owned by a large syndicate which had branches all across Spain — quite unlike the smaller, mainly family-run massage parlours that the old man frequented just across the border in the Campo de Gibraltar. He also knew that a large number of girls plied their trade in them under the most exploitative of conditions, constantly rotating from one brothel to the other so that the punters never got bored with what was on offer. You'd find all kinds of nationalities involved in this circuit of concupiscence — Brazilians, Uruguayans, Russians, Rumanians, Estonians — in addition to all manner of colours, shapes and sizes. Prices were fixed across the entire nationwide chain: 2000 pesetas for a blow job, 3000 pesetas for a fuck with blow job included.

'Is it true what he's saying, *Viejo?*' Harry asked Mario shortly afterwards. 'Are we really going to a brothel?'

'Don't listen to anything he says,' *el Viejo* calmly replied. 'I already told you: the guy's full of shit. He's just trying to get everyone to do what he wants, like he always does, *el cerdo asqueroso.* But I don't think it will happen this time. At the end of the day, this is George's night. That means that we'll all do whatever Georgie wants to do. And, if there's anything I know about that kid, it's that he's so in love with Romina that he won't even want to set foot in a place like that.'

**

About fifteen minutes later, Harry found himself squashed in the back of the Civic again and on the way to the *Club Flexo* brothel in Benalmadena. All four of his companions were pretty pissed by this stage — waving towels and T-shirts out of the window and pulling grimacing faces at all the cars they overtook. Throughout the journey Harry kept thinking about the brothel and what would happen there. Would the others make fun of him when they realised that he had never been with a woman before, he wondered. Would they joke about it in front of the whores? Would they try to cajole him into having sex with one of those Brazilian hookers that Mario always talked about? 'This is going to be terrible,' Harry thought, shaking his head. 'Absolutely terrible!'

They arrived at the brothel just after sunset. It was situated off the N-340 motorway, next to one of the many high-rise hotels that litter the coastline all the way from Estepona to Málaga. Directly above the entrance there hung a bright fluorescent sign: a bare-breasted mermaid with the words '*Club Flexo*' flashing in blue lights next to her tail. The whole ensemble reminded Harry of a documentary he had recently watched on TVE about tourist brothels in Thailand — bright lights and the promise of cheap sex wherever you looked. It was hard to believe that an establishment like this — so squalid, so downright tawdry — existed less than an hour's drive away from safely middle-class and sanitised Gibraltar. If anything, this idea was reinforced by the presence of an armed security guard by the doorway. With his left hand resting on his revolver holster, the guy chewed gum and joked with a young hooker in a long fur coat. He even lifted the girl's coat at one point and playfully reached for her legs. *'Pero qué haces?'* the girl laughed, covering up her exposed thighs. *'Qué clase de guarda eres?'*

'Come on,' Mickey joked when he saw Harry lagging behind the others. 'Time to lose your cherry, *pimpollo.*'

'Leave Harry alone, Mickey,' *el Viejo* barked back. 'The kid's not as innocent as you think.'

Passing through the doors, Harry entered a large and ill-lit hall. Loud techno music was being pumped out from somewhere. Clouds of artificial smoke floated over a tiny dance floor. To create the illusion of a subterranean chamber, everything had been painted in black: the walls, the ceiling, the floors, even the metal doors of an elevator squeezed into a corner. At the far end of the hall stood a small drinks bar; on the wall behind it hang a large ornamental mirror. One or two antique pornographic prints could be seen on each side of the mirror's gilded frame — half-torn snapshots that must have shocked our forefathers' delicate Victorian sensibilities, but which in their current setting only looked grotesquely eccentric and comic. Harry calculated that there were fifteen or twenty girls scattered across the place. Sipping fancy cocktails. Smoking cigarettes. Lounging around in various states of undress. Some had their breasts exposed and at least one of them wasn't wearing a G-string. Despite the relatively early hour of the evening, there were already quite a few punters on the premises. Mostly little men with Pancho Villa moustaches and tanned faces. Spanish right down to the bone. There were also a few Gibraltarians here and there. Among them he spotted an old teacher of his from Bayside school. He was standing next to a tall black woman in white lingerie, his wizened bald head positioned just inches away from her silicone-inflated breasts. 'So *el Viejo* was right,' Harry thought, momentarily amused by the idea that a married History teacher should have driven an hour and twenty minutes on his own to come to a place like this. 'All kinds of men are hooked on this shit.'

'What do you think, kiddo?' *el Viejo* said, coming to a stop next to the bar. 'Pretty crazy place, huh?'

'Mmmm.'

'It always gets like this up here on a Saturday night. Whores-galore, if you know what I'm saying.... Anyway,' the old man said, suddenly rubbing his palms together, 'what can I get you, kiddo? Whisky? Beer? Cuba libre?'

'A beer's fine, thanks.'

El Viejo shelled out a thousand pesetas for two bottles of San Miguel and then handed one of them over to Harry. 'If there is any girl you fancy,' he said after taking his first swig, 'just go up to her and tell her. Don't be shy or anything. This is a business transaction we're talking about, remember. She'll take the stairs and you'll take the lift over there. That's the way it's always done. She'll then meet you by the landing upstairs and take you to her room. You'll get twenty minutes with her, maybe twenty-five if she likes you. Then she'll lead you back to the lift and you'll both come down together.... By the way, have you seen any girl that you fancy yet?'

Harry looked at *el Viejo* for a second and then shook his head. 'I'm all right for now,' he said, turning towards the bar and focusing on the veiny swirls on the marble counter. 'Don't worry about me, *Viejo*. Just go ahead and do your own thing.'

El Viejo patted him on the back and then started walking off, glad that Harry didn't need 'mothering.' 'Don't forget,' he said, turning around after a few paces. 'If there's any girl you fancy, just go up to her and tell her. That's how it works here. Don't be shy or anything like that. *No hay que tené vergüenza* in this sort of place, brother.'

The teenager nodded and carried on focusing on the counter. Some moments passed in silence. 'Look, look,' Manolo suddenly chortled by Harry's side. 'The old bastard's already found himself a bird. He doesn't hang about that one, does he, Ticker?' Gazing up from the counter, Harry saw what Manolo was referring to: Mickey and a leggy blonde, walking hand-in-hand away from the bar. The sight made the teenager's stomach churn, even though he had not been expecting anything less from Mario's son-in-law. Just then two of the girls strode towards the bar. Closer and closer they came, thrusting their chests forward and swaying their hips from side to side. The first of them came to a stop near

Sammy and began to dance suggestively before him. Meanwhile, her companion walked over to Manolo and yanked aside her G-string: 'Hey, *hombre*, do you like *mi concha? Mi concha* want your *bicho* in it!' It happened just like that — without preliminaries of any kind. Standing two or three paces away, Harry could only watch the double scene unfold with a mixture of shock, disgust and wide-eyed fascination, unable to decide exactly which emotions best fitted the events before him. Then, just as Sammy and Manolo were being led away by their vanquishers, another girl started to walk in Harry's direction. She advanced slowly and seductively, both hands resting on her hips. Quickly turning to the person next to him, Harry blurted out the first words that came into his head:

'Are you going to go up, then?'

'I don't know,' George replied, bashfully shrugging his shoulders. 'I've never done something like this before.'

It took Harry some time to register what *el Viejo's* grandson had said, but when he did he immediately felt better. So George, muscle-bound George who had slept with tons of women before and had had loads of girlfriends, had never been with a whore until now. The thought reassured him, made him feel as if he were not the only one in such a quandary. But the sense of comfort did not last long. Merely a fraction of a second later, the girl who had been heading in Harry's direction suddenly planted herself in front of George. She smiled, she pouted, she shook her breasts like two pendulums of flesh: '*Hola, cariñito*. What is your name?' And *that was that*. Before Harry realised what was going on, the two of them were already walking off — a seventeen-stone blond-haired giant and a mulatto girl in a micro thong, looking every inch like an advert for some sleazy Caribbean holiday resort....

Harry turned around once more and gazed down at the marble counter. He tried to make himself look small, to shrink into inconspicuousness, to think about his Airfix models and his little pots of paint and forget about what was happening around him. But the tactic did not work. Within seconds there was another girl by his side — stroking his legs and pressing against him, trying to reach for his trouser fly.

'Come on, honey,' the girl said with a Hispanic accent. 'You want a nice time, don't you? You want some suckie-fuckie now?'

'No, not-not really,' Harry stuttered back, still looking down.

'What's wrong with you?' she snapped. 'You're not *marica*, are you? You like men's *culos* or something?'

'No, no, no,' he replied uneasily, clutching his bottle tightly to his chest. 'It's just that I don't feel like it today.'

She walked off soon afterwards and he was left alone again. A few moments passed. Anxious, testing moments during which many of Harry's adolescent convictions were being ripped out of him and slowly smothered by the black, cavernous space that spread like a hangman's blindfold around him. One by one, he then watched them all go off upstairs — Joe, Ticker, the Spaniards standing by his side. Seeing them all go like this was hard, intensely disorientating. For some reason Harry found himself remembering his old RE lessons at Bayside Comprehensive and the sorts of things they taught back then about sex and relationships. He remembered how uncomplicated it had all sounded, how laughably unproblematic. You either had sex with someone because you were married to them, or you didn't have sex at all. That was all there was to it — with none of this wishy-washy middle ground you sometimes encounter in life where morals dissolved as easily as the bubbles in a bottle of San Miguel.

'Listen, kid,' *el Viejo* said, suddenly appearing by his side. 'I'm going to go upstairs now. Don't go with a girl if you don't want to. Don't feel pressurised. I'll be back in a little while. Remember,' he added just before he sauntered off into the semi-darkness, 'whatever you decide is cool. If you want to go with a girl, that's fine. If you want to stay down here, that's also cool. The trick is to be positive about whatever you decide, *no te se olvide, vale?*'

Soon only Willy and Harry were left by the counter. They stood with their backs against each other, like two strangers drinking at a bar. The irony of the situation did not escape Harry. There they were, a twenty-four-year-old who needed a new kidney and a frightened young virgin who was probably suffering from leukaemia, both of them surrounded by a dozen scantily clad

Eastern European and Latin American hookers. A more tragicomic scenario was hard to imagine. If Willy had been anyone else, Harry could have at least drawn a bit of solace from his presence, maybe shared a few words about the predicament that faced them. But, Willy being Willy — well, there was not much that anyone could say to him, was there? Not that Willy's weirdness was such a bad thing, mind you. At least with someone like him the teenager could feel sure that he'd never be left alone at the bar....

But Harry was wrong. Only a few minutes later, a blond girl came up to Willy and started dancing in front of him. She moved slowly and sinuously, thrusting her pelvis with shameless abandon towards him. Meanwhile, Willy stood there without doing anything — staring blankly into space, his lips slightly parted like always. It was almost laughable. Anyone seeing the dumb jerk would have thought he was a wax dummy, a statue unearthed out of the Roman ruins just down the road at La Bahía de Claudio and put on display as a stripper's stage accessory. Still, as we know from many a fairy tale, statues sometimes come to life — and this one proved to be no exception. Suddenly, without warning, without so much as a single word, Willy took the girl by the arm and then marched her away, almost making her drop an empty glass she was holding. It was so dramatic, so unexpected. All that Harry could do was stand by the bar and watch the pair disappear together into the darkness, unable to dwell on anything except the grim and rather unpalatable thought of what they'd look like 'doing it' upstairs.

And so he was left alone. Alone in a room with a dozen hookers. 'Jesus Christ,' Harry thought, 'what am I going to do now? What am I going to do?' A terrible fear suddenly descended upon him. Panic scorched his insides. Should he go up with one of them — or should he just stay there and do nothing? If he did the former, he would probably have to undergo the trauma and humiliation of explaining to a whore that he hadn't done 'it' before, that he was as pure and virginal as the Holy Mother of God. He could almost imagine her laughing at his words, shaking her head with mocking disregard. She would probably even come down after it was all finished and tell everyone how she had deflowered him. On the other hand, if he stayed downstairs and didn't do anything, the guys would tease him and laugh at him for the rest of his life — that much was clear. Jesus, what could one do? Already there were one or two rumours going around the incineration plant that he was gay. Although these cut right through to Harry's heart, he could not exactly complain about them. He was nineteen years old and no one had ever seen him with a woman before. If he didn't go with a girl now, *Jesus Christ, what would they start saying about him when word of this got back to the plant?*

And then it happened. Afterwards he could not remember exactly how. Maybe the woman who appeared by his side jiggled her breasts; maybe she stroked his crotch — he was not sure. All he could recall was a voice, a blur of flesh, the sensation of skin touching skin. And then — almost before he knew what was happening — he was already in the lift and on his way to meet her upstairs. He stood there twitching his hands under the glaring fluorescent lights. He wondered whether she was pretty or not. As the lift slowly whirred its way to the first floor, he could feel his throat go dry and the sweat drip into his eyes. 'So I am finally going to do it,' he told himself. 'The moment that I have been waiting for so long is about to happen.' He tried to cheer himself up with the thought, to dredge up some masculine pride within him, but the sordidness of it all cut into him like a knife. 'This is wrong,' he thought, looking down with his chin digging into his sternum. 'So wrong.'

At length the lift came to a stop and Harry walked out. She was waiting for him on the landing, leaning back against a whitewashed wall. For the first time that night, he was able to see her properly. She was about twenty-four or twenty-five, not particularly pretty but with lovely skin the colour of cinnamon. Large silver hoops hung from her ears. Her eyes were small and drowsy, reduced to two narrow slits. He guessed that she was on drugs.

'Through here, *cariñito mío*,' she said.

He followed her down the corridor until they got to room number 26A. It was a small and poorly lit cubicle, with a dirty paper lampshade hanging down from the ceiling. Cheap lime green wallpaper covered each of the four walls, scattered here and there with dirty red and brown stains that came from God knows where. The only visible items of furniture were a small single bed and its accompanying chest of drawers. Through a small window to the side Harry could see the high-rise hotel across the road. He could even hear the cars zooming along the highway below. He wondered if it was possible to feel more *exposed* to the outside world.

'Well?' she said, unfastening her bra and slipping out of her panties. 'Aren't you going to take your clothes off?'

Harry did as he was told and then stood silently in front of her. Although he had seen plenty of porn mags at the yard before, he was still surprised at how much better 'the real thing' looked. From her flower-like breasts to the curve of her hipbone: everything seemed in its right place, endowed with an indefinable sense of proportion that almost brought tears to his eyes.

'You're beautiful,' he whispered hoarsely.

'You're not so bad yourself, *cariño mío.*'

Harry smiled, then looked away. A naked woman in her prime was standing before him and yet he did not feel the slightest pang of desire. Even worse: all that he could think about was the low number of platelets in his blood. The timing of his thoughts pissed him off, filled him with a maddening sense of disbelief. For the last day and a half he had not wasted a single second thinking about the idea of disease and death — so why did it have to come now, now of all bloody times?... 'Only a loser like me could manage this,' he thought. He then looked down and shivered. To think that everything he was — his struggles at school and his difficulties at the plant, his Monday morning encounters with *el Viejo* and his shyness with girls, his sleepless nights at home and his prayers to God to help him find a woman — to think that it could all end just like that, so suddenly, so abruptly, as if it had all been lived for no reason at all: it was strange, unsettling, profoundly discomforting. For a second he tried to disconnect from what he was thinking, to focus on the soft brown skin of the girl's abdomen or the delicate folds of her shaven pink genitals. But it was no use — the same thought kept pushing into his head: to live, to die, to let go of everything you were. For the first time since being told he was ill, the idea of death appeared not just as a distant, meaningless abstraction, but as an event waiting to happen, a very real possibility that loomed darkly and threateningly over the horizon. Recognising this was like having a shot of reality injected into his veins. With a crippling pang of emotion, Harry realised that he did not want to be separated from his parents. He realised that he did not want to lose *el Viejo*. He realised that, come to think of it, he did not even want to leave behind the stupid bastards who poked fun at him in the plant. That's how scared, how *absolutely, goddamned fucking terrified*, of dying he suddenly felt.

'What's wrong?' she asked.

'It's too complex to explain.'

'Don't you like me?' she said, holding up her breasts and squeezing them together.

'No — it's not that.'

'Are you gay?'

'No.'

'What, then?'

'I don't know how to explain it.'

She looked at him for some seconds, a flicker of incomprehension shining in her contracted almond eyes. Then she walked to the chest of drawers and took out a packet of cigarettes. Lighting herself one, she sat down on the bed.

'Would you like a cigarette, *cariño mío*?'

'No, thanks.'

Harry looked at the girl and then at his clothes scattered in an untidy heap on the floor. 'This has got to be one sick joke,' he thought. For close to five years now he had been waiting for a moment like this — hoping that it would come, praying fervently for it, dreaming about it every single goddamned bloody night. And now this happens!... Really, he was not sure whether to laugh or burst into tears!

'I'm very sorry about this,' he finally said, putting his trousers back on again.

'It's all right,' she said, yawning. 'Don't worry.'

'It's just that.... I don't know. All this.... I don't really know how to put it into words.'

'Don't worry about it,' she again repeated. 'It's better like this for me. You're my dream kind of customer, if you know what I mean.' She smiled rather drowsily. 'What's your name, by the way?'

'Harry.'

'My name's Maria-Luisa. You're not Spanish, are you?'

'No, I'm from Gibraltar.'

'Ah, the famous Rock.'

'Yes, the famous Rock.'

She paused and took a long drag on her cigarette. 'Tell me something about yourself, Harry,' she said.

'There's not much to tell, really.'

'Tell me anything — where you work, what you get up to, what your friends are like.'

'I work in a refuse incineration plant.'

'Ah, *um incinerador do lixo.*'

'Yes, *un incinerador de lixo.*'

'And what do you do when you're not working?'

'Not much, really. I like to watch movies. I like to build airplane models.'

'Do you have a girlfriend?'

'No.'

'Would you like one?'

'Yes.... Very, very much.'

She smiled and brought her cigarette to her lips. 'You're a sweet kid. You remind me of my younger brother. He's a bit younger than you, though.'

'What's his name?'

'Ruben.'

'That's a nice name.'

She smiled again. 'Look, I'll show you a picture of him.'

She pulled out another drawer from the bedside table and produced an album of photographs. It was bound in imitation Morocco leather and had the words '*El Álbum de mi Vida*' stamped across the front cover in curvy Arabic lettering. As she started flicking through its pages, Harry noticed that the skin on the back of her hands was covered with tiny purple ulcers — a constellation of sickly purple marks that stretched all the way from the tips of her fingers to the middle of her forearms. He assumed that they were insect bites.

'Here he is. That's my Ruben.'

He looked at the album spread across her naked thighs and saw a picture of a smiling adolescent. He was standing next to a barbecue grill, wearing a Yankees sports cap and a Manchester United T-shirt. In the background you could see a clothesline and a small mound of toys draped with a towel. The normality of the photograph shocked Harry, assaulted his eye like an intruding foreign body. That look of mischief on the kid's face, those clothes billowing out in the wind, that red towel carelessly thrown over a plastic bucket and some Lego bricks — he did not know what he had been expecting to see, but he was sure that it was not this. There was something so mundane about it all, so *recognisable*. It was hard to mentally combine the scene in front of him with the naked prostitute by his side. For some reason he had been expecting to see a picture of a half-starved kid, a dirt-streaked scavenger. The fact that he didn't really bugged him.

'I'm flying back to Rio on the twenty-seventh of December,' Maria-Luisa said at last, closing the album. 'I can't wait to see him again.'

'I'm sure you can't,' he replied.

She put the album back in the chest of drawers. A long silence followed. Then, rising from the bed and slipping her bra and panties on:

'Can I have my 3000 pesetas now?'

'Yes, of course.'

He took out two creased bills from his wallet and placed them on her palm. '*Muchísimas gracias*,' she said, scrunching the notes into a ball and stuffing them into her bra. Then she opened the door and led him to the landing.

While they waited for the lift, Maria-Luisa began to arrange her bra so that the top of her nipples could just be seen. Harry watched her from two or three paces away, totally captivated by the way she kneaded her *pezones* with her fingers to make them erect. After a few moments, Maria-Luisa saw what he was doing and threw him a friendly wink. Just then a metallic chime was heard and they both walked into the lift.

El Viejo and the others were already downstairs. All the Gibraltarians in the group were standing by the bar, looking satisfied and relaxed. A few yards away Sammy and Ticker were having their usual ding-dong. Sammy: 'I tell you what, boys, all things considered, it's a miracle that the bedspread didn't go up my arse!' Ticker: 'A miracle? The only miracle was that she dared blow your disgusting rank knob at all, if you ask me.' Only Mickey, out of the eight of them, seemed to have noticed that Harry was back. As soon as he saw Maria-Luisa and the teenager emerge from the lift, he left his drink on the counter and walked over to their side.

'So what was the kid like?' Mickey asked the prostitute in an annoyingly loud voice. 'Did the little boy pop his cherry or not?'

Maria-Luisa eyed him scornfully for some moments and then turned to face the teenager. 'He was one of the best fucks I've ever had,' she said, putting an arm around Harry's shoulders and kissing him softly on the lips. 'I loved every fucking minute of it. If every customer was like him — and not ugly bald *pendejos* like you — this job would be the best in the world!'

It was an instant of pure magic. A moment worth savouring. The off-duty police sergeant stared dumbly at Maria-Luisa for a few seconds, then turned back to the nineteen-year-old. For a moment he looked about to say something — his jaw dropping open and his mouth puckering up in anticipation of the words to come — but then he thought twice and took a step back. He gazed down. He slowly scratched the side of his neck. Then, like a man who knows there's nothing left to be done, he turned around and rapidly retraced his way to the bar. '*El muy idiota calvo,*'

Maria-Luisa said abruptly, sauntering off towards the other side of the hall.

**

As he walked back to the car park, Harry Pozo lagged some ten or twenty yards behind the others. It was a cold and breezy summer's night, the kind you sometimes get in the middle of a Mediterranean August. Car fumes rose from the nearby highway and filled the air with the smell of nitrogen dioxide. Seagulls glided slowly and almost indolently through the midnight sky. In between the high-rise blocks that dotted Benalmadena's coastline, the moon could be seen reflected on the sea — a splash of red in a cauldron of darkness. '*Joder*,' Harry thought, surveying everything around him with a wry grin, 'what a strange night this has turned out to be!' As he carried on walking, he remembered *el Viejo's* welcoming wink at the bar, the congratulatory slaps on the shoulder from the others, the look of new-found respect in Mickey's eyes. He also remembered the words that *el Viejo* had used that morning: 'Life is about taking risks, it is about moving forwards and never looking back.' That was *so true,* wasn't it? If you never took any risks, you insulated yourself from rejection and avoided the laughter of those who would gladly mock your efforts. That is what he had been doing all his life: not talking to girls in case he got blown out, never revealing his feelings for fear of being picked on, never risking, never taking a chance, never reaching out for his hopes and dreams simply because he was scared of getting hurt along the way. Yet, compared with the prospect of falling sick and dying of leukaemia, what did all these imaginary fears amount to? Not a lot, that's for sure. That is why you had to take risks in life, why you had to ask girls out, why you had to force yourself to open up and make friends. Because if you didn't — it was clear to him now — you sacrificed the opportunity to develop as a human being, to become everything you could have become had you only been willing to try. And there is nothing more heartbreaking, as *el Viejo* always kept saying, nothing sadder and more goddamned bloody tragic, than giving up on everything you could have become simply because you never had the balls to reach out for it. With this thought in his head, the young man tucked his hands deep into his pockets and tried to catch up with the others. Meanwhile, the moon continued shining like a blood-filled ulcer in the sky....

3. Timeshare

I.

It was just before last orders at the Blue Lion. Taffy and I were sitting somewhere within its smoky, burgundy-wallpapered interior (William Morris, with gristly lumps of wallpaper adhesive and a few dead insects pushing out here and there). If my memory serves me right, he was wearing a T-shirt saying 'Fuck the Queen' or 'Fuck the System' or 'Fuck the Pigs' or something along those lines. Probably some moth-eaten residue from his days as an affiliate overseas member of the Socialist Workers' Party of Great Britain, you'd have safely guessed. Being the beginning of the nineties (and Taffy being the addict to popular trends that he's always been) I found myself listening to some rambling exposition on the proleptic, intra-diegetic structure of *Reservoir Dogs* (or something along those lines). Not my luckiest of nights, to be sure.

'You see, Rodriguez,' Taffy said, puffing on his cigarette. 'Tarantino does not need to explain the sense of loss and frustration that his character is going through. That is because it is already there, embedded in the film, ingrained within the script — between the lines, so to speak — a sort of latent subtext that we must unravel for ourselves — do you know what I mean, Rodriguez?'

Okay, okay — so maybe those weren't his exact words and maybe I'm indulging in a little bit of verbal exhibitionism myself. (I don't have a CSE in Film Studies for nothing, do I?) But, hey, they are pretty close enough to what he said. You know — the usual student bedsit spiel about what a genius Tarantino is and how his films capture the current *zeitgeist* and all the rest of that postmodern rubbish. Quite depressingly clichéd stuff, to be honest. Especially when you have some pimply, curly-haired megalomaniac regurgitating the same old shit for close to one and a half hours. 'Surely there must be something that interests him more than Tarantino?' I thought, looking around the room and racking my brains.

Then a miracle happened.

Yes: a miracle.

Namely: the answer that I had been looking for sauntered in through the door and sat on one of the stools at the bar, one leg crossed over the other, exposing seven or eight pounds of supple, gym-toned flesh under the slit which crept up the side of her skirt.

'Listen, Taffy,' I said, leaning sideways. 'I don't want to interrupt your proclamations on Tarantino, but turn around and look at what's just come in. Check the quality of that specimen.'

'Specimen?' he immediately blurted out. 'What specimen?'

'That one over there — the one lighting herself a cigarette just now.'

'That's nice,' Taffy said seconds later, his eyes slightly dilated under the smoky fluorescent light filtering down from the ceiling. 'But not as nice as your ex-girlfriend, Rodriguez.'

It was not exactly what I had been anticipating. My ex-girlfriend, Taffy's paragon of femininity, the yardstick by which all other daughters of Eve were to be measured — what the hell had she got to do with this?

'I still can't believe you didn't bring her back here while you were together,' he went on, drawing stylishly on a half-smoked cigarette. 'Man, you did yourself a terrible disservice.'

This was more than I had bargained for — an ex-SWP activist (and member of the Quentin Tarantino International Fan Club) counselling me on how I should have conducted my last romantic relationship! Christ, the plan had been to get the horny little runt singing the praises of mid-thigh miniskirts, not for him to ramble on about the woman who had recently broken my heart in a thousand different places!

'I don't know how you can say all that, Taffs. You didn't even get to meet the girl, for God's sake!'

'That's not the point, Mr. Rodriguez,' he answered with a mischievous smile. 'The point is you should have brought her back here with you — just like you should have continued studying and got yourself a decent job. I've told you once and I'll tell you again — you don't get larger tactical blunders than that, mate. I saw that picture of you two at that pier in Blackpool or wherever it was. In a small place like this you'd have been universally envied.'

'*Universally envied?* What's the point of *that*, if I may ask?'

'What's the point? I'll tell you what's the point, Peter. Begins with R and ends with T. *Respect*, that's what the point is.'

He leaned back and took another puff from his cigarette, letting the smoke escape in slow grey swirls from the sides of his mouth. Taffy: the motherfucking nigger with attitude, the gun-toting, cocaine-sniffing hoodlum from the run-down suburbs. Matters were definitely *degenerating*.

'That's the way it works in a small town like ours, brother,' Taffy continued moments later in his finest Italo-American rasp. 'It's not who you are, but who you *appear* to be. You know: the clothes you wear, the car you drive, and, especially, especially, above all, the company you keep. That's the real big one, my friend. The one that really makes or breaks you. "Tell me the company you keep, and I will tell you who you are." I take it that a learned fellow such as yourself must have heard that old popular refrain.'

'What's the use of telling me all this?'

'Not much use, really,' el *Taffy* admitted with a careless shrug. 'Anyway, on the subject of keeping up appearances — how do you fancy going to Bahía Beach after this place? Haven't been there for ages.'

'Why do you ask me that?'

'I don't know. It's just that I thought it'd be nice to go there. You know, check the women out and have a laugh.'

I put my glass down and looked at el *Taffy* without saying a word. Clubs, I must confess, have never been top of my list of ideal places. They make me feel small and engulfed, hopelessly hemmed in among a sea of writhing, perspiring bodies. I also knew that Taffy was perfectly aware of this.

'I don't suppose this is your idea of a joke, is it?'

'My friend,' Taffy replied rather sarcastically, 'have I ever joked with you about anything?'

'Besides,' I added with a despondent shrug, 'we won't be able to get in. You need a membership card to get in that place.'

'Don't worry about that,' he said, rising from his armchair and bringing out a tattered leather wallet. 'I know the guy at the door. Used to sell timeshare up the coast with my brother Jake.

He'll let us in without a card, our Paulie will.... Let's just have another quick drink here first and then we'll go, shall we?'

Five minutes later he was back with four tequila slammers on a waiter's tray. Each of them was poured into a different coloured shot glass. Fluorescent green. Bright orange. Saffron yellow. Shocking pink. As soon as I saw him with the tray, I just had to laugh.

'It'll be great,' Taffy said after quickly downing a slammer. 'I've been told that the place is wall-to-wall with fanny these days! You can almost smell it as you go in!'

'You think so?'

'Yeah,' he replied, reaching for another glass. 'I got a mate who works for Norwich Union and goes there every week. Says it's full of hot bitches all gagging for it. What could be better than that?'

The walk to Bahía Beach took about ten minutes. Most of the time *el Taffy* talked about the 'well-known concupiscence' of the establishment's patronesses, reciting a veritable litany of sexual escapades to back up his words. One-night stands, marital split-ups, *casos de cuernos*, even clandestine finger-fucking in the bogs — he went through the whole gamut of carnal misdemeanours with the practised detachment of a Gibraltarian divorce lawyer, patiently and painstakingly explaining the exact meaning of 'irreconcilable differences' in front of a hushed courthouse: 'And now to exhibit B: the dirty trollop loitering outside the men's toilets.' To make things even more interesting, he would occasionally pull a face and release a sonorous belch or two. In the beginning I thought that this was quite funny — in the same way, I suppose, that misbehaving little kids can sometimes be considered mildly entertaining. But after twenty or thirty belches (and at least one shouted complaint from somewhere in the neighbourhood: *Callarse ya, coño — que hay gente durmiendo!*), I began to have serious reservations about the former Burger King worker's behaviour ... not to mention his psychological make-up.

'Listen, Taffers,' I finally said as he knelt in the middle of the road to tie his shoelaces. 'Do you know that in the Middle Ages there was a festival dedicated solely to belching and farting?'

'What was that again?' Taffy replied with an ugly grimace. 'A festival dedicated to what?'

I said, 'If only I had a camera now.'

'You what?'

He was still kneeling on the ground, his features bathed in the light of a nearby lamppost. At that moment I realised how silent and empty everything was around us. It was almost like a revelation — something that suddenly and unexpectedly encroaches upon one's consciousness. Apart from the humming of the lamppost next to us, nothing could be heard. No wind, no voices, no movement. It was eerie, kind of oppressive.

'Difficult to believe,' I blurted out the first thing that came to mind, 'but only three weeks ago these same streets were full of three or four thousand lager-swilling, kebab-eating Englishmen.'

'You mean those *guiri* bastards on the way down to fight Arabs in the Gulf?' *el Taffy* replied without much interest. 'By the way, what did you say that festival was called again?'

I looked at Taffy, but did not say anything. For a people who are supposed to be fiercely British, I thought to myself, Gibraltarians have a very strange relation to the 'Mother Country.' We tell the Spaniards that we are proud to be British, we stick George Cross stickers on our windscreens and we support football teams like Manchester United and Liverpool, we even send our kids to British universities — but the moment we actually come face to face with a Brit all this seems to disintegrate, suddenly and without warning, dissolving into empty semantics as quickly as an effervescent lozenge liquefying in a glass of water. It is no longer a matter of being British then — but a case of 'Gibbos' and '*Guiris*', '*llanitos y ingleses*', 'us' and 'them', as if our Britishness were no more than a disposable mask we put on from time to time to convince ourselves that we are not just a cluster of newly emancipated colonials.

'It occurred on Shrove Tuesday every year,' I resumed after a rapid intake of breath, 'and the person who broke most wind and belched loudest was crowned *Rex Stultorum* — or "King of Flatulence".'

'That must have been pretty cool,' *el Taffy* replied, standing up and belching yet again. 'I'm sure I'd have been one of the favourites for the title, don't you think?'

By the time we got to the club, there was already a line of ten or twelve non-members outside its glass doors. Mostly adolescent ruffians and prepubescent girls. Big he-man attitudes and lashings of crimson lipstick. Plus a token drunk or two, of course. The usual array of provincial freaks, I reflected as we took our places at the back of the queue — either too young or too fucked up to receive their gold-embossed membership cards.

'Listen, Taffy,' I whispered, suddenly swamped by our combined lack of social standing, 'let's just leave it, shall we?'

'What are you talking about, my friend?' Taffy said, grimacing angrily beside me. 'Just take it easy, all right? We'll be in in a second.'

I nodded half-heartedly and shoved my hands into my pockets. I have to confess: I was not in the best of spirits. At my age, I thought, every single mug has one of those cards — every single mug, that is, except Taffy and me and possibly the scruffy drunken middle-aged bum three places in front of us. Instead there we were — a pair of unemployed losers about to queue with a bunch of sixteen-year-olds who chewed bubble gum and smoked Marlboro Lights and talked about the latest single by Take That as if it were the most important thing on the planet. The realisation did not exactly flatter my ego.

'Look, Taffy,' I once again whined. 'Let's just leave it, shall we? We'll never get in anyway.'

I shook my head and turned to walk away — but Taffy grabbed my arm and pulled me back, sharply and violently, with an almighty tug that brought us right to the front of the queue. Eye to eye, I should perhaps add, with a bloke who looked like he'd just come down from the podium of the Suited Simian of the Year competition.

'Excuse me, sir,' Taffy began in his finest BBC English, 'could you please tell me how much it is to get in?'

'Have you got a membership card?'

'No, but...'

'Sorry, mate,' the giant quickly interrupted, 'this is a members' club.'

'I am, my friend, perfectly aware of that,' Taffy answered with a fawning smile. 'I just wanted to know whether me and my friend here could pay to get in.'

'Look,' the seven-foot bouncer said, taking a threateningly purposeful step forward, 'I haven't got time to play games with geeks like you. Just fuck off, will you?'

And then he slammed the door shut. Angrily and without warning. Sending the 'Members Only' sign into a pendulous frenzy behind the plate glass window....

'Did you see that?' Taffy said as the sign slowly stopped swinging in front of us. 'Did you see the manners of that oversized buffoon?'

'Let's just go, Taffy. We'll never get in with this guy behind the door. Be reasonable for once, will you?'

But Taffy, of course, was in no mood to be reasonable. 'Shut up, Peter!' he shouted. 'Just shut up. Let me do things my way.'

And, true to his word, he turned around and did it *his way*: kicking the ceramic flowerpot by the entrance, banging his fists on the door, shouting, spitting, swearing at the doorman, *cagándose en su madre, en su puta madre, en la guarra que lo parió*....

It continued like that for about thirty seconds, possibly forty at the most. Then the bouncer came out, grabbed Taffy by the scruff of the neck and threw him on top of me, after which both of us crashed violently — and rather humiliatingly — to the ground.

'Now get the fuck out of here, you fucking fools!'

That was it. Curtains down. Denouement over.

'I thought you told me the guy sold timeshare with your brother?' I said as I tried to extricate my legs from under Taffy's torso.

'That wasn't him,' he replied, wiping a streak of blood from his mouth. 'Must be his day off.'

II.

It didn't end there, of course. Not on a night like *that*. As I lay there on the ground, I could not help thinking that the grey clouds drifting in front of the moon looked a little too ominous, a little too sinister. Like a nebulous mist forming over a trachomatous eye, I thought. A wound filling up with coagulating blood. If I hadn't been so drunk (and hadn't had Taffy tugging at my shirt like a maniac trying to get up) I think I'd have been *seriously distraught*.

'Thanks, Rodi,' Taffy mumbled softly after I had lifted him to his feet. 'You're a good pal, you are.'

He dusted his clothes under a nearby lamppost and then wiped his arm slowly across his mouth, leaving a thin trail of blood smeared on his sleeve. In the background you could hear assorted laughs and giggles, sounds of people cheering, one or two taunting claps. *Rodriguez and Calderon*, I thought — *Cabaret artists extraordinaire, court jesters for hire, undisputed Kings of the Festum Stultorum.*

'Are you all right, Taffers?'

'Yeah.'

'Sure?'

'Yeah, don't worry about it.'

'Are you really sure? You've got blood all over your mouth.'

Taffy shook his head. 'Listen, let's just go somewhere else and have a drink. Stop worrying about me, will you!'

'I assume you're joking.'

'Joking? About what?'

'About having another drink.'

'No — why should I?'

'But it's almost half past twelve!' I protested in a voice speckled with minuscule particles of spit. 'Everything will be shut now.'

Taffy smiled impishly. 'Not to worry,' he said, opening the front of his jacket and revealing the nose of a pewter hip flask protruding from an interior pocket. 'I always carry emergency rations. We can go to the usual place and have a drink!'

'But I don't feel like it!'

'Why not?'

'Because I just don't!'

Taffy shook his head and swallowed hard. I could see his jugular bulging out of the side of his throat, proudly and defiantly, almost as if it had an autonomous existence of its own. It was one of those things that kind of *get at you.*

'Okay, then,' I muttered under my breath, not quite sure how else to deal with the sight of that bulging vein, 'but only for a short while — is that understood?'

About fifteen minutes later we found ourselves at the end of Main Street and climbing the two-foot wall that enclosed Trafalgar Cemetery. It was very dark around us and only the murky light of some distant lampposts guided our movements. I could hear Taffy swearing next to me in the heavy gloom: '*Me cago en la puta leche*, the things you have to do *en este puto sitio* to have a bloody drink!' Once the wall was successfully negotiated, we weaved our way past the gravestones until we reached a large memorial that stood in a hidden corner of the cemetery. It was composed of a slanted marble slab and a pair of ceramic orbs, the latter having been reduced to two mutilated stumps over the course of the years. Past experience had taught us its value as a tolerable backrest.

'Do you know,' Taffy rasped out as soon as we sat down, 'three weeks ago we'd have been arrested just for being here.'

'No, I didn't know — why's that?'

'We were in "Rock Red" back then because of all those Royal Navy ships,' he replied, taking a sip of brandy. 'The highest security state laid out by Gibraltar Fortress HQ. When that happens there's all sorts of intelligence guys checking out places like this. You know, just in case of a terrorist bomb. Anyone caught idling around here would have been arrested on the spot.'

I raised an eyebrow in amusement — not only because some of the worst acts of drunken hooliganism I had ever seen were perpetrated by Royal Navy sailors during this 'Rock Red' period, but also because of the secretive, almost *film noir* tone that Taffy had used to relate his anecdote. To stop myself laughing aloud, I quickly asked him how many different security states there were.

'Three, of course,' he answered with an extremely deadpan expression. 'Rock Red — which means maximum alert, Rock

Yellow — which means a state of increased vigilance, and Rock Black — which means the same old shit as always.'

'And in which one are we now?'

'Now?' he said, pausing for a second with the flask against his lips. 'Rock Black, I'd imagine.'

He continued sitting there for some moments without moving or saying a word. Somehow I got it into my head that he was about to spew. I could almost visualise the parabolic trajectory of his vomit, could almost smell the godawful pong of regurgitated cocktails and beer. Very discreetly I moved a couple of inches away.

'Do you know,' Taffy suddenly began again, 'that some twenty French and Spanish ships were destroyed or captured by the time the Battle of Trafalgar finished, but not a single British vessel was lost?'

There he goes again, I thought — about to start telling me how many people died in the battle, how many of them are actually buried in this cemetery, and what state of decomposition Nelson's body was in when they brought it into Rosia Bay. The guy's incorrigibility knew no bounds!

'That boy Nelson sure knew what he was doing,' Taffy added moments later and then became quiet again, perhaps put off by my lack of reaction.

I prised the flask away from him and took a long swig of brandy. If there was something I disliked about Taffy it was his puerile obsession with war. The Second World War. The Vietnam War. The Napoleonic War. He knew them all inside out. Battles, campaign strategies, weapons used, casualties — the works. If that wasn't bad enough, the guy was obsessed with the Nazis. I mean, totally entranced by the fuckers. He had books on them, he collected their memorabilia, he was even saving up for a trip around Europe to see the sites of their crimes. (He had saved two hundred and sixty pounds so far — not bad, considering that the former Burger King worker had been unemployed for the last sixteen months!) Once he even bought an old SS dagger from a mail order catalogue. It came in a shoebox stuffed with yellowing copies of the *Daily Mirror* — together with a note attached to the handle saying it had seen 'active use' in the Battle of Stalingrad. Taffy kept it on his bedside table, next to a framed photograph of Jim Morrison and a half-rotted Waffen-SS armband. He even had a pet name for the dagger: he called it 'Stormbringer'.

'Taffy,' I mumbled innocently after a while, having decided to engage him on my own terms, 'have you got a lighter on you?'

'No, but I've got some matches. Do you want some?'

'Yeah, that'll do.'

He delved into his pockets and threw a box of matches into my lap. I immediately turned to face the gravestone behind me.

'What on earth are you doing, Rodriguez?'

'Just trying to read what it says on the gravestone,' I replied as I lit one of the matches but saw it go out with a soft hiss.

'Are you joking? You won't be able to read a thing!'

'You can still see the words chiselled into it,' I answered while lighting another match. 'The grooves run deep.'

'Suit yourself,' Taffy said, reaching out for the flask by my side.

With great difficulty this is what I read:

Sacred to the Memory
of Joseph Puttnam
Seaman on His Majesty's Ship
Experiment
Who died of wounds sustained at the Battle of Algeciras
On the 6th of July 1801
Aged 22 years
R.I.P.

'Sad, isn't it?' I said.

'He was a soldier and he died a soldier's death,' Taffy replied rather testily, 'there's nothing sad about that.'

'Still, it makes you wonder.'

'Wonder about what?'

'About life and mortality and all that shit.'

'If you say so.'

'I mean, think about it — one moment the kid is running up and down the deck of his ship covered in sea-spray and soot and that kind of thing, the next he's been dead and buried for almost three hundred years and serving as a backrest to two drunken Gibraltarian fools like us. Quite ironical, that, don't you think?'

Taffy shook his head grimly. 'That depends on how you would define irony.'

That was it — I was starting to annoy him. I decided to go straight for the jugular.

'Who do you think was a better commander, Taffy?' I said, laying out the bait irresistibly before him. 'Napoleon or Nelson?'

'Oh, Napoleon,' he replied with sudden interest, hardly noticing the change in conversational direction. 'Definitely Napoleon. Although Nelson was a useful commander too. That I am obliged to recognise as well.'

'Better than Villeneuve?'

'You mean Nelson? Yes, of course. What sort of a question is that?'

'And what about the Spanish commander at Trafalgar?' I asked, reaching out for the hip flask. 'The one who fought alongside Villeneuve? How would you rate him?'

Taffy snorted contemptuously. 'You mean Federico Gravina? He was a cunt. A yellow-livered, arrogant little dago bastard who ran away when the chips were down. Like all Spaniards. Useless as fuck.'

Ironic, don't you think? A man with a surname like Calderon — dark eyes, raven hair, olive skin, unshaven *nearly all the time* — slagging off Spaniards in such a racially motivated way? But anyway....

'Why do you ask?' Taffy said after a short while.

'Nothing. I was just thinking.'

'Thinking about what?'

'Films.'

'Films?'

'You know, all those black and white films made in the thirties about Nelson and Drake and Blackbeard and other seafarers. *Captain Blood* and the rest of them.'

'What about them?' he asked.

'Well ... how can I put it?... Haven't you noticed how the good guy is always clean-shaven and nicely dressed? Blond hair, blue eyes, fair-skinned? Your paradigmatic Aryan, wouldn't you agree? So goddamned milky-white, in fact, that his goddamned face seems to shine right out of the goddamned screen, don't you think?'

'What are you trying to get at?' Taffy asked with growing suspicion.

'*Characterwise*, he is reliable, honest, trustworthy, noble, brave, loving, gentlemanly and, of course, kind-hearted. Anything else I've left out?'

'That's the way all heroes should be,' Taffy replied with a defensive edge creeping into his voice, 'shouldn't it?'

'Perhaps,' I said. 'But now think of your average villain. Tell me, what do you see?'

'I don't know,' he replied, no longer hiding his irritation. '*What am I supposed to see?*'

'Treachery, perhaps?' I answered in the sweetest tones I could manage. 'Violence? Lustfulness? Meanness? Avarice? Pride? And — of course — braggadocio. Let us not forget braggadocio.'

'What do you mean?'

'Let me ask you this,' I said, adopting the same secretive voice that Taffy had used only a short while ago. 'How would you describe your average pirate Captain? Dark hair? Dark eyes? Unshaven? Olive skin?'

'Meaning?'

'Well ... let me put it this way ... have you ever looked into a mirror?'

'You little fucker,' *el Taffy* muttered softly under his breath.

Silence. You could almost hear the sound of Taffy's cerebral gears turning within his head. Tick-tock, tick-tock, tick-tock.

'By the way, Peter, I almost forgot. How's that thing going that you were writing?'

'What thing?' I asked.

'That thing you were telling me about recently. *A vindication of the rights of spics and wops in history*. That's close enough to what it is, isn't it?'

'It's not a vindication of anything,' I replied stiffly and somewhat annoyed (even though I knew that I shouldn't have been). 'It's an essay on anti-Spanish sentiment throughout the ages.'

'Yeah, whatever. How's it going? You think you stand any chance of winning that competition in the *Chronicle* you were talking about?'

'I don't know,' I admitted rather too candidly. 'It's a bit long-winded and not very well structured. I'd like to write less about literature and more about history in general.'

Taffy nodded. 'Must be quite a difficult thing to write about, I guess.'

'Yeah, it is.'

'I mean, at the end of the day, *a spic's a spic and a spade's a spade*. Must be hard convincing people otherwise.'

I shook my head and looked down in disgust. 'Can I ask you something?' I said. 'Why are you so fanatically anti-Spanish?'

'Can I ask you something, too?' he replied in turn, relishing every second now. 'Why are you so fanatically pro-Spanish?'

'I'm not,' I answered, somewhat wounded by the accusation. 'I don't even like the bastards. It's just that I hate to see any manifestation of fanaticism around me. It's what leads people to burn launches and overturn cars, what makes them slit each other's throats and gas their enemies with Zyklon-B. Fanaticism, in my opinion,' I concluded with an absurdly over-poetic flourish, 'is the secret whispering of the devil in our inner ear.'

For the next few minutes we sat there without saying a word. From time to time people could be seen walking past the cemetery gates — talking, laughing, shouting, drifting towards Bahía Beach in different states of drink-fuelled elation. For a second I gazed up and saw that the sky was covered in stars — little pinpricks of gold on an ever-spreading slick of tar. Looking at them, I remembered how I had once snogged a girl not far from where we were now sitting. It happened seven or eight years ago, back in the days when I was still at Bayside Comprehensive. We had curled up together on a tombstone nearby, two bashful and apprentice lovers, two clueless souls lost in a whirlwind of gropes and fumbled caresses. *Just let me feel your tit once more, anda — just once more, por favor — and then we can go, vale?* Not much had changed in this place since those days, I reflected. The shrubbery looked just as overgrown and untended; the surrounding medieval ruins continued reeking of damp; and the back of the bus stop on Trafalgar Road still bore the same faded graffiti — 'Manolito sucks dicks.'

'It wouldn't have been any good, anyway,' Taffy suddenly mumbled. 'No good at all.'

'What's that?'

'Just a load of silly girls dancing on their own,' he drawled, 'and all the guys standing around the dance floor like vultures.'

'You mean Bahía Beach?'

'You know — what usually happens in Gibraltarian clubs.'

I looked at Taffy and saw that his chin had sunk to a point just off his sternum. He seemed *dangerously wasted.*

'Isn't it strange?' I suddenly began, partly in an attempt to revive him and partly to stave off any more nostalgic thoughts. 'Even before the English came here, this place was being used as a cemetery.'

He grabbed the flask at that moment from my hands and brought it to his lips. For a second or two I could hear the drink swirling down his throat, as well as the sound of flexing and relaxing neck muscles. Instinctively, I pulled a few more inches away from him.

'I mean, look at that wall over there,' I continued, already running out of things to say. 'Do you know that it was built in the second half of the sixteenth century?'

I looked at Taffy again and then at the heap of old bricks on the other side of the cemetery. Five hundred years ago some Castilian architect must have stood on a spot nearby trying to figure out how to erect a wall on the rocky promontory before him. I could almost visualise him — loosening his ruff and shaking his head, wondering what on earth he must have done to be sent to such a remote and inhospitable outpost of the Hapsburg Empire. 'What's the world coming to?' he must have thought. 'Why am I stuck here in this hole of holes?' The answer, of course, was that the wall was being built to protect the city from marauding pirates (such as the infamous brothers Aruj and Khayrad'din Barbarossa) who would frequently land on the beaches of the southern side and then proceed to loot, rape, burn and generally take all sorts of liberties with the local citizenry. The plan was simple: split Gibraltar in two (with the city in the North, and an unpopulated waste ground to the South) and thus insulate the local population from any unwanted alien incursions. Not that this knowledge would have placated the mercurial humours of our Spanish friend one vaporous jot. 'Madre de Dios,' he probably thought with legendary Castilian disdain even as the wall was being erected around him. 'Let them fall into the hands of pirates — they are all thieves and cutthroats here, anyway.'

'Funny, isn't it, Peter?'

'What is, Taffy?'

'Us two, sitting here.'

'What do you mean, Taffers?'

'Look at us,' he croaked drunkenly. 'Just look at us. Two grown men drinking in a cemetery. Two guys without girlfriends who can't even get into a poxy, chicken-shit club like Bahía Beach. Two absolute, goddamned fucking losers. What's wrong with us, Rodi? Can you tell me? Is there something that someone didn't tell us? Did we miss out on one of life's vital lessons somewhere along the line?'

He began to laugh at this point. At first it was just a quiet titter, an almost involuntary chuckle. But as the seconds passed and I made no effort to reply, his laughter became louder and more aggressive, acquiring a distinctly maniacal edge. This made me so angry that I wanted to say, 'No, I'm not like you. I never will be. I don't admire the Nazis and I don't hate the Spanish and one day I'll find a girlfriend again and have a Bahía Beach membership card and do all the things that will prove to you that I'm no fucking goddamned loser!' But instead of saying any of this I remained there without speaking a word. I remained there staring into the darkness — without moving a muscle, without so much as batting an eyelid, listening to the obscene cackle that came out of his mouth and echoed noisily through the cemetery....

'Do you know,' Taffy added with a yawn moments later, 'I think *I'm well and truly fucked!*'

I tell you what: I could have cried then. I could have laid my head on the slanted gravestone behind me and shed tears for the unlived life I carried inside and which at that moment seemed as unreachable as the stars flickering in the night sky. I could have cried for Taffy and for myself, for the souls of the dead men buried under us, for the drunken revellers on their way to *Bahia Beach*, for the hundreds of couples that must have made love through the years in the cemetery, for the rotting trees and the desiccated bushes and the odour of damp soil that assailed our nostrils, for the life of unimaginable intensity that I knew was out there, but which I, *goddamned fucking loser that I was*, had not even attempted to grasp for fear of trying....

'What do you say to a nice take-away?' Taffy suddenly snorted by my side. 'I don't half fancy one of those nice, big, juicy Cajuna burgers!'

It was a godsend. A piece of divine intervention. Even though I'd have probably spewed at the mere sight of food, I readily agreed to his proposition!

'Okay, matey,' Taffy replied, struggling slowly to his feet. 'Let's go get that juicy burger before Tatties closes.'

III.

We arrived at Tatties Take Away House fifteen minutes later. The place was empty except for the small Moroccan who worked there and two drunken squaddies sitting on the varnished wooden stools next to the counter. One of them had a close-cropped head with various bands of flesh enfolding the back of his neck. He wore a long-sleeved Queen's Park Rangers top and his compact but muscular appearance made him look like a prize Pit Bull. The other was tall and wiry and had greasy ginger locks hanging down the sides of his neck; I could not help thinking he was Irish.

'Come on, son,' the Irishman was saying to the little moustachioed Moroccan. 'Hurry up with them kebabs. We don't have all day, matey!'

'Oh, no,' Taffy sighed under his breath as we took our place behind the two soldiers. '*Dos ingleses de mierda.* Two *guiri* soldier boys they forgot to take down to the Gulf.'

The little Moroccan was visibly stressed behind the counter. Lines of sweat criss-crossed his face and then dripped from his chin on to the food he was nervously wrapping, a never-ending stream of drops issuing from him with the metronomic regularity of a leaking bathroom tap. As he finished wrapping one of the kebabs, he suddenly froze in mid-movement and scratched his head:

'I am so so sorry, my friend. Di ju sayee tomateh sauce on both kaybab or only one of kaybabs? I ehaver forgot, my friend.'

'Are you listening to that, Reg?' the Irishman said to his friend. 'Mr. Shit-for-Brains here is trying to be funny with us. Thinks he can take the piss now, like, does he? My, my, he's got something coming his way, hasn't he?'

The Irishman turned back to the Moroccan at that moment and smiled — a cruel, mocking smile that exposed swollen gums and a row of crumbling urine-yellow teeth under his upper lip. Not knowing exactly what was going on, the little Moroccan did the worst possible thing he could have done: he smiled back.

'Listen, mate,' the Irishman suddenly said in a much fiercer tone of voice. 'Stop smiling like eh fucking imbecile and get 'em kebabs ready before me and Reggie-boy here decide to turn your stinking little pigpen upside down. I said chilli sauce and no salad on one of 'em, and no chilli sauce and salad on the other one. Is that fucking clear? Fuck's sake's, can't you wogs speak any English? Don't you realise you're in eh British colony now or what?'

The Moroccan nodded and threw the newspaper-wrapped kebab into a metal bin. It struck against the inside with a muffled clang. Switching on his electric carving knife a second time, he cut some more kebab meat off the skewer.

'Why don't you just give him a fucking break?' Taffy abruptly mumbled by my side. 'Jesus, are you guys getting regularly bum-fucked or what?'

I turned around and this is what I saw: Taffy, his eyes half closed and his chin glistening with spittle, resting his arms and head in a state of semi-collapse on the counter. 'Oh, shit!' I thought. 'Here we go again!'

'Excuse me, boy,' the guy in the Queen's Park Rangers top suddenly said. 'What was that again?'

'I said I'm going to gouge out your eyes and skull-fuck you if you don't shut up, *guiri de mierda!*'

The guy in the Queen's Park Rangers jersey looked at his mate and then looked back at Taffy again.

'Listen, guys,' I quickly interjected. 'Don't take any notice of him. He's totally gone. Legless. Kaput. Doesn't know what he's saying — do you, you drunken sod?'

'Look, Reg!' the Irishman said to the guy in the Queen's Park Rangers top. 'Another little dago who *speaka dee good English.* My, my, my — these must be the two most intelligent spics in the whole of the island, don't you think so, Reg?'

He smiled and nodded to himself, obviously pleased with the profundity of his repartee. Meanwhile, the guy called Reg slipped off his stool and stood up, all two hundred pounds and five IQ points of him, clenching and unclenching his fists with malevolent vigour.

'Look,' I replied, swallowing hard. 'He's drunk and I apologise for his behaviour. We don't want any trouble — what do you say, Taffers?'

'I say they can fuck off back to where they came from,' Taffy bleated drunkenly with his head still on the counter, ' — back to get sodomised by all those Pakis and Niggers running their goddamned country.'

I closed my eyes in despair. *Taffy, you dumb shit! What the fuck are you trying to do — get us both killed in a kebab shop?*

'Look,' I stuttered quite noticeably. 'I'm s-sorry. I r-r-really am. He's just p-pissed. Rat-arsed. Doesn't even know what he's s-say-saying.'

'These spics are a funny lot, aren't they, Kev?' the Queen's Park Rangers fan said, this time prodding me roughly on the shoulder. 'Don't you think we should teach them a lesson, eh?'

'Sure, Reg,' the Irishman replied. 'Let's teach 'em both a lesson, like — especially that piece of shit lying on the counter. I say we *pummelise* the pair of 'em, don't you?'

The guy with the Queen's Park Rangers jersey smiled and pushed me even harder. At that moment I realised that there was no getting out of this one. The realisation braced me, took away part of my fear — even though by this time he was pushing me straight against the wall behind me. 'Very soon he will hit me,' I thought, quite surprised by my dispassionately cold logic. 'He will hit me hard and I will fall.' To stop that from happening I had to hit him first, had to discover a way of catching the bastard by surprise. Instinctively, I looked around to see what I could find and my eyes fell on an empty gallon bottle of whisky standing on the counter. There was a label stuck on its side — Staff Christmas tips. Without thinking what I was doing, I grabbed the bottle by its neck and swung it against him. An enormous crash followed. Crunching glass. Clouds of smoke. A string of angry words in Arabic. All of a sudden it dawned on me that the bottle had missed my antagonist and hit a one-armed bandit behind him. Luckily, though, the sound of shattering glass stunned the Englishman briefly and I used the opportunity to punch him in the stomach. At that point something quite unexpected happened: my would-be assailant's legs gave way and he dropped like a sack of potatoes to the floor. I actually remember seeing him lying there, moaning sonorously and clutching his belly. Not, alas, that I had much time to fully register what was happening. Before I could even check if Taffy was all right, the other guy pounced on me and sent me crashing against the wall behind us. 'You fucking cunt!' he shouted in my ear, smothering me with a repellent blast of alcohol fumes and bad breath. 'I'm going to kill you! I'm going to kill you!' He then pinned me against the wall and tried to stick his fingers into my eyes, grazing my lower eyelids with his fingernails in the process. 'Get him off me, Taffy!' I croaked hoarsely. 'For fuck's sake, get him off!'

IV.

What happened over the next few minutes I cannot really say. I remember parts of it — vaguely, indistinctly — like some half-remembered dream that slides in and out of focus. Sirens, screams, arms grabbing me from different directions — these are some of the parts I have managed to salvage. Other than that, I'm afraid, there is not much else to relate....

By the time I finally came round again, I was alone in the back of a police car. My hands were tied behind me and a sharp pain was digging into my wrists. Two coppers occupied the front seats — one was driving and the other had his face turned towards me. The interior of the car — I remember this very clearly — smelled of disinfectant and piss-stained upholstery. Kind of like it smells in hospitals. From where I sat, I could see the eyes of the driver reflected in the rear-view mirror. They kept flickering nervously from side to side — little slivers of foil glistening in the darkness.

'*Cabrón?*' the policeman in the passenger seat screamed. '*You* are going to call *me* a *cabrón? Aquí no hay má cabrón que tú, te se ha metío en la cabeza, cabrón?* You and only you are the only *cabrón* around here, *te se ha metío en el coco?* Is that understood, *cabrón?*'

Was it true that such a terrible insinuation had passed my lips? Had I really implied that the gentleman's wife was sleeping with someone behind his back? To be perfectly honest, I'm not sure. As I sat there with the handcuffs cutting into my wrists, I had trouble remembering when exactly the police had arrived at Tatties, let alone whether I had called the guy a '*cabrón*' or not. Still, that did not prevent me from realising how weird the bloke looked wearing an English bobby's uniform and speaking Spanish at the same time. There was something quite incongruous about the fact, fundamentally oxymoronic — like seeing a donkey wear a bishop's mitre or a pig sitting on a throne or something of that sort. For a second it even crossed my mind to tell him that '*Se te*' is infinitely preferable to '*Te se*' in Spanish (the latter expression being generally considered a sign of ill-breeding among the educated Castilian classes), but in the end I resolved not to. At the back of my mind I kept thinking about all those stories that Taffy (where was that clown, by the way?) used to tell me about policemen beating people up with towels wrapped around their fists. Until then I hadn't given much weight to his claims (a word of advice: never trust a lapsed anarcho-socialist — or whatever the guy called himself — on matters of law and order), but as I sat there listening to that constant barrage of abuse ... well, I just wasn't sure what to think any more. 'All they want is one word,' I finally reasoned with myself, alarmed at the sudden clarity of my thinking. 'Just one word. Then they'll have their beach towel party.' The thought sobered me up rather considerably.

Once we arrived at the police station, I was led into a room that smelled pretty much like it had smelled in the car. It was brightly lit and as I walked in I momentarily found myself squinting against everything around me. A short while later, seven or eight policemen traipsed in and surrounded me in a large, well-rehearsed circle. Five of them were in uniform, the rest were in plain clothes. One of the latter asked me what had happened; he was tall and thin and his face had an ashen pallor to it that looked reasonably honest. As soon as I opened my mouth to speak, however, I was told to shut up by the fat little guy next to him. '*Aquí el que habla soy yo, vale?*' he screamed, making me start in spite of my drunkenness. Okay, dude, I thought, whatever you say.

The Fat Little Policeman: What's your name*?*

Peter Rodriguez: Peter Rodriguez.

The Fat Little Policeman: Well, Rodriguez, tell us what happened.

Peter Rodriguez (confused): I don't really know.

The Fat Little Policeman: *Cómo qué* — you don't really know? Are you crazy, Rodriguez, or what?
Peter Rodriguez (even more confused): Well, I....

Five minutes elapsed, possibly ten. They asked me where I lived, where I worked, whether I owned a car, who my father was, what I had been doing that night, whether I took drugs and whether I knew that I had broken the law by smashing the Tattie's Christmas tips bottle. All the questions were asked by my pot-bellied, goggle-eyed nemesis. He stood there with his thumbs tucked into his belt-hoops, a fragment of white shirt peeping sloppily out of his navy blue jumper. Put it this way: it was not exactly textbook interviewing. Every now and then the lardy buffoon would ask me a question in a perfectly serious manner — only to interrupt me with an ear-piercing scream as soon as I made an attempt to answer: '*No hables hasta que yo te lo diga, vale?* Meanwhile, the others started laughing behind him — hahahaha hahahaha hahahaha. 'Can this really be happening?' I thought with a mixture of sadness and alarm. 'Is this really the Gibraltar I know? The one where everyone is known for their friendliness and generosity? Where Hindus, Muslims, Jews and Christians all live harmoniously together in an area not much larger than twenty football pitches? Where no murders or rapes are ever committed and where tourists are always welcomed with open arms?' In the meantime a weird thought came into my head. A real *headwrecker.* Even though my hands were trembling in the cuffs and I was close to vomiting with fear, I began to remember a text I had studied during my short time at uni. It had been part of a module called 'Propaganda and race: anthropological representations of foreignness in the Middle Ages' — or something like that, at any rate — and its author was the venerable anti-Catholic and anti-Spanish propagandist Antonio Del Corro. I can't recall the exact title of the pestiferous little pamphlet, but I know that it dealt with the Spanish Inquisition's methods and practices, detailing, among other things, how the inquisitors poured water into their victims' throats without drowning them and how they enjoyed seeing young maidens stripped naked on the torture rack. 'Del Corro was right all along!' I suddenly thought to myself, observing all the laughing, suntanned faces around me. 'He was right about all you bloody lot!'

When the questions eventually came to an end, I was told to stand still and wait until my handcuffs were removed. I was subsequently asked to take off my shoelaces and hand them over to a bearded policeman beside me. Such was my state of disorientation, however, that I took off my shoelaces *and* my shoes.

'You're a clever arse, aren't you?' the fat little guy immediately shouted from the other side of the room.

'Excuse me?'

'You, *listillo*,' he said, approaching with a ridiculous, chest-inflated swagger. 'You think you're very clever, don't you?'

He carried on strutting down the room until he was just inches away from me. I could feel the sickening graze of his breath against my cheek, a rancid, garlicky stench that came mixed with the stink of his overpoweringly strong BO.

'Don't I know you from somewhere?' he said, breathing yet another cloud of foulness into my face. '*Esa cara de cabrón la he visto yo antes en algún lao.*'

He clasped his hands behind his back and carried on looking at me from up close, still breathing hard on me, still trying to belittle me in front of all the others. Thankfully, it was at this point that the tall and honest-looking policeman intervened:

'Leave him alone, Joe. Can't you see that he's drunk?'

'Drunk?' my antagonist sneered. 'He's not drunk. *Lo que es, es un cabrón como tó los niñatos ahí fuera* ... aren't you, you little shit?'

He then raised a hand as if he were going to hit me, but quickly brought it down again, grinning with self-satisfaction, clearly relishing that he had almost made me jump out of my skin.

'You see?' he said, shaking his head. 'He's not so drunk, is he?'

Everyone laughed; my antagonist turned away. For an uncomfortably tense moment, I wondered whether it was now time for the coppers to bring out their beach towels.

'Well, Mr. Rodriguez,' the bearded policeman said in a voice that was not too unkind. 'Time to go to sleep.'

Shortly afterwards the circle of policemen began to disband. They did so slowly and with great reluctance, like a crowd dispersing after a public commotion. A surge of relief coursed through my veins. With a rare sense of gratitude, I found myself thanking God that I was in Gibraltar after all!

'Well, my lad,' the policeman muttered, leading me away. 'Time to sleep it off. *A dormí la mona hasta mañana.*'

V.

My cell couldn't have been larger than twenty or twenty-five square feet. Once my eyes got used to the dark, I could make out three wooden benches screwed into the surrounding walls — with a lidless toilet bowl rising like a broken tooth in the centre between them. Each of the benches had been padded around the edges with oddly shaped balls of rubber, probably with the intention of stopping the detainees from slitting their wrists or gouging out their eyes or doing whatever it was they were capable of doing with sharp wooden corners. Two other men shared the cell with me — a drunken, heavily clothed tramp who lay snoring loudly on one of the benches; and a younger-looking guy who stood in a corner staring in my direction. The place only stank of one thing: shit.

'Hello,' I said to the guy standing in the corner, not knowing what else to say under such circumstances.

'What are you in here for?' my new cellmate asked in a distinctly northern English accent.

'I don't know,' I replied. 'For causing a drunken disturbance, I guess.'

The young man smiled. 'Have a seat, mate. Have a seat.'

I sat down and remained silent for a while. Through the darkness I could see that the guy was about my age. He was dressed in a loose black shirt and tight jeans and had long, curly hair that reached halfway down his neck. He was also very thin. Seeing that he didn't appear much of a threat, I decided to carry on speaking to him.

'What do you think I'll get?' I asked.

The guy still looked in my direction. 'For being drunk and disorderly?'

'Yeah.'

'Do you have any previous convictions?'

'No.'

'Not much, then,' he replied in a casual tone. 'A fifty-pound fine, perhaps. Maybe a seventy-five-pound one, if you're unlucky.'

'That's not bad,' I said.

'Mind you, you'll have a criminal record and you won't be able to emigrate to Australia later on in life.'

'No, of course not,' I replied, wondering why he had come up with such a strange observation. 'I never thought of that.... By the way, where are you from?'

'Manchester. And you?'

'I'm local.'

'You don't sound it.'

'That's because I lived in England for about a year,' I said.

'Whereabouts?'

'Manchester, actually.'

'Really — which part of Manchester?'

'Rusholme.'

He shook his head slowly, as if not believing what he was hearing. 'I come from Didsbury, just up Oxford Road.'

'Do you? That's quite a coincidence. A friend of mine lived there.'

'What was his name?'

'Martin.'

'I don't know any Martins,' he said thoughtfully.

'He was a Communist,' I replied.

'I don't know any Communists either. What were you doing in Rusholme?'

'My university residence was there.'

'You were a student?'

'Yeah.'

'Poly or University?'

'University.'

'What were you studying?'

'Medieval History.'

'Did you quit your studies before you finished?'

'Yeah, kind of — how do you know?'

'You just said you were there for about a year, didn't you?'

'Yes, of course. I said that, didn't I?'

'You should have continued studying, mate, if you ask me.'

'You're probably right.'

'You could have been somebody one day with your degree.'

'Yeah, I guess you're right.... By the way, who's he?'

'This guy? Not a fucking clue, mate. Not a fucking clue. They brought him in a few hours ago. He was already asleep when they chucked him on that bench. He's been farting all night, the dirty bastard.'

'I already kind of noticed.'

'I'm just scared he's gonna shit himself, me.'

'Fucking hell, that would be a laugh!'

'Not a laugh, mate. A stink: that's what it would be. Get it right. A proper awful fucking stink.'

I shook my head and smiled. 'Why are you here? Do you mind if I ask?'

'I beat up my dad.'

'Why?'

'I don't know. A silly family argument — what usually happens.'

'I'm sorry to hear it.'

'That's not the worst thing, mind you.'

'What is then?'

'The worst thing is I'm supposed to be getting married in two days' time and, according to the *oinkies* outside, I'm staying in here for four nights at least.'

'That's bad. What you going to do?'

'I don't know. Cancel the wedding, I suppose.'

'Shit! That's awful!'

'It's all Samantha's fault. She's fucked up big time on this occasion.'

'What do you mean?'

'Samantha's my girlfriend. She and my dad have never got on well and yesterday they almost came to blows at the Queen's Hotel where we're staying. Being the fool that I am, I came down on her side and hit my dad in front of all the family.'

'Are you all here for the wedding?'

'Yeah. We all flew together to Málaga and then hired a couple of cars to get here.'

'I'm sorry to hear that.'

'Don't be. It's my fault. I should never have listened to her in the first place. Women are such bitches. Do you know what she was arguing about? She was complaining that my dad never lets her watch *Blind Date* back at my parents' house, the silly brainless little slut!'

'If it's any consolation, I was ditched by my girlfriend earlier this year.'

'What do you mean?'

'She was a second-year language student. We lived in the same student residence in Rusholme.'

'Was she a good fuck?'

'What?'

'Was she a good fuck?'

'I don't know — I guess so.'

'What was her name?'

'Marsha.'

'I had a girlfriend called Marsha once. She was Scottish and had really large tits. What made it all go pear-shaped between you and your Marsha?'

'It happened just a few months ago. I had just quit university and come back to Gibraltar. She phoned me from Manchester one night — I think she was a bit pissed at the time — and said it was all over. "I'm having doubts about our relationship," she said, "and I don't think things will work out in the long run." The usual rubbish.'

'Like I said, mate — women are all bitches.'

'Maybe — but I should never have fallen for any of that long-distance romantic shit, should I?'

'Heard anything since then?'

'I've tried calling her on a few occasions, but she's always put the phone down on me. Except one time when this bloke took the phone off her and told me to fuck off. Just as you hear it. *Fuck off, you foreign bastard. Leave Marsha alone.* (That's my impression of an Irish accent, by the way.) I guess it was her new boyfriend.'

'You shouldn't phone her, mate. Let the bitch rot in hell with that Irish wanker.'

'I know.'

'Why'd you do it then?'

'What do you mean?'

'Why'd you keep calling her like that?'

'I don't know.'

'You mean you still want her back or something?'

'Yeah, something like that.'

'But why?'

'I don't know. I guess I miss her or something.'

'That's no good, mate. No good at all. You know what I'm saying?'

'Yeah, I know what you're saying.'

'So then why do you keep on calling her?'

'I don't know. I guess that's just the way I am.'

VI.

Yes, that's right — that's just the way I am. That's why I quit university and why I still haven't been able to find a job. That's why I have friends who admire the Nazis and why I've never been able to get my Bahia Beach card. That's why I get arrested when I'm plainly innocent and why I've been humiliated by some moronic little shit who's probably being two-timed by his wife. That's why my girlfriend dumped me telephonically and why she's probably cavorting around this very minute with some racist Irish twat. Peter 'Shoots himself in the Foot' Rodriguez — that should be my name. Tattooed on my forehead for all the world to see what a sad joke I am. The undisputed king of the Festum Stultorum.

VII.

It all ended in a small, windowless courtroom about three weeks later. I stood in the dock dressed in an old cotton suit that I had borrowed from my father, wiping away the beads of sweat that streamed down my forehead. When the judge asked me whether I had anything to say, I told him that I was very sorry and that I never intended to get drunk again. I also let him know that I had once been a student of Medieval History at the University of Manchester and that I had no previous convictions. For a moment or two the old fellow looked at me without saying a word. Then he raised his gavel and brought it crashing down against the circular mat on his table. I had been found guilty of being drunk and disorderly, he said. I had a choice of paying a fifty-pound fine or spending ten days in prison. If I didn't have enough money to pay the fine in its entirety, I could apply for a special dispensation that would allow me to pay in two separate instalments. Naturally,

I told him that I would pay the fine in one lump sum. As I left the courtroom moments later, I had only one thought in mind — *what a shame it was that I could no longer emigrate to Australia.*

4. The Passion of Gilbert Spiteri

Our story starts on the thirty-first December, 1984. Like many Gibraltarians who worked in the naval dockyard, Gilbert was made redundant that day. That is to say, he was given a cheque for three thousand pounds and a consolatory handshake by an English guy with a double chin and a navy blue pin-stripe suit: 'Thank you for your help, Mr. Spiteri. Here's a little something to show our appreciation.' For a thirty-five-year-old boiler fitter who used to earn eighty-nine pounds and seventy-eight pence a week, this 'little something,' it can be imagined, did not seem that little at all. 'Three thousand pounds,' Gilbert thought, holding the cheque that evening under the bare light bulb in his Glacis kitchen. 'Three whole bloody grand!' If it took his fancy, he could go out next morning and buy that Pioneer with the eight hundred-watt speakers that sat triumphantly behind the plate glass window at Rock Electronics. Alternatively, he could go on that holiday to Florida that he had been saving for during the last two years. (Giles Gonzalez, one of the boys from the hull-scraping section who had won the lottery with a group ticket some months ago, had gone there recently and said it was 'chock-a-block with American totty.') Come to think of it, he could even buy himself that second-hand Honda Prelude parked outside the used car showroom at Corral Road. 'Just take your pick!' Gilbert thought, throwing the cheque into the air and watching it spiral slowly to the floor. 'Take your pick!'

For the next few days Gilbert Spiteri couldn't control his consumerist instincts. By this it is meant that he bought anything and everything that captured his interest — a Sega Master System, an assortment of Van Halen and Kiss CDs, a life-size replica of Tutankhamun's death-mask, a four-lane Scalextric, a collection of Jacques Cousteau videos with an accompanying set of leather-bound books. Finally, towards the end of that same week, Gilbert made his biggest purchase yet: he walked down to the second-hand car dealers and wrote them a cheque for two thousand four hundred pounds in exchange for the Prelude parked outside.

It was like something out of a television advert, like a dream come true. For three days and three nights Gilbert sat in the leather bucket seats of his Prelude and drove through every single goddamned road and alleyway stretching across Gibraltar's six and a half square kilometres. He revved his engine down Main Street; he spun his alloys at the second Queensway traffic lights; he performed hand-brake turns outside Eastern Beach — in other words, he did all the things you'd have expected from an ex-boiler fitter whose previous car was a second-hand Mini bought from a sixty-five-year-old Moroccan rubbish collector who was retiring back to Tétouan. Then tragedy struck. Tragedy of tragedies — the cheque bounced and he had to return the car to the garage!

'One thousand eight hundred and eighty-seven pounds?' Gilbert now thought, examining his bank statement under the (still naked) light bulb in the kitchen. 'What happened to the rest of it?'

It was a big blow — not exactly terminal, but quite painful all the same. For a whole week all Gilbert could think about was the Prelude's bucket seats and its retractable sunroof (as well as the number of chicks that, theoretically at least, he could have screwed on the back seat). 'If only I hadn't bought all this rubbish,' he once or twice reflected, kicking whatever electronic object — a Donkey Kong mini games console perhaps, a battery-operated toothbrush — lay stranded across his way. At last, after much internal deliberation, Gilbert became philosophical about his loss. 'Oh well,' he now thought, stoically resigning himself to a Prelude-less existence, 'I still have a lot of money left.' And with this he began to think of other ways to spend the one thousand eight hundred and eighty-seven pounds (or a little bit less by this stage) that still remained in his bank account.

It was during this period that Bryan rang Gilbert for the first time. Bryan had been a G3 electrician at the dockyard until he was made redundant too. He had been part of the RFA workers' unit at the Little Patio. Some of the guys at the yard had nicknamed him 'MacGyver' because no one understood how he could drink so much without ever getting himself sacked. Though it was only midday when he called that day, the ex-electrician already sounded considerably under the influence.

'Listen, Gillie,' MacGyver spluttered out on the other side of the line, 'I'm at the Venture and I'm bored out of my head. Fancy coming for a drink, *compadre*?'

Gilbert held the receiver between his shoulder and the side of his face — in a posture he adopted when uncertain what to say. 'Should I carry on playing Pac-Man,' he wondered, staring at the flashing television screen, 'or should I go down to the pub for a few drinks?' On any other day, Gilbert would have baulked at the idea of drinking on a weekday and in the company of a notorious lush like MacGyver. But on this particular day — the twenty-third since he had been laid off — Gilbert Spiteri was caught somewhat off guard. Boredom, that old foe of the unemployed, was already gnawing at his resolve.

'Okay, MacGyver,' Gilbert finally replied, nodding and taking the receiver into his left hand, 'I'll see you there in half an hour.'

From that day onwards Gilbert and MacGyver would meet every morning at the Venture Inn. It was not so much something they had specifically agreed upon — more of an unspoken understanding between them. This arrangement might strike the reader as something of a surprise, considering the antipathy that Gilbert had previously shown both to MacGyver and his dipsomaniac vagaries. But, in the words of the old Spanish proverb, *las circumstancias cambian igual que el hombre*. For Gilbert, in any case, the arrangement had a practical side — a pint or two at the pub serving to break up his daily trudge to the Employment and Training Board and back. 'What better way, after all, to finish your job-hunting than by having a couple of bevvies?' the ex-boiler fitter figured. It was just a shame that MacGyver always preferred to meet him at the Venture instead of coming with him to the ETB.

Like most Gibraltarian pubs, the Venture Inn traced its origins to the nineteenth century and the days when Gibraltar had been one of the most important naval bases in the British Empire. *El Venture,* as it was commonly known, was situated at the beginning of Main Street, curiously ensconced between a pharmacy and a family-run electronics store. Dozens of wooden crests and black and white photographs of Royal Navy ships covered its interior walls — a testimony to the bar's popularity with scores of Navy men during the rowdy days of the fifties and sixties. There were even a few photographs here and there of the servicemen themselves — yellowing, damp-eaten pictures with little cardboard labels that could hardly be read without straining your eyes. All the fellows in them had similar names — Archie, Jamie, Stevo, Bazza. And almost all of them looked the same — close-cropped heads and drunken leers that still bristled with defiance all these years later. On his second or third visit to the Venture, Gilbert had even met a Costa del Sol expat who claimed to be in one of the pictures. His name was Norman, he said, and he used to serve on board the *Ark Royal* as a helicopter mechanic's assistant. 'That's me,' Norman declared, pointing himself out among a bunch of similar-looking youths with their arms interlaced. 'That nipper with the cheeky little grin. Hard to tell, innit, looking at the balding, pot-bellied old fella in front of you!'

Gilbert never forgot his encounter with the retired sailor. Some of the older regulars had told him that *el Venture* was a 'no-go zone' for locals back in those days, a place where you were as likely to get your head kicked in by some ex-Borstal kid as anywhere in London. Although Gilbert had only been a little boy at the time, he still remembered how frightened he used to get whenever he walked past the boozer's entrance, how terribly terribly scared. From the pub's interior, meanwhile, you could hear the singing of thirty or forty drunken Englishmen, stamping their feet and banging on the tables under the admiring glance of half a dozen 'loose' women and one or two local homosexuals: 'Who the fucking hell are you? We're the boys from forty-two!' It was strange to think how much the pub had changed since then. To imagine that it had once lived a past whose only remnants lay in the dusty, yellowing photographs hanging on its walls. But that's the way it went. Ever since the British military had begun to pull out of Gibraltar and the colony was forced to stand on its own feet, *el Venture* had changed from a den of depravity to a quiet little bar that made most of its money serving tea and all-day breakfasts to the English and German day-trippers who traipsed in from across the border. Some bright spark had even introduced a few tauromachian objects into the décor for the tourists' benefit — a blood-red cape here, a stuffed bull's head there, one or two bullfighting posters. The Venture was still open at night, but now it tended to be empty except for two or three middle-aged drunks, usually very red in the face and discussing local politics, and the odd, Koran-flouting Muslim who wandered in from the Moroccan workers' hostel just down the road at Casemates. Times they are a-changing, as Bob Dylan says.

On his first few visits to the Venture Gilbert rarely drank more than a pint or two. But as the days passed (and the ETB counsellor's 'Sorry, *pero* there's no vacancies today' became more and more securely fixed in his head) Gilbert Spiteri, moderate drinker and Gibraltarian nice guy, slowly began to slip. First of all, it was just one or two extra pints ('No harm in just one extra pint of Boddies, is there, eh?'). Then it was another three or four ('All you'll get is a slightly drier throat tomorrow morning, that's all.'). Finally, a short while after that, he was mixing spirits into his beer and belching into his glass, just like MacGyver.

What happened next was sadly predictable. Within a few weeks the money in Gilbert's bank account ran out. At this point he began to steal, to beg from passers-by, to harass old acquaintances for a pound or two — anything just to get his hands on a drink. Also during this time he started to regularly visit his parents' flat in Laguna Estate. There the thirty-six-year-old would often be seen balanced on the ledge of his elderly mother's balcony, threatening to kill himself if she did not come up with the cash he needed. '*O me das el dinero* or I throw myself!' he would shout at the top of his lungs, hating himself for what he was doing but unable to stop all the same. And, of course — faced with the prospect of an imminent tragedy — Gilbert's mum, like most Gibraltarian mums had they been in a similar situation, would always give in and hand over the dosh.

This pattern of events carried on for a long time without any major alterations. Gilbert would drink till he had no money, stagger to his parents' flat, threaten to commit suicide, receive some cash in the see-through money bags in which his mother kept her lifelong savings, go back to the pub and then repeat the whole process again when he ran out of money three or four days later. Within this chain of events, nothing of significance happened — unless we count the night that Gilbert downed two bottles of Famous Grouse and ended up sleeping with *Shirley la puerca* (she who drank out of an old Wedgwood china cup that accompanied her wherever she went and whose clothes always stank of the thirteen cats she kept at home) or the times he would end up in court for the various sundry misdemeanours you would normally associate with out-and-out alcoholics. Once, for example, he was thrown into jail for pissing in Main Street against a lamppost in broad daylight. Another time for walking into Tatties Take Away House and stealing three vegetable samosas (Please note: this did not indicate a preference for vegetarian Indian dishes on Gilbert's part — just the fact that they were the nearest thing within reach in the display fridge.). On another occasion for throwing a watermelon at a street entertainer who stood outside the cathedral pretending to be a statue. (Don't ask where he got the watermelon from — because even Gilbert couldn't say when they interviewed him down at the station.) The usual stuff. If you'd have asked Gilbert why he did these things — and many a copper and social worker, believe you me, did try — he would probably have told you that he was not sure. It was just one of those things, you know. You got drunk because you had nothing to do, and then you did the things a drunk did because you were utterly and totally off your head, you know what I mean?

**

Time passed. Gilbert had been a drunk for close to three years by this stage, scrounging money from his ever-suffering mother on an almost weekly basis. There was no MacGyver by then — his former partner in crime having been shipped off to a rehab clinic in Bilbao after a sudden bout of hepatitis that nearly killed him. Not that Gilbert cared much about his mate's departure. Whenever anyone asked him about the ex-electrician, he would look at them through foggy eyes and dismissively shake his head. 'Magy's gone on holiday again,' he would say, two small balls of spittle glistening around the edge of his lips like they usually did.

'He'll be back soon.' *Poor drunken sod*, you'd think to yourself. *He's off his head again.* Not that what Gilbert said was entirely groundless, mind you. Ten months earlier, MacGyver had suffered a similar attack and been taken to some ranch run by the Opus up near Ronda. He had come back three weeks later, Bible in hand and hair shorn down to a thuggish grade one. *'Qué pasa,* Magy?' Gilbert said upon seeing him strolling down Main Street with one of the local priests. 'Joining the Gibraltar Regiment, mate?' MacGyver did not answer just then — he only smiled awkwardly and looked away. But later that same evening he was back at *el Venture* again, fervently reciting the hymns he had been taught at the ranch with sixteen shots of gin arranged in a row by his side. *Alcoholism is a disease*, so they say, *not a disgrace.*

**

And so we reach Christmas Eve 1987. The time is a quarter to nine. The temperature is around eleven degrees. The Main Street bars have already shut and there is no one walking under the flashing Christmas lights. Here and there one can observe a few remnants of the day's revelry — a couple of broken beer bottles, one or two paper streamers, a patch of coagulating vomit. Everyone is at home now — either sleeping off the day's excesses or sitting around a table next to a half-cut leg of Serrano ham. A few hours from now, no doubt, one or two good souls will shrug off fledgling hangovers and force their way down to the Cathedral of Saint Mary the Crowned to hear Midnight Mass. ('If only Midnight Mass were every Sunday,' his Lordship the Bishop is always sadly reminding us *feligreses*, 'we wouldn't have empty churches during the rest of the year!') But at the moment there is not much happening. An alley cat brushes itself against a lamppost. A pair of Persian shutters creak open somewhere. Hidden within a shadowy doorway, a young policeman smokes a furtive cigarette and wishes that he was spending the night with his girlfriend. *'Valiente mierda de Nochebuena,'* he thinks, edging further back into the darkness.

Gilbert Spiteri is also having a bad night. At eight o'clock the Venture closes ('Sorry, Gillie,' Ali the barman says, 'but I've got a family to go to') and he finds himself out in the streets, rubbing his bare arms and wondering why on earth he has not brought a jacket with him. His first thought is to walk over to his parents' place in Laguna. It is always warm and cosy there at Christmas. Plus he could get himself a decent hot meal. However, after remembering last year's disaster, he decides that perhaps this is not such a good idea. Gilbert hasn't quite forgotten *that charade*. From the moment he first entered her flat, his mother had refused him access to any form of alcohol, claiming (quite correctly) that he was already substantially inebriated. 'But can't you see that you're *borracho, niño?'* the old woman cried shrilly as she walked up to him with a tray of freshly baked vol-au-vents. 'What do you want to do — get even more drunk?' Sound as this advice was, of course, it was of little consolation to a drunk like Gilbert. Having already been deprived of any alcoholic refreshment for the larger part of an hour — and having, what is more, spent the last few minutes listening to his seventy-year-old dad's extemporised speech on why he should stop drinking — Gillie needed a drink and he needed it quick. A shot of whisky, a swig of rum, a sip of port — anything would do for the time being. Taking advantage, therefore, of a moment when his mum and dad were both in the kitchen, Gilbert smuggled a bottle of liquor out of the drinks cabinet and carried it under his coat to the bathroom. It was a bottle of Teacher's too, Gilbert's favourite whisky. Once safely locked in the room, he downed about half of the bottle in one swig and then rinsed out his mouth carefully with water so that his parents would not notice the tell-tale aroma of whisky on his breath. He even spread some Colgate Extra Minty toothpaste on his teeth just to make sure. Unfortunately, none of these precautions did Gilbert much good. Why? Because, as soon as he returned to the living room, the hastily imbibed liquid shot back up his throat and made him vomit all over his mother's brand-new fitted carpet. Not just the half-bottle of Teachers, one should perhaps mention, but also the free canapés offered to him at the Venture that afternoon, all of it splattered across the dark crimson carpet in a large viscous heap out of which one or two undigested olives and a couple of cocktail sausages could still be seen. *Un verdadero pastizo,* to use that old favourite Gibraltarian phrase.

**

Standing outside the locked doors of the Venture, Gilbert finds himself caught in a quandary. It is not the fact that he has no coat and is rapidly losing heat through his upper extremities that most bothers him, but what to do now that all the bars are closed. To put it in simple terms, he can either walk back to his unfurnished bedsit in Glacis Estate — or he can potter around Main Street in the hope of finding something to drink. A most difficult choice, considering the irrepressibly manic MacGyver is not there to goad him on to a quick decision. Finally, after reflecting a few minutes on his predicament, Gilbert plumps for the second course of action. This decision is taken on the twofold assumption that (a) someone must have left a half-drunk can of beer somewhere during the course of the day's revels and that (b) Gilbert, being an expert in matters like these, will be able to sniff out the said can and summarily drink its contents.

Not long afterwards, Gilbert finds five half-empty cans beside the wrought-iron benches opposite the Cathedral of Saint Mary the Crowned. They are closely and symmetrically bunched together, like the 5 on the face of a die. Gilbert immediately guzzles them down and then, not knowing why but still doing it all the same, places the cans on the ground in a vertically stacked tower of five. Following this, he belches aloud. 'If only Midnight Mass didn't start so late,' he thinks, gazing at the locked doors of the cathedral across the road. That would have put an end to his present troubles. He can almost imagine himself sitting at the back of the building, next to the portable electric heaters that are sometimes wheeled in during the winter months. Gilbert sits there almost every day from November to February — despite the occasional frowns and reproving glances from some of the ageing *beatas* around him. Funerals, baptisms, marriages, marriage rehearsals, holy communions, remembrance services, rosary recitations — he goes through them all with his hands tucked into his pockets and his eyes half-closed, always hunched there on his own at the back of the building. *In the name of the Father, and of the Son, and of the Holy Spirit. Amen*: it is a phrase that Gilbert has heard more times than he can possibly remember. Only a few days ago there was a memorial service for some twenty-year-old kid who had died of leukaemia or something. The church had been packed with fainting, red-eyed women and sombre men in black suits who kept loosening their ties and gazing uncomfortably around them. That had annoyed Gilbert very much, left him cursing under his breath during the entire service. *Cry as much as you like, you pathetic, snivelling fools. Don't you know that no amount of tears will bring him back?*

Not surprisingly, Gilbert prefers going to the cathedral during the early hours of the morning. He is then able to sit there in almost total peace, surrounded by nothing except the smell of incense and burning candles and the half a dozen old people who can usually be found praying at that time. He does this regularly when he gets up early and has a couple of hours to while away until the Venture's doors open at eleven. It is always a good and fairly trouble-free way of starting the day. Sometimes this old woman with a lace shawl wrapped around her head comes up to his pew and brings him sandwiches and teacakes. He does not know her name, but he likes her all the same. Gilbert finds this odd because normally he does not like do-gooders at all. He hates the way they make it their mission in life to save his soul, to wheedle themselves into his personal affairs. Priests, social workers, justices of the peace, random strangers who offer him advice on how to run his life — they are all the same, Gilbert thinks. *Convincing themselves they are acting altruistically, yet only feeding their own cravings for personal redemption.* Even those who despised drunks openly were preferable to these do-gooders. At least with people like that all you had to do was swear an oath or two and they would go away, nodding their heads and muttering harsh words as they walked off: 'Useless, good-for-nothing drunks. Why can't they just get a job like everybody else?' But with the do-gooders there was never this guarantee. You could swear at them. You could spit at them. You could curse them and damn the no-good bitches who had spawned them. You could do all this and much, much worse ... and still the damn fools wouldn't stop breaking your balls.

This woman is different, though. Gilbert realised that much the first time he saw her. She is so simple, so devoid of artifice.

She does what she does because she thinks Gilbert is hungry, not because she feels she has to save his soul. Gilbert likes that. He likes it very much. Most of the time he does not eat the sandwiches themselves — they almost always contain pâté of some sort and Gilbert absolutely hates the damn stuff — but he still likes being given them all the same. It always ignites a light within him, always makes him smile for a few moments no matter how depressed or hungover he may be. Not that Gilbert ever tells her any of this. For some reason he has trouble uttering anything other than a few grunted syllables to her. There is always something stopping him from expressing his real feelings, an invisible emotional barrier that he finds hard to cross. One morning, still drunk from the night before, he even started swearing and shouting at her and the old dear quickly retraced her steps and fled. When Gilbert woke up the next day and remembered what had happened, he was immediately overcome with shame. For six or seven days he avoided the cathedral, preferring to drift through the freezing, rain-soaked streets of town rather than face the prospect of seeing his spurned benefactress again. *Why did I have to behave like that with her? What the hell got into me?* She was the only person who cared for him in this whole goddamned town and he had ended up treating her like filth. Was it because deep down he didn't want to be helped, like people always kept telling him? Once, for example, a young American missionary had approached him as he sat boozing at the Alameda gardens and had told him that he should stop drinking because alcohol only brought the worst out of him. 'It is the devil's way of poisoning your mind,' the American said, standing opposite him in an immaculately ironed white shirt and with a Bible in his hands. 'In the name of Lord Jesus Christ, let go of this self-sabotaging demon before it takes over the rest of your soul....'

It took Gilbert eight whole days before he finally mustered enough courage to return to the cathedral. He was destined never to forget the experience. He had been up most of the previous night trying to drink himself to sleep and, by the time he got out of bed and staggered towards the front door, he had already polished off a bottle of Jim Beam and six Pernod miniatures that he had stolen from a wine and spirits shop the day before. It was around half past seven, well before the city of Gibraltar comes to life. A cold westerly wind was blowing in sharp, merciless gusts, shaking rooftop aerials and disgorging the contents of rubbish bins through the empty streets. Bulging rain clouds loomed threateningly over the horizon. As he stumbled out of his bedsit, Gilbert breathed a little warm air on his hands, then locked the door behind him and set off towards the Venture with the intention of sitting on its doorstep for a couple of hours. He had been doing this for the last few days now — sitting there on his own, with his hands tucked into his pockets and his jacket collar turned up, waiting for Ali the barman to arrive and unlock the door behind him. But that morning Gilbert was not counting on the diabolical state of the weather. Trees swayed. Lampposts shook. Clouds of dust kept blowing into his eyes. '*A toma por culo con esto*,' Gilbert soon thought, shaking his head and digging his hands deep into his pockets. 'It is no weather to be sitting on a doorstep!'

Gilbert did not stop that morning at the Venture, but carried on walking down Main Street instead. He walked quickly, purposefully, every inch of his being pulsating with the desire to escape the growing tumult around him. But when he arrived at Saint Mary the Crowned the old apprehensions returned: should he walk into the building and risk meeting the old lady with the shawl — or should he just turn around and go back to *el Venture's* doorstep? Sweat drops collected on his forehead at the thought; a knot formed in his stomach. Gritting his teeth, he wished that he had saved at least one miniature bottle of Pernod; it was at times like these that a man needed a little alcoholic sustenance to pull him through life's problems! 'Oh, what the hell!' he thought in the end, clenching his fists in his pockets. 'Chances are she won't even be in with weather like this!'

But Gilbert was wrong: the old woman was in. And, what is more, she was soon walking down the aisle towards him. 'Where have you been?' she said, stopping in front of Gilbert with the usual bundle under her arm. 'I've been bringing you your sandwiches, but you never came.' For a moment Gilbert looked up and tried to say something, but quickly discovered that he was too overwhelmed to speak. Then he buried his face in his hands and started to sob like a child.

**

Gilbert is looking up at the cathedral's clock tower. He is trying to determine what time it is. From what he can see, it is almost ten past ten. That is to say, over forty-five minutes before the cathedral's mahogany doors will be swung open for the arriving faithful. Thinking about this depresses Gilbert, makes him wonder whether he should just turn around and walk back to his damp-ridden and cockroach-infested bedsit. What else could he do? The streets are totally empty and the bars are all closed and he knows no one brave enough to let a hardcore drunk like him into their home on a night like this. However, just as he is about to start the long walk back to Glacis, Gilbert catches sight of the cathedral's external side chapel. 'Isn't that where they put up that charity crib every Christmas?' he thinks, recovering his composure. 'Doesn't the place usually stay open all night?'

Though there is nobody inside, the chapel is illuminated by three powerful spotlights. Two of its walls are covered with collages and crayon drawings done by the children of Saint Mary's Primary; the other two are plain and unadorned. The crib itself is located at the far end of the chapel and contains six or seven wax figures just under life-size, along with one or two farm animals made out of papier-mâché. A heavy mahogany balustrade closes it all off, presumably to stop drunken hooligans entering inside and vandalising the wax figures. (Wasn't it last year that someone had sliced off the Virgin's head? Or was it the year before? Try as he may, Gilbert cannot remember.) Hidden somewhere behind the wax figures, a speaker is playing a looped excerpt from Handel's *Messiah:* 'For unto us a child is born, unto us a son is given, and the government shall be upon His Shoulder....'

Gilbert brings up some phlegm and spits it on the marble floor. He has noticed that the Virgin has very sad eyes. Far too sad and dolorous for a woman who has just given birth, he rapidly decides. He wonders whether this is because she is suffering from the sense of anti-climax that women reputedly suffer after childbirth (like his own mum claimed to have suffered after he himself was born), or because she has already gained some knowledge of the fate that awaits her son. It is difficult to say. To be perfectly frank, Saint Joseph does not look much happier either. He is hunched over his staff, quite uninterested in what is happening around him. He looks tired and spectacularly fucked-off, a man who'd rather be somewhere else if given a choice. He has not even noticed that one of the wise men is eyeing up his wife with more than just a passing interest. *Poor old sod*, Gilbert thinks. He reminds him of someone, but he is not sure who. He wonders whether it is the look in the saint's eyes or his big muscular appearance that gives him this impression (or even, for that matter, the fact that he is about to be shamelessly cuckolded). In the cradle, meanwhile, the little baby Jesus smiles and gurgles noiselessly, a rosy pink cherub entirely oblivious to the sad world that engulfs the grown-ups around him....

'That's it!' Gilbert suddenly cries, gripping the wooden balustrade with wild-eyed enthusiasm. 'That's who you remind me of!'

Gilbert releases the balustrade, quite astounded by the mental connection he has just made. Normally, he does not think much about the man or the proposal he made that fateful night. Gilbert simply laughs the whole thing off, views it as something that he managed to clamber out of at the very last minute: 'Jesus Christ, Ali, the things that one almost gets into after a few bevvies too many!' But as he stands there facing the seven wax figures in the crib, he cannot stop blushing at the memory of the man and the debacle that followed. He had met him at the Venture one night about a month and a half ago, a tall German in a sheepskin coat — bearded and broad-shouldered like the statue of Saint Joseph in the crib — who sat down beside him and casually asked him if he wanted a cigarette. *Here we go again,* the ex-boiler fitter thought at that stage. *Another do-gooding martyr intent on saving my soul!*

Gilbert went on to accept the stranger's offer without smiling or saying anything. It was his policy never to refuse a proffered cigarette — something that wouldn't have changed had it been His Excellency the Governor of Gibraltar extending the packet of Fortuna towards him that evening. He then turned his back on the German and rapidly finished the drink in front of him. 'Pour us another J & B, Ali, will you?' he calmly asked the Moroccan barman, totally ignoring the stranger by his side. 'I'm starting to get thirsty again.' It was a trick that Gilbert always employed to deal with situations like these — a mechanism of self-protection that was, in addition, a way of telling others that he wanted to be left alone. A kind of symbolic V-sign, as it were, to the League of Temperance or whatever they called themselves....

Nevertheless, that evening Gilbert found it harder than usual to disengage from what was happening around him. For a long time he could feel the German's eyes on the back of his head, boring into his thoughts, trying to determine exactly what was going on in his brain. The experience unsettled Gilbert, made him even more paranoid about foreigners than he normally was. Taking a long swig of whisky, he remembered the moment their eyes had met as the German had lit his cigarette. He had looked so quiet and so respectable, Gilbert thought, by now extremely aware of the man's presence behind him, *almost priestly*. And yet there was something about him that seemed out of place, something that wasn't quite right. You could almost sense an interior toughness, an aura of hard-fought worldliness that was at odds with the idealism and naivety that frequently plagued most men of the cloth. If anything, this was complemented by the way the guy carried on sitting next to him — without saying a word, without ordering a drink. It was odd, Gilbert thought. Very odd. After nearly three years of heavy drinking, he knew that whenever someone asks to sit beside you at a bar they usually want to tell you something. Some terrible secret they're carrying inside, perhaps. Some cheap lie that will make them look good in your eyes. What they *never did* was to sit there without saying anything.

'Is there nothing you have to say, then?' Gilbert finally said, turning around. 'Are you just going to sit there like a dumb fuck all evening?'

'I just wanted to spend some moments in silence with you,' the German replied calmly, 'that's all.'

Gilbert pulled a disgusted frown. 'You're not gay, are you?'

The German smiled. 'No, not at all.'

'What do you want, then?'

'Have you never walked into a room before and felt that someone needed your company? That something drew you towards them? Made you want to get closer to them? Kind of like an invisible magnet, something you could not explain?'

'No,' Gilbert replied curtly. 'Don't know what the fuck you're on about, mate.'

The German smiled again, this time with a hint of sadness. 'Can I ask you a question?'

'Depends on what you ask.'

'What would you do if you knew you couldn't fail? If you knew that whatever you decided to do would always end up the way you wanted it to end?'

'What would I do?' Gilbert replied, trying to emulate MacGyver's legendary bluntness with people he did not like. 'I'd wish you'd fucking go away and stop wasting my fucking time! That's what I'd fucking wish for!'

'Really?' the stranger asked sombrely. 'Is that what you would *really* wish for?'

For a moment Gilbert looked at the bottles lined up behind the bar and found himself thinking about what the German had said. *What would he wish for? What would he wish for if he knew that his wish would always come true?* He thought about this for some seconds, but — to his annoyance, to his great sense of frustration — realised that he didn't know the answer. More than that: he simply didn't have a clue.

'Who the fuck are you, anyway?' Gilbert suddenly exclaimed, swinging around on his stool. 'You're not a religious freak or something, are you? For fuck's sake, can't a man have a drink without some no-good, Bible-waving *entrometío* coming up to him and trying to save his soul from the fires of perdition!'

'I'm not a Bible-waving whatever-you-call-it,' the German replied, taking out a small card from the inside of his sheepskin jacket and laying it on the counter. 'I'm just someone who wants to help.'

Gilbert looked at the German for some seconds and then at the business card lying between them:

Frank Voss
Spiritualist and Healer
Calle Los Claveles 33a
Jimena, Cadiz
Tel: 9567-333-4354

'I knew it!' Gilbert shouted, almost knocking his glass over with a flailing hand. 'I fucking knew it! You're just a fucking do-gooder like the fucking rest of them!'

The German picked up the card from the counter and put it back into his coat pocket. 'Why are you so scared?' he said calmly.

'I'm not scared!' Gilbert replied angrily. 'I'm just pissed off! I've met plenty of people like you! Loads and loads of them! All of them coming here and trying to save me, all of them convinced that the lives they lead are so much better than mine! You know why you all come here? I tell you why: you come here because it makes you feel better comparing yourselves with grade-A fuck-ups like me!'

'Is that what you think?' the German responded sadly.

'Just fuck off, will you?' Gilbert immediately snapped back. 'Just fuck off and leave me alone!'

The German found it hard to disguise his disappointment. 'If you're angry with me, I will get up and go,' he said. 'I cannot change your feelings if you feel them so strongly. But before I go,' he added with a forced smile, 'I'd like to do something for you.'

'What's that — you're not going to hand me a Bible like the rest of them, are you?'

'No,' the German said. 'I'm going to tell you a story.'

'A story?' Gilbert replied with an angry frown. 'What the fuck are you on about, mate?'

'Twenty minutes,' the German continued without taking his eye off him, 'that's all I'm asking. Once I finish, you can send me straight to hell if you want. You can swear at me as much as you like. Seems like a fair deal, don't you think?'

Gilbert looked at the German in silence for a few seconds and then picked up his tumbler. 'Do me a favour, mate,' he finally said. 'Give us another fag, will you?'

The German smiled brightly and brought out his packet of Fortuna.

'Ten minutes,' Gilbert said. 'I'll give you ten minutes to tell your story. I suppose it'll do no harm. Everyone ends up telling their stories in a shithole like this.'

For the next half hour Gilbert sat on his stool listening to the German's story. In many ways it was not unlike some of the morally instructive tales that Gilbert had been told in the past by other do-gooders, and, for the first few minutes at least, he listened on with a barely concealed scowl on his face, bringing his whisky angrily to his lips every twenty or thirty seconds. Essentially, the story revolved around a drunk like Gilbert, the kind of man who'd lost all hope in life and cared about nothing except his drink. 'Not that it had always been like that for him,' the German said, smiling sadly. A few years before all this he had been a different man. A totally different man, as a matter of fact. He used to have a lovely wife and two beautiful teenage daughters, plus a well-paid job with a large corporation that brought him the respect of all his colleagues. But then, in the German's own words, 'something went wrong, a glitch suddenly arose out of nowhere.' It started at his place of work, where the man had just been promoted to the top echelons of his corporation. With his promotion came new responsibilities and new pressures, new burdens that he had to assume. Thinking it would help him cope better, the man began to indulge in the occasional drink. At first it was just one or two whiskies with soda — just enough to make him relax and forget about things. 'Nothing wrong with a couple of highballs a day,' the man would think, sinking back into his favourite armchair each night. 'Every man deserves a couple of whiskies after a hard day's work at the office — doesn't he?' Gradually, however, these one or two whiskies increased to three or four. Then they became six or seven. Then, a few weeks later, he was going through a whole bottle a day. From that point onwards everything began to fall apart. First, he was sacked from his job after repeatedly turning up drunk to the office.

Next, his wife left him for one of his friends. And finally, to cap it all off, to really turn the knife inside him, the law courts ordered that he could only see his children once every month.

'All right, all right,' Gilbert said, unable to repress a contemptuous smile. 'I think I've more or less sussed this one out, haven't I? The man loses everything and then gradually wins it all back after he stops drinking, right? That's what you're going to tell me now, isn't it?'

'Not quite,' the German said, slowly lighting himself a cigarette. 'Returning home one evening, the man found one of his teenage daughters waiting for him like she always did when she came on her obligatory once-a-month visits. The girl was standing on his porch, trembling and pale. Smiling drunkenly, the man let her in. He locked the door. And you can more or less imagine the rest.... Suffice it to say that, by the time he woke up a few hours later, the man found his daughter huddled in a corner, holding her face in her hands and crying softly. Suddenly the man realised what he had done. The thought sickened him, brought tears to his eyes. "How could I have done this?" he asked himself, remembering how proud he had been at his daughter's birth and how he would have once done anything for her. Mentally, he decided that this was the end, that he had reached the bottom of the abyss. Full of self-disgust, unable to believe that he had sunk so low, he left his house and walked to a motorway footbridge with the intention of killing himself. "This is the end," he thought, staring at the cars speeding along the road below. "This is the end." '

The German took a puff of his cigarette and then put it down on an ashtray. 'What do you think happens next, Gilbert? Do you think a man like this deserves a second chance? Do you think he can turn his whole life around? Picture him with your mind's eye standing there on the bridge, Gilbert — alone and dishevelled, a bottle of whisky still poking out of his pocket, a man who has not seen a bar of soap or a razor for weeks, a foul-mouthed drunk who has just sexually abused his own daughter. Try to visualise him in your head. This is no James Stewart in *It's a Wonderful Life;* this is a tramp, a filthy drunk, a man who has just committed the unpardonable sin. Can you see any hope for him, Gilbert? Is there any way this man can redeem himself?'

Gilbert Spiteri shook his head.

'Well, then, Gilbert — listen to this.... Just as the man was about to throw himself off the bridge, a little kid who was passing by stopped at his side. "Excuse me," he said, tugging at the man's sleeve. "Excuse me, you've dropped something." Grunting to himself, annoyed that he could not even get this last moment right, the man looked down and saw a broken doll lying on the ground. A cheap, smiling, blond-haired Barbie, the kind you can get from any toy shop for a couple of marks. Now, to most people, a cast-off doll may not mean anything, but to the man it reminded him of something that happened to him many years ago. He had been a kid then, not more than ten or eleven years old. He had been teasing his younger sister about a doll she had got as a present. "Farty Pants, Farty Pants!" he shouted while trying to pull the doll away from her. "Your doll's name is Farty Pants!" As he was engaged in doing this, his sister wrenched the doll away from him and its head fell off. Immediately the young girl broke into tears. Much worse — she became totally inconsolable. "Don't worry, sis," the boy said, full of guilt. "Even if it takes me a whole day, I'll fix your doll for you!" Now, all these years later, the words came back to the man and filled his eyes with tears. It was like some secret button had been pressed within his heart that enabled him to gauge things properly at last. During the entire span of his life, he suddenly realised, he had broken many dolls — the dolls that represented his wife and himself when they were happily married, the doll that stood for himself when he had been successful at work, even the sad, trampled doll that he had abused only the night before and that stood for his teenage daughter. He had broken all these dolls and had never tried to fix them, preferring to throw them away like the Barbie doll that currently lay discarded in front of him. The realisation hit the man hard; it made him understand just what a fool and a loser he had been. "From this time on," he promised as he picked up the broken doll and put it in his pocket, "I will dedicate myself to fixing dolls. I will do whatever it takes to repair them." '

'What occurred after that?' Gilbert asked, setting his glass down on the counter. 'Did he go to jail?'

The German nodded. 'Yes. He went to the nearest police station and gave himself up and was sentenced to ten years in jail.'

'And is that where "he" decided to become a spiritualist?' Gilbert asked with a slight hint of mockery in his voice.

'He didn't decide; he was chosen.'

'What do you mean?'

'That day at the bridge he made himself a promise to turn his life around. That promise was *a sacred promise*, it came from the innermost core of his being. When you make yourself a sacred promise like that, God always bestows upon you a gift to help you achieve it. My gift was my mediumship, my desire to heal the lives of others.'

'I still don't understand.'

'Let me put it another way. You see the person sitting here in front of you? He was convicted of sexually assaulting a minor and he spent eight years in jail. He was constantly threatened by his fellow inmates during this time and also taunted by most of the prison officers. Every single night he used to write a letter to his wife and his daughters — but these were always returned to him, unopened and unread, a pile of cheap brown envelopes that grew larger and larger by the side of his bed with every passing day. Now, you tell me, do you think a man in that kind of situation could have been happy?'

Gilbert shook his head slowly.

'*Well, I was,*' the German said, smiling. 'Very happy too. Happier than I had ever been in my life, as a matter of fact. And do you know why? Because that day at the bridge I asked God to take control of my life and do with it whatever he chose. That is why. Because I surrendered to him, because I placed my trust wholly and totally in him — and in so doing was given the gift that I had been searching for all my life without even realising that I was searching for anything.'

Gilbert stared at the German for some seconds, then looked down suddenly at the bar counter. 'I wish I could be as happy as that,' he said softly.

'Then come and meet me tomorrow morning at the Gibraltar-Spain border,' the German replied with a gentle smile. 'I will introduce you to some friends of mine who can help you. They're all volunteer workers and they won't charge you anything. It's time you let go of this life and became everything you were meant to be.'

The German placed his hand on Gilbert's shoulder and smiled again. For a second Gilbert looked up at him in silence, overwhelmed by the simple goodness that radiated out of the man. Then, typical of the emotional wreck that he was, the ex-boiler fitter began to cry. He just could not stop himself. He could feel the tears streaming down his face — hot, uncontrollable tears that stung his eyes and almost burned his skin as they slithered down his cheek. With each tear he shed, something was being dislodged inside him, taken by the root and then slowly ripped out — pieces of himself that had been stuck for a long time inside but which now rose painfully to the surface. He was not exactly sure where these pieces came from, but he knew damn well why he was crying. He was crying because he was thankful. He was crying because he realised that he was being given a chance that he did not really deserve. But more than anything else, he was crying because he suddenly found himself vowing that he would change, *he would change no matter what*, whether he would have to go to the ends of the earth to do so. '*Yes, yes, yes!*' a voice inside him cried. '*I want to be saved! I want to turn my life around! I want to be everything that I was meant to be in life!*'

**

But Gilbert never went to the border the next morning. To this day, he cannot understand why. Frank's story had made him cry, he had felt genuinely moved and had convinced himself that the time had come for him to change — but when the opportunity arose Gilbert just let it slip like sand through his fingers. Something inside had stopped him from taking it, a self-sabotaging streak that suddenly emerged from nowhere and made him spend his morning at *el Venture* instead, sipping brandy and feeling the low, indefinable weight of guilt gnawing at his conscience. 'Is that what life is all about?' Gilbert now wonders, clutching the crib's balustrade and shaking his head. 'An endless stream of contradictions, of doing one thing but meaning the other?' Certainly, that is the pattern that his own life appears to follow. All he has to do is think about that accursed morning at the pub. With a burning sense of shame, he recalls how he had carried on drinking shot after shot of brandy until his guilt faded and he even joked about the German with the other Venture regulars. 'Just imagine, Khalid' — he remembers telling one of the Moroccan drunks — 'I was about to be persuaded to leave you guys by an incestuous, paedophilic Kraut in a sheepskin jacket. Jesus, what the fuck possessed me?' Remembering all this depresses Gilbert; it fills him with tremendous self-disgust. Once again, he tells himself, Gilbert Spiteri had spat into the face of goodness; once again he had scorned the hand stretched out towards him. *Is it any wonder that my life is as fucked up as it is?*

'Hey, you!' a woman's voice suddenly shouts. 'What are you doing there?'

Gilbert turns around and sees an old woman standing by the chapel's entrance. She is carrying a wooden broom in one hand and a rosary in the other. She is also dressed in black from top to toe. She looks like some kind of witch, Gilbert decides. All that she needs is for a black cat to materialise from behind a pillar and start circling around her legs. *Abra-cad-abra. If you don't listen to my words, I'll turn you into a big fat turd.* Within seconds Gilbert forgets about the German spiritualist.

'Have you got no sense of respect?' the old woman continues in the croaking tones of a lifelong spinster. 'Coming to Our Lord's birthplace as drunk as that, *borracho como una cuba?*'

It must be her whining voice — or the fact that she is barely three and a half feet tall. Whatever it is, Gilbert cannot stop himself from laughing. It just tumbles out of him, spontaneously and without check — the uncontainable laughter of a hysterical drunk. 'What am I doing?' he thinks as the tears stream down his cheeks. 'What the hell am I doing?' He knows that it is wrong — laughing in a site of veneration of all places. But at the same time Gilbert Spiteri cannot help himself. Meanwhile, the old woman is getting more and more annoyed. 'You young people have no respect for anything these days!' she hisses, vainly trying to shoo Gilbert off with the broom. 'No respect!' Her words, invariably, make Gilbert laugh even louder.

Gilbert Spiteri leaves the chapel a short while later and walks back into the street. It is still cold and empty out there. Across the road a stray dog is poking his snout into an overturned rubbish bin. The poor animal is twisting and turning on its back, attempting to pull out a large plastic bag stuffed into the bin. Already Gilbert feels bad about laughing at the old woman. He feels terribly, terribly ashamed. Probably the old dear was there to sweep the chapel before Midnight Mass, he thinks. A lonely old spinster, with no family reunion to attend and no friends to cook for. Come to think of it, she even looked similar to the old woman who sometimes brings him sandwiches in the mornings. Shuddering, Gilbert digs his hands into his pockets and walks over to the metal bench where he had earlier found the beers. The five cans are still stacked on top of each other, glinting faintly in the darkness. For a few seconds he stands silently in front of them, swaying on his feet, trying to keep himself steady. Then he prods the tower with the tip of his boot and watches it come tumbling down. *So this is what it means to be alone*, Gilbert Spiteri thinks as the cans rattle on the ground around him. *So this is what it means to have no one in the whole wide world to turn to.* And with this knowledge, with this dark and terrible gleam of self-understanding, he turns around and begins to walk back home.

5. Death of a Tobacco Smuggler

His name was Manuel and he was my best friend at school. He lived about ten minutes away from me and we played together every afternoon. His parents were going through a divorce (I discovered this from a mutual friend, although I wasn't exactly sure what the term meant) and he lived alone with his grandmother, a small, sparrow-like woman with grey hair and nicotine-stained hands that trembled slightly whenever she lit a cigarette. The first time I met him was down at the American Boulevard, a raised concrete promenade with a few potted trees and rickety wooden benches where we kids used to gather after school. I was only eight years or nine years old. As I entered the Boulevard one afternoon, this freckled, ginger-haired kid came up to me and nonchalantly tapped me on the arm. He looked mean and intimidating, a proper little Gibraltarian tearaway. He was also carrying a Dana Point Longboard, one of the most expensive skateboards you could buy at the time.

'You're from Bishop Fitzgerald's Middle, aren't you?' the ginger kid asked, looking me up and down.

'Yes, I am,' I replied, nervously taking a step back. 'Why do you ask?'

'What's your name?'

'Peter.'

'Peter what?'

'Peter Rodriguez.'

'I'm from Bishop Fitzgerald's too, Peter Rodriguez.'

'Really?' I said softly. 'That's strange! I've never seen you before.'

'My grandmother's just moved from Glacis to Arengo,' he said, calmly picking a bogey from his nose. 'I've been taken out of Saint Anne's and put in that shitty school of yours so that I don't have to walk so far. Anyway,' he suddenly said, flicking out the skateboard from under his arm, 'enough of all that shit. You want my skateboard or not?'

'You what?'

'I said you want my skateboard or not?'

'Wha-what do you mean?'

'I said you want the Longboard, dumbo. Are you kids at Bishop Fitzgerald's all a bunch of retards or what?'

'But I have nothing to give you for it,' I feebly protested.

'Don't worry about that,' he replied with a dismissive shake of the head. 'I don't want anything for it. Just promise me that you'll join my gang and that I'll always be your leader, that you'll stand by me and follow my orders no matter what — and you can have it. Deal or no deal?'

I looked at the sparkling combination of aluminium and orange plastic in front of me and then I looked back at him. 'Deal,' I said.

**

When my mother found out how I had got the Longboard, she grew very cross. She told me that it was wrong to take things without paying for them and that I wouldn't get far in life if I carried on acting like this. I remember feeling pretty stupid and sheepish as I handed the skateboard over to Manuel the next day — almost like I had committed a crime and was now being forced to apologise to my victim. Despite this, Manuel and I became good friends and began to meet at the Boulevard every afternoon after school. We did all the things that eight-year-old Gibraltarian kids used to do in those days — we smuggled our way into MOD sports pitches to play football, we went skateboarding in the *piazzela* beside the old Theatre Royal, we'd trek up to the Upper Rock and pretend that we were American soldiers making our way through the Vietnamese jungle. Once we had a fight and Manuel wrestled me to the ground and pinned my arms behind my back. For the next two or three days I stayed at home, too embarrassed to leave the flat. Then one afternoon someone knocked on our front door and to my delight I found Manuel standing on the landing outside. 'Fancy coming out, Peter?' he said, grinning mischievously. 'There's a big football tournament on at the Boulevard between us and *los ingleses.*'

There is one memory, though, that stands out from the others. It dates back to our first or possibly second year at Bishop Fitzgerald's, and it occurred in the Regal II, an old movie house on Reclamation Road that was knocked down many years ago.

Manuel and I used to go there regularly to see the Saturday afternoon matinee. We'd normally sit at the front of the hall, eagerly clutching our Coke cans and our packets of jelly babies as we waited for the show to begin. I can't remember what film they played that day, but it must have been some godawful American B-movie — *20,000 Leagues Under the Sea*, *The Revenge of the Mutant Alligators* or something of that nature. As those were the days before the British government banned tobacco advertising in cinemas, adverts for cigarettes and alcohol were regularly screened during the intermission — even though the average age of the audience wasn't higher than nine or ten. Among those they played every week was one for Piccadilly cigarettes. It was actually quite a funny advert — a guy with a handlebar moustache hops out of a red Lamborghini, calmly strolls up to some girl in a skin-tight dress, lights her a cigarette and then disappears with her back into the car while a chorus of girls start chanting 'Piccadilly, Piccadilly' in the background. An example of seventies machismo at its worst! Anyway, when the advert came on that day, Manuel did something that no one had ever done before: he stood up on his seat and started chanting 'Pica-willy' instead of 'Piccadilly'. It happened just like I am relating it — entirely without warning. For a moment he stood there silhouetted against the screen behind him, screaming at the top of his lungs and thrashing his arms about like a conductor directing an invisible orchestra. Then all the other kids joined him in a cacophonous chorus that swept across the entire *Regal II:* 'Pica-willy, pica-willy, for that long, long moment of pleasure!'

For the next couple of years things remained more or less the same. I'd meet Manuel practically every day after school and together we'd get up to all kinds of mischief — ringing doorbells and running away, playing football in *la piazzela*, dropping homemade stink bombs in crowded public areas. At one point we even decided to form our own under-elevens football team — the *Bishop Fitzgerald's Skywalker's Eleven* was the somewhat unfortunate name we chose for it — but quickly gave up on the idea when we could attract no one to our ranks save my tomboyish next-door neighbour Mariella and one of Manuel's sissy second cousins.

Another time we tried to construct a raft with the planks of a broken wooden pallet — but saw it sink less than ten yards from the shoreline at Eastern Beach. It was one glorious catastrophe after the other, but we always had great fun anyway, always ended up laughing so much that we came close to wetting ourselves. '*Son como dos hermanos,*' all the adults around us would say, smiling with amusement at our 'inseparability'. And they were not far off the mark either: on the third of March, 1979, on a blustery, grey day that both of us swore never to forget, Manuel and I cut our thumbs with a penknife and mixed our blood in the name of eternal brotherhood....

Then the unthinkable happened: our paths started to diverge. It began in September 1980, when my dad had to attend a mechanic's training course in England. Not knowing how he'd cope for six months without anyone cooking and cleaning for him, my father did what most Gibraltarian men would have done under the circumstances: he decided to take his family with him. It was, of course, a really big step for us all and I spent our last few weeks in Gibraltar dreaming about how exciting it would be to live in a land where I could play football on a proper grass pitch instead of the cinder shambles that we had down at our own Victoria Stadium. I made plans for it all — the high street sports shops I'd visit, the Division One football matches I'd force my dad to take me to, the autographs of famous Liverpool players I'd somehow obtain and in this way become the envy of all my mates back in Gibraltar. For about three months, it is fair to say, I could hardly think of anything else.

Then came the evening before we headed off to the UK. I don't think I will ever forget that day. Every man, they say, carries a book of memory within him. Inscribed within this book are key dates and phrases, mental photographs of people and places, events that have long since gone but which will remain with him to his dying day. That last evening I spent with Manuel in Gibraltar was very much like that for me. It was a warm September afternoon, I remember, and the Levanter cloud was suffocating the whole town with a cloak of humidity. (For those who don't know what I'm talking about, the Levanter cloud is a stubborn, stagnant mist that forms over the top of the Rock when pockets of warm, moist air rise up its eastern face and come into contact with the colder fronts near the summit. People say it is just another facet of Gibraltar's *Britishness* — the fact that we sometimes get grey skies while it continues bright and sunny across the border in Spain.) After sharing a bag of doughnuts that Manuel had brought with him, we went skateboarding next to the old Theatre Royal and then we bought some football stickers from the little corner shop at the bottom of Valdayo's Ramp, the one owned by the balding, gap-toothed guy who was said to look at girls from our school in a way that wasn't really acceptable. I remember drawing Joe Jordan out of my packet, a player that I hated as much for his association with Manchester United as for his thuggish appearance. For a while Manuel and I sat on some railings outside the shop, swapping stickers and shooting the empty wrappers into a manhole that some PWD worker had forgotten to close off. It was just like any other day — only this time the thought that I'd be flying to England in less than twenty-four hours loomed at the back of my mind. Tons of stuff needed to be done before then. Bags had to be packed. Posters had to be taken down from walls and inserted into protective cardboard tubes. Addresses had to be copied into my brand-new address book. Consequently, I got up after a short time and said that perhaps I should be going. At this point Manuel slid off the railing and proceeded to stretch his arms behind his back. He then yawned aloud. For a few unsettling seconds he stood there without saying anything, smiling and looking every inch the street urchin that he was, almost as if he were trying to devise one last valedictory prank to play on me. 'Good luck, Peter,' he finally said, stepping forward and embracing me in a show of affection that took me totally by surprise. 'Make sure you show those English kids what Gibraltarians are made of.' Then he turned around and walked away, without once looking back.

It is not my intention to include much here about those six months in England. What I will say is that things didn't quite go as I expected and I ended up discovering, possibly for the first time in my life, that even the best-laid plans can sometimes go astray. On my first day at school, I was called a 'dirty foreigner'. A couple of days later, I was pushed to the ground and spat upon. By the end of the week, I got kicked in the stomach and pelted with empty crisp packets in the playground. From then on it was a constant stream of abuse — racist insults, random beatings, unexpected provocations. For an eleven-year-old not used to any kind of victimisation, the strain was enormous to bear, crushing in its intensity. With tears in my eyes, I would lie awake every night in bed, grinding my teeth and counting the days left before we flew back to Gibraltar. Back to Manuel and to the American Boulevard. To the beach and to skateboarding in *la piazzela*. To playing football at the Victoria Stadium and going fishing from the North Mole. To all the things, in other words, that I had known for the first ten and a half years of my life, but which had suddenly been taken away from me during those six godawful months I spent in Pontefract, South Yorkshire.

But when I got back things had changed: Manuel was no longer the same Manuel that I once knew. He smoked now and hung out with girls and kept using really bad Spanish swear words like *coño* or *puta*. It was a dramatic transformation, although not, I must confess, entirely unexpected. Some of the kids in my English school, you see, had already been acting in a similar manner — drinking beer, smoking cigarettes, constantly swearing, swapping porn magazines, talking about the girls they had 'snogged' at the youth club the previous evening. At the time I regarded all this as an Anglo-Saxon phenomenon, something that couldn't possibly happen in my beloved Gibraltar. But now that I had come back I realised that such raffish behaviour wasn't such a singularly English thing after all. For example, whenever I now phoned Manuel to ask him if he wanted to play football, he would always claim that he had something to do. 'Not today, Pete,' he would say, sounding quite irritated. 'I've got lots of homework.' Or the other classic response: 'Maybe tomorrow, Rodi. I've got to help my Gran with the shopping this afternoon.' At first I took him at his word, unable to believe that my best mate could have been lying to me. But then one day I found him smoking with a group of older kids by a street corner at a time he was supposed to be helping his Gran paint the kitchen ceiling. 'Hi, Peter,' he said, calmly taking a drag. 'Awful bastard fucking weather we're having, bro, don't you fucking think?'

From that day onwards things were never the same between us. I stopped phoning Manuel, while he never made any effort to get in touch with me. In fact, by the time we moved into Bayside Comprehensive School a few months later, the break was virtually complete — Manuel was moved into a lower band class, while I got put into one of the higher ones. We still said 'hello' when we saw each other in the playground, but it was never like it used to be. I was your typical bookish student, quiet and lost in my own thoughts, often reading subjects outside the curriculum and lagging behind in my academic studies as a result. Peter 'Swotriguez' — that's what everyone called me. The class bookworm. The resident nerd. By contrast, Manuel was your typical classroom thug — uninterested in anything except sex and drugs and overturning whatever rules could be overturned. Even now I can remember all the shit he got up to: setting off the corridor fire alarms, climbing the school gates, flooding the toilets, smoking in the science laboratory. Then, just before our second year at Bayside was out, Manuel went a step too far: he threw a chair at a teacher during Group 8's RE class and was immediately expelled from school. The teacher's name was Mr. O'Sullivan and he had been brought over from Ireland on a year's contract to neutralise the dearth of local RE tutors. I can't recall the exact circumstances leading to the event itself — I think that Mr. O'Sullivan had just told Manuel to stop digging his ruler into another kid's ribs or something like that — but I do seem to remember that the Irishman had to be taken to Saint Benedict's Hospital and given six stitches above one of his eyes. Definitely not what poor old Paddy must have envisaged when hearing about his dream Mediterranean posting some months earlier!

Over the next couple of years I did not see Manuel much. I was busy studying for my A-levels and only caught sight of him every now and then, usually out in the streets with the older guys that he hung around with. Sometimes he would say hello to me; but other times, especially when he was with his friends, he would just carry on walking past and totally blank me. Often I found myself wondering what he was up to, trying to figure out how things would eventually shape up for him. I did not have to wait long to find out. Sitting in the sixth-form common room one afternoon just before my A-levels, I read in the *Gibraltar Chronicle* that a juvenile had been arrested for assaulting a Moroccan fishmonger. The victim had suffered numerous facial lacerations and had to be taken to Saint Benedict's Hospital. Taking into account that the accused was only eighteen years old, the judge sentenced him to only twenty months in jail. His name was Manuel Sciandri.

Things moved very fast at this point. My A-levels came and went and before I knew it I was doing a History degree at the University of Manchester. There I became involved with a second-year Modern Languages student by the name of Marsha Marsden. A buxom, red-headed, emotionally volatile, somewhat uncommitted feminist whose two great obsessions were Lindt chocolates and Californian Cabernet Sauvignon, the delightful Miss Marsden had such a powerful effect on me that I quickly forgot all about Charlemagne, the Black Death, the High Gothic Style, the Spanish Inquisition ... or anything else that I was supposed to be studying. A classic case of first love infatuation, no doubt. Soon I began to receive written warnings about my non-attendance in class. Finally, one day I was called before the university's disciplinary board and told to pack up my bags and go back home. This was not a course of action I was particularly keen on. To begin with, I would have to face the unpalatable task of explaining to my parents how I had squandered my hard-earned government scholarship. Secondly — and more importantly, as far as I was concerned — it would tear me away from the side of my beloved Miss Marsden. Therefore, I decided to stay in Manchester as a 'non-student.' The plan was to get a job and rent a flat somewhere near the university campus. To live on my own until Marsha finished her second year and moved in with me. Here fate threw a spanner into the works. Although I religiously applied for every admin vacancy that appeared in the *Manchester Evening News,* I was never granted the privilege of a job interview. And when a company called Balban's Chemical Solutions asked me to attend what they described as 'a pre-interview information session', I duly bottled it and stayed in the Student Union playing *Asteroids* and *Space Invaders* instead. So in the end the inevitable happened: I ran out of money and was forced to return to Gibraltar with my tail between my legs.

The next couple of months were testing ones. Out of all the kids in my old sixth form who went on to college, I was the first to abandon his studies and come back to Gibraltar. This rather singular honour pissed me off considerably. More than that: it seriously undermined my morale. Loser. Failure. Has-been. It didn't take an overly paranoid mind to work out what names people must have been calling me behind my back. If that wasn't enough, my slim-waisted, ginger-haired Miss Marsden — who only a few weeks earlier had been pledging her undying love for me — suddenly phoned me one evening and said it was all over between us. She gave no real excuse or explanation as to what had precipitated this decision; just that things would have never worked out and, of course, that I deserved *something much better* than what she could offer me. The usual break-up spiel, I suppose — with the only difference that this time it was being relayed from a distance of some eight hundred miles away. On top of that, around this time I had to endure the indignity of being thrown into jail for a night after an unsavoury episode with a fruit machine and two drunken English squaddies. (What can I say? Bad luck seems to follow me around!) It was partly to forget about all this that I took the first job that came my way — driving an ice cream van for a local food and drinks supplier. It was not the most challenging of jobs, but at least I was my own boss and I could do more or less what I wanted. My daily routine was much the same each day: I would drive my van around the different housing estates in the mornings and then, following a short lunch composed mainly of ice creams taken from the van's fridge, I would roll down to Eastern Beach and park in a lay-by next to the seaside promenade. There I would remain until six or seven in the evening, enduring the howling screams of the little kiddies and the angry recriminations of one or two mums who had convinced themselves that I had sold half-melted lollies to their precious darlings. Wonderfully thrilling stuff!

For a few weeks I shunted every day between my parents' flat and Eastern Beach, only taking a break when there was a strong Levanter wind and there was no point in going out in the van. Then there were the sundry inconveniences that I had to put up with as a teenage ice cream seller. Not only, for example, did my customers grant me all the respect normally allotted to a dog turd, but rare indeed was the day when another member of the ice cream vending fraternity wouldn't accuse me of encroaching into his territory or undercutting the price of his Strawberry Splits. *Vamo, la verdadera poca vergüenza que tiene el niño!* As if all that wasn't humiliating enough, I also had to deal with the steady stream of young smugglers that came down to the beach every afternoon. That was another story altogether. First, the cocky shits would pull up abruptly next to your clapped-out van in their brand-new Mercs or Beemers. Then they'd throw a tightly rolled-up twenty- or fifty-pound note through your open window. '*Dame dos* Calipo and one Strawberry Split, *vale, tío.*' Finally, after you handed over their order, they would tear open their ice creams, throw the wrappers on the ground and then rev off without even bothering to say thank you, *without even acknowledging you.* Clearly — whichever way you looked at it — it was not the most inspiring of scenarios. After almost a whole summer enduring such affronts, I decided that I couldn't handle it any longer. I *had* to quit that job for the sake of my sanity. I simply had no option. So one day I drove my Bedford Rascal van back to my employers on Devil's Tower Road and told them that I had had enough of screaming kids and overprotective mothers and adolescent smugglers and that I'd rather go on the dole than sell another Orange Maid again. That done, I walked out of the building and screamed at the top of my voice with sheer happiness.

It only took about three days before I regretted my decision. I was alone in my parents' flat at the time, watching some mid-morning discussion TV programme about heroin on the streets of Edinburgh. 'Life,' some pallid guy was saying in a near-incomprehensible Scots accent, 'used to be a rainbow full of colours for me until I met heroin — then it all changed.' The moment I heard this, something inside me went cold. I can't describe precisely what it was, but it felt almost as if a shadow had passed over me, a wave of acute self-consciousness that almost left me gasping for breath. Suddenly I began to think about my university days and how things would have shaped up had I not been thrown off my course. More particularly, I thought about Marsha and how we'd have probably still been together had I not scampered off back to Gibraltar. That cut me up badly, I must admit. Really, really badly. For a while I just sat there in my dressing gown, still watching the Scottish guy speak but without registering anything that he was saying any more. Then I got up, went to my room and climbed straight into bed.

It must have been only two or three weeks after this episode that Manuel re-entered my life. To this day, I still wonder what strange power brought us together a second time. Two lines, drawing away from each other with each passing year, following their respective courses in total counterpoint to one another, suddenly and without warning begin to converge inwards again. Must have something to do with destiny, don't you think?... But to return to my story — coming out of my block of flats one morning, I discovered Manuel standing on the opposite side of the street. He looked fatter and older, his once hairless chin now hidden under a layer of thick ginger fuzz. 'Hello, Peter,' he said, smiling and taking a puff from a cigarette. 'Fancy seeing you again.' He then told me that he had recently been released from jail and that he was living with his new girlfriend in a flat just down the road at *la Calle Comedia*. He said that he had had a rough time in jail, but that he had learned his lesson and was going straight. 'Don't wanna go through all that re-ha-bil-i-ta-tive bullshit all over again,' he assured me, laughing. As he talked, I noticed several gold chains and religious medallions bulging under his half-open shirt. I also spotted the talon of a dragon or some other mythical creature etched across his left collarbone, the only visible part of a tattoo that must have stretched all the way down to his chest.

From then on I'd often catch Manuel hanging around our estate. He was always smoking and always on his own, a lonely and friendless ex-con (I assumed) with nothing better to do. Once, as I was returning home from yet another fruitless trip to the Employment and Training Board, I briefly caught sight of his girlfriend. She was standing at the top of *la calle Comedia*, waiting for him to throw her a beach towel from their first-floor balcony. She had cinnamon skin and shoulder-length black hair and looked a little bit like a young Sofia Loren. Her name, Manuel told me when I saw him again some days later, was Lydia and she was a Spaniard from the border town of La Línea de la Concepción. Lydia Maria De Los Angeles y Tortosa — to use the whole Roman Catholic and Apostolic shebang. Manuel had met her at the Acropolis Piano Bar in Fuengirola just after his release and she had moved in with him some weeks later. When I first saw her I could not believe that a drop-dead gorgeous bit of stuff like her could be with someone like him. She looked so elegant, so sophisticated — almost the exact antithesis of the washed-out character that Manuel had become. Something told me that Manuel was up to his bad boy tricks again.

It was around this time too that I began to go metal detecting at Eastern Beach. Looking back on the whole enterprise, it was quite an insane idea, a typically hare-brained scheme of mine. But as the Spanish proverb says, *cuando el pan falta, la mente siempre salta* (or, in a less poetic, anglicised version, 'when you are desperately short of funds even the most pathetic of glimmers will resemble the shine of gold'). It all started back at my parents' flat one evening, halfway through a conversation I had with my dad. We were watching a TVE documentary on buried treasure at the time. I still have a vivid mental picture of it — sand-encrusted emeralds and misshapen doubloons being sucked into a giant rubber aspirator while Bach's 'Air on a G-string' played atmospherically in the background.

'I once found a gold ring at Eastern Beach,' my dad suddenly said.

'How exactly did you come to find it, Dad?'

'It was just lying there,' he replied without taking his eyes off the screen.

'What did you do with it?'

'Took it to Cohen and Massias and sold it for thirty pounds,' he said, calmly stroking the side of his nose. 'Bought myself my first ever television with the money.'

What my father said about the ring didn't really surprise me. Us Gibraltarians have never been the most careful of people with our jewellery. Every summer we all go down to the beach draped in gold: chains, earrings, bracelets, anklets — anything that will show off and confirm our wealth to those around us. It's just like in any other small Mediterranean town — natural Latin ostentation combines with a practically crime-free environment to make the beach as good an exhibition ground as the trendiest of jet-set salons. Thinking about all this, I suddenly had an idea. A really brilliant and original idea. What if I now bought a metal detector and started combing the beach for lost items of jewellery? What if I did that faithfully and conscientiously every day? Surely, it'd be next to no time before I made enough money to fly back to the UK and reclaim my estranged dolly bird in Manchester!

It was called a Goldak Commander and I bought it with the little cash left over from my ice cream vending days. For the next few weeks I took it with me every morning to Eastern Beach, but I never found anything. Or perhaps I should rephrase that — I never found anything other than a few rusty coppers and a handful of ring-pulls. It was, of course, a major disappointment. A bitter pill to swallow. As I shuffled my way through the damp, grey sands, all I could think about was the one hundred and fifty-eight pounds that I had so foolishly wasted on that useless heap of junk!

I must have been metal detecting for about a month by the time I stumbled upon Manuel at Eastern Beach one afternoon. Summer had already ended and the beach was now empty except for a few die-hard sun-seekers, desperate to soak up some last rays before the onset of the autumn Levanter. After sweeping the shoreline in a slow zigzag, I noticed a group of men crouched near the wall that separated the beach from the adjoining road. They all wore baseball caps and dark sunglasses. They also looked very menacing. Obviously tobacco smugglers, I thought, catching sight of the walkie-talkies hooked on their belts and the binoculars hanging from their necks. As I turned back towards the shore again, one of them stood up and began to run in my direction. For a moment I stood still, my heart pounding against my ribcage. As the figure came closer, though, I realised that it was none other than my old friend Manuel Sciandri.

'*Qué pasa*, Peter,' he wheezed out with considerable effort as he finally came to a stop beside me. 'What you doing, man?'

I removed my metal detecting headphones and looked at him with an embarrassed smile. 'What was that again?'

'What are you doing with that thing, man? You look like something out of *Star Trek*, *tío*.'

I gazed disconsolately at the metal detector for some seconds and then looked up at him. 'It's supposed to be my ticket to fame and fortune,' I said.

'Your what?'

'It's what I try and do for a living, Manuel,' I said, retracting the detector's telescopic stem and then slinging the entire apparatus over my shoulder. 'It's better than going down to the Employment and Training Board every morning and being told the same old "no vacancies today" rubbish.'

'And do you ever find anything valuable?'

I unzipped my waistpouch with my remaining free hand and brought out a cluster of ring-pulls. 'Does this answer your question?' I said.

'Do you want to earn yourself a few quid, mate?' Manuel replied, smiling incredulously. 'One of our guys has let us down big time and we're looking for someone to replace him. Come with us, *anda, Pete-ito*.'

In this way began my career as a tobacco smuggler. It was not a very long career, I hasten to add, and it was not something that I am particularly proud of, but it happened so there is no point in denying it either. As for my actual work as a smuggler, there is hardly anything glamorous to relate. Nine times out of ten, you find yourself sitting with two guys and a quarter ton of cigarettes in a Volkswagen van just next to Eastern Beach. You sit there at night, with your lights and engine switched off, smoking cigarettes and drinking cups of thermos coffee. Out in the Bay, meanwhile, there is a launch with another two guys waiting to come inshore.

They are waiting to receive a signal from the lookout (who is normally perched somewhere near the top of the Rock with a pair of infra-red binoculars) saying that there are no Gibraltar police in the vicinity. This is because, contrary to what most tobacco smugglers may claim about doing nothing illegal within Gibraltar itself, exporting tobacco from the Rock is hardly a *bona fide* activity. Although anyone can buy cigarettes in large quantities in Gibraltar, you can only export the damn stuff with a valid merchant trader's licence and, as virtually no one in the contraband trade possesses the document in question, 'legal tobacco exportation' is really not that legal at all. You therefore have two simple options. You can either raise your middle finger at Providence and load up your launch at the marina where it is berthed — or you can go down to one of the beaches where things are generally a bit quieter and do it there. If you decide to go for the second option (which is what we almost always did) you are obliged, as I have already said, to spend some time smoking and drinking coffee in the van until the lookout tells the boys at sea that it is safe for them to steer inshore. You then have to get out of the vehicle and run with the 15 kg boxes across the beach to the waiting launch. This is not usually a difficult process — although sometimes, because you are working under such accelerated conditions, accidents can happen. Once, for example, I tripped over one of the boxes and banged my head against a stone lying on the beach. Another time this massive wave caught us by surprise and sent us all sprawling into the sea! However, most of the time we *did* manage to pack the boxes into the launch and then push it safely away from the shore. Moreover, once this phase of the operation is out of the way, there is not much left for us box loaders to do. Yes, you do carry on smoking cigs and drinking coffee in the van for a bit longer — but this time you are only there in case the merchandise cannot for some reason be dropped off on the Spanish side and it has to be hastily brought back *into* Gibraltar....

On the face of it, it all sounds quite simple, an easy way to make a few hundred bucks without too much effort. But tobacco smuggling, like all things in life, also has its flipside. Going out on the boat, for a start, can be a really risky affair. I only went out to sea three times during my entire smuggling career, but on each occasion I was half-scared to death. You sit there completely enveloped in darkness, about a mile or two away from shore. Your engines have been switched off because your lookout has told you that the drop-off point on the Spanish side is presently crawling with *guardias civiles*. You have already been stationary like this for forty-five minutes, maybe an hour. Meanwhile, you rub your gloved hands. You listen to the murmur of the waves lapping against the launch. You look at the orange and yellow lights of the mainland flickering in the distance. If you are of a sentimental disposition — and floating aimlessly at night like that, let me tell you, has a tendency to sentimentalise all but the most simple-minded of men — you wonder what your friends and family are currently doing. You wonder if they are thinking about you like you are thinking about them. From time to time you can hear the engines of other speedboats zooming past you. You cannot see them — because all tobacco launches travel with their lights switched off — but you can sense their presence as a result of all the shaking and rattling around you. *Jesus Christ! Did you hear that? How bloody close was that?* It is principally for this reason, I believe, that the call from the lookout to move on is always greeted with such a sense of relief. Although, objectively speaking, it is hard to see why, you somehow think you are safer when you are moving than when you are totally stationary. Maybe it is because you no longer feel you'd be a sitting target in case of an accidental collision; maybe it is because you think you are in control of your own destiny — I don't know. Anyway, things don't really improve once you get going. Your bow rises to a crazily high position and every medium-sized wave feels like a sledgehammer going through the side of your fibreglass hull. Even if you are only a co-driver and don't have to do any actual steering, you are forced to cling to your seat if you don't want to get tossed overboard. Not, it has to be said, that this is the worst of the problems facing you. Remember, you are navigating without lights or any other form of guidance, so you can't see where you are going and no one can see you in turn. Ultimately, this is what makes the whole experience so scary, what really gets your adrenaline pumping. Although you try hard not to think about it, at the back of your mind you know that almost anything could be out there: submerged rocks, fishermen's nets, hidden sandbanks, stationary tobacco launches. The same applies to all those items of waste that passing oil tankers dispose of illegally in the Straits — oil drums, wooden pallets, broken-down washing machines, old mattresses. Crash into any of that shit at seventy miles an hour and you'll soon be feeding the fishes....

Not that visibility is always as bad as that. Sometimes a full moon hangs in the sky and you can see everything around you — oil tankers, floating mattresses, wooden pallets, as well as the other launches, all of them laid out like pieces on a giant black marble chessboard. It is actually quite a sublime sight, the kind of moonlit seascape that would surely make a fantastic poster. But such picture-postcard prettiness also has its price. Just as the moon shows you what is out there, so too it can alert the Spanish authorities of your presence at sea. That, it goes without saying, is not good. More accurately, it is absolutely disastrous. Once, I remember, I was sitting in the van with my partners Big Gonzo and Master-Blaster when we heard the rotating blades of a *guardia civil* helicopter about half a mile away. Moments later, a solitary speedboat appeared against the horizon, its small black hull illuminated by a single shaft of grainy light. Shots rang out, shouts were heard. 'It's all right, it's all right,' Manuel's voice suddenly crackled out of the radio. 'It's not us in that launch. We're about two miles away. We can hear the shots and see the helicopter's beam on the boat, but we're a long way away....' Even so, you still felt for the poor unknown buggers who were out there getting shot at in the darkness. Alone inside that fibreglass shell, screaming impotently as the bullets hailed down on them....

All in all, I must have worked as a smuggler for some twelve or fourteen weeks. Contrary to what I thought that first day at Eastern Beach, the guys were a decent and friendly enough lot. It seems to me that people have these fixed ideas about smugglers — inasmuch as they are all, without exception, seen as obnoxious, mindless degenerates who persist in squandering away their money on cars and cocaine without the slightest scruples of conscience. This may be true of some of the young kids who get involved in the contraband trade — I had seen as much during my ice cream selling days — but there are also many others who are not like that at all. Get close to this last group and you will realise that they are just ordinary human beings. People who are fed up with earning one hundred pounds a week and want to achieve something more in life, that's all. Look at me — I was just an ordinary guy with ordinary concerns, the kind who would have run a mile to avoid any trouble. I read novels by Graham Greene, I listened to China Crisis and Duran Duran, I liked architecture and museums — not exactly the sort of things you would associate with a smuggler, are they? And yet people, not just in neighbouring Spain but in Gibraltar as well, seem to have this idea fixed in their heads — as if every smuggler has to conform to their own preconceptions. I was able to experience this phenomenon several times during my short smuggling career. Time and again, we would get people looking at us with undisguised disgust as we drove past in our battered Volkswagen van, the twin flames of hatred and suspicion flickering in their eyes, as if we were no better than rapists or child-murderers. Although there was obviously an element of self-defence in this — in the sense that they were placing what they saw as an aberrational form of behaviour into a reassuring frame of reference — there was also something cruel and tragic about these folks' actions. Regardless of the wrongs and rights of smuggling, people should realise that it is just ordinary guys who are engaged in this sort of activity, ordinary guys who breathe and laugh and clown around and sometimes, when things go wrong, die in the nastiest possible circumstances. Of course, that does not mean that all these pre-conceived ideas are always mistaken. Sometimes, evidently, you do get those who live up to the stereotype. Our own lookout, for instance, was this guy whose nickname was *el Follador*. Earrings on both ears, hair greased back with *brilliantine*, shirt always opened down to his navel — he was the living reason why certain North Europeans still carry on maligning us Latins over four hundred years after the repulse of the Armada. A real dago scumbag, if you know what I'm getting at. Whether he talked about sniffing cocaine with his mates or screwing Scandinavian girls at the Costa del Sol, there was always the same look of mischief in his eyes, the same posturing swagger. 'They're all the same,' he once said to us halfway through a late-night fry-up at *El Martillo*. 'Buy a Scandinavian bitch a few drinks and she's as good as in your bed. Either because they like getting fucked or because the stupid bitches just can't say no.'

El Follador, though, was just an exception. It is important to stress this — just as it is important to note that none of the others really had that much to do with him, only tolerating him because he made them laugh with the sheer ridiculousness of his sexist and homophobic opinions (a wonderful antidote, I must nevertheless admit, in situations of extreme pressure). Take Fitoman, for example, the guy who led the operation and the co-owner of the launch along with Manuel. On the outside, he looked like the most fearsome guy imaginable: six foot three, with jet-black hair to his shoulders and a Celtic armband tattooed around his gym-trained biceps. Yet behind that rough, deliberately provocative façade, Fitoman was actually one of the nicest, kindest, most genuine guys going. A joiner by trade and the father of three kids, he was always there with encouraging words — reassuring you, inspiring you, promising that the job would get done without complications and that we'd all be having a lardy fry-up together before we knew it....

Big Gonzo and Master-Blaster, my two companions in the van, were also decent enough. Big Gonzo was a part-time corporal with the Gibraltar regiment — a squat, crew-cutted guy who was always talking about Manchester United and eating Pot Noodles. *El Master*, his best friend since school, had once been a panel beater's apprentice at the dockyard, but had been unable to find a job after the yard partially closed down. Like 'Fitoman' and '*el Follador*', 'Big Gonzo' and '*el Master*' weren't real names — only verbal tags given to them on account of personal idiosyncrasies. Although these were primarily used to disguise our identity when we talked over the radio, they also reflected the great camaraderie between us, the close fraternal bonds that held the group together. My own nickname was '*el Estudiante*' (or 'the student'). The others got this moniker from a *teleserie* they used to show back in the eighties called *Curro Jiménez*. A typical TVE production, it was about some nineteenth-century Spanish bandit who operated in the Sierra near Ronda — fighting the French, mobilising the peasantry, robbing the rich, giving money to the poor and generally doing all the things that noble, big-hearted Spanish outlaws were supposed to have done during the Peninsular War. '*El Estudiante*' was one of the members of Curro's band of gallant ruffians: a young, skeletally thin guy with a goatee beard and a half-rusted musket who was supposed to have studied at the University of Salamanca before turning to banditry....

Last but not least, there was my mate Manuel — or *el Puffy*, as he was now known because of his bloated, puffed-out features. He was one of the two regular drivers in the gang, alternating at the wheel with Fitoman every two or three journeys. Always quiet and taciturn, never sharing his thoughts with anyone, the guy had clearly changed a lot since our time at school. Back in those days, he had been such a carefree and lively spirit, always outspoken and rebellious, ready to challenge everyone and push things to their limits; now he rarely talked about anything other than the job at hand. He was still ready to take risks, don't get me wrong. That streak within him had probably intensified with the passing of the years. But, alas, it was no longer accompanied by that irrepressible sense of energy that had once crackled through everything he did. A light had gone out within him, a part of his old personality appeared to have died — as if all those months in prison had subdued an essential element of his being. Only very rarely would he stop and talk about something that we had done in our younger days — some prank we played on one of our classmates, some middle-school football match in which both of us had scored goals. And even then you got the feeling that he looked back more with a sense of puzzled curiosity than with any real nostalgia. Possibly the longest 'conversation' we ever had happened outside the tobacco retailer's depot, halfway down the old North Front Road. It was a mild autumn afternoon and Manuel and I were loading boxes of Winston into the van while the others carried them out to us. I was not exactly in buoyant spirits at the time: I was trying to re-establish some form of amicable contact with my ex, but the heartless woman was having none of it. As we toiled together in silence, I noticed that most of Manuel's medallions were hanging out of his half-open shirt. Nearly all of them were engraved with the same figure — a stooping, sad-eyed Madonna with a crown of gleaming stars on her head. Some were no larger than five-penny pieces; others — I don't exaggerate! — were the size of Olympic medals. Intrigued, I set aside my usual reserve and asked him whether the medallions had any religious significance.

'It's *la Virgen del Carmen*,' he said, holding out the largest of the medallions. 'The patron saint of Andalusian fishermen. They say that if anyone believes in her with all his might they will always be protected at sea.'

'And do you really believe in any of that Andalusian peasant rubbish?' I asked as I carried on loading boxes by his side.

Manuel's swollen features twisted into a sarcastic grimace. 'Not me, mate. I just wear them to keep my Lydia happy, know what I mean, Rodi?'

Ironically enough, it must have been three or four weeks after this episode that our smuggling days came to a sudden end. We were parked at Eastern Beach in Fitoman's van at the time, Big Gonzo, Master-Blaster and me, the three of us having a smoke while we waited for the guys to make the drop-off on the Spanish side. I was trying to read the *Gibraltar Chronicle;* Big Gonzo and *el Master* were listening to a tape by Ace of Base or some other early nineties band. So far it had been an unsettled day. For most of the afternoon we had been sitting with Fitoman and Manuel outside Terry and Mandy's Tavern down at the marina, enjoying a pint and killing some time before the start of the evening operation. Not a single cloud could be seen in the sky and, after a couple of drinks, everyone in the group had taken their shirts off to enjoy the glorious November sun. Then, quite unexpectedly, the weather changed. The sun slid away behind some clouds; the temperature, in turn, dropped by several degrees. 'For fuck's sake,' Big Gonzo cursed as the first drops of rain splattered on our plastic table, 'they said it was going to be sunny in the *telediario!*'

There was some debate as to what to do next. Fitoman wanted to call everything off because of an advancing easterly wind that would render the circumnavigation of Europa Point more difficult than usual, but Manuel, impervious to risk as always, argued that if they steered the launch a mile or two away from the lighthouse they would miss the worst of the ten-foot waves being swept inshore. 'All we have to do is set off earlier than usual and load the boxes this time from the marina,' he reasoned, taking a drag of his cigarette. 'That way we can navigate better and won't have to come too close to the coastline as we make our way round the Point.' After some further deliberation — and a slight improvement in the weather conditions from eight o'clock onwards — Manuel had his way and they finally set off from the floating pier at Sheppard's Marina just after half past.

There are tactical errors in smuggling, and there are big major fuck-ups. This was one of the latter. Although we got away with loading the boxes in full public view, it wasn't long before the weather began to turn inclement again. Moreover, radio reception was so poor that *el Follador* was having trouble contacting the guys on our radio channel:

> Calling Fitoman, calling Fitoman. Do you copy, baby? I repeat, do you copy, *hermano?*

Then, just before nine o'clock, the situation took a turn for the worse. Thunderclaps now ricocheted through the Bay. Ten- or twelve-foot waves leapt out of the sea. 'Sweet merciful Christ,' I thought, unable to stop myself mentally recreating what Fitoman and Puffy were going through in the centre of that hellish vortex. 'What in God's name is happening?'

The last we heard from them was at twenty past nine. In a rasping voice Fitoman told us that they had just delivered the boxes and were about to head back to Gibraltar. 'Everything's fine,' he shouted defiantly above the shrieking wind. 'Gonzo and company: you boys go back home now if you want. We'll be going through *la bocana* in just a few minutes. And *Follador: a ver si* you show *un poco de estilo,* brother, and get the food in tonight, no?'

After that, nothing. We must have sent out some two or three hundred messages during the remainder of the night, but each time our efforts met with the same results: *Follador* had seen nothing from the top of the Rock, and all we got from Fitoman's radio was a low crackling buzz. By this stage the mood in the van had become extremely sullen and oppressive — the Ace of Base tape was no longer on and six empty packets of Marlboro lay strewn across the dashboard. All sorts of thoughts kept entering our heads: *had the launch broken down? had they been captured by Spanish Customs? had Fitoman and Puffy crashed against another launch? were they floating somewhere out at sea?* At around half past one we called Fitoman's landline in the forlorn hope that they had already returned home without letting us know — but, of course, Fitoman wasn't there. ('Fito?' the joiner's wife slurred back on the other side of the line, obviously half asleep. 'No, he's not here. Isn't he working tonight?') Finally, just before three o'clock in the morning, we decided to call the local police and tip them off about the missing launch.

I didn't sleep at all that night. I couldn't stop thinking about Fitoman and *el Puffy* in that goddamned boat. 'Will they be all right?' I wondered as I tossed and turned in bed. 'Will I ever see the pair of them again?' Only a few hours earlier, Fitoman, Puffy, Big Gonzo, *el Master* and me had been having a beer at Terry and Mandy's Tavern at the marina, waiting for *Follador* to let us know from his perch half a mile up when there were no Spanish Customs boats operating in the Bay. It was difficult to believe that all that had happened less than a day before — the clinking of beer glasses, the smell of grilled *calamares* coming from the kitchen, the typically Gibraltarian jokes about *cabrones* and *maricones*, Fitoman's comment about what *Follador* would have said had he seen the size of the English barmaid's tits. It all seemed to belong to another era now — like a black-and-white snapshot of something that had happened in the distant past. With a mounting sense of dread, I remembered how only two weeks ago a young guy had lost a leg when his tobacco launch had crashed into some rocks near Eastern Beach. It had been all over the news. *Young Gibraltarian in tragic accident. Condition still critical after amputation.* 'Could something similar have happened?' I wondered, still turning fretfully in my bed. 'Could they have suffered an accident of some kind?' At last, around eight-thirty, the phone rang. Quickly, with my heart in my mouth, I dashed across the living room and picked up the receiver.

Straight away I knew that it was going to be bad news. On the other side of the line Big Gonzo was crying, his gruff, forty-a-day voice reduced to a series of broken, high-pitched sobs:

'Our launch ... it's been rammed.... Those fucking Spanish bastards.... It's not fair.... Fitoman has been captured.... Puffy is still missing.... It's just not fair.... A search party is out there looking for him now.... What are we going to do now, *Estudiante?* What are we going to do?'

My first reaction was to shake my head and put the phone down. Manuel, missing at sea? What on earth was Big Gonzo talking about? Had the guy taken leave of his senses? Had he been overdoing it with his *porros* again? Or was this one of *el Follador's* half-witted jokes? That could be it, couldn't it? Anyway, you can't just disappear at sea like that, can you? Not in this day and age, not with satellites and radars and the rest of it.... Someone was having Big Gonzo on, surely.... They had to be, hadn't they?... I mean, people don't just disappear like that ... do they?

The next few days were extremely hard. Every morning I'd wake up with the hope of hearing that Manuel had been found, of learning that he was back in Gibraltar safe and sound again, of finding out from Big Gonzo how the gritty little bastard had survived against all the odds and how we would all go in the afternoon to Terry and Mandy's for a celebratory pint of San Miguel — but, of course, there was never any news. It was like a recurring nightmare, a cyclical exercise in self-delusion. Finally, after about three days, what I most dreaded came to pass: Manuel was assumed to be dead and the search party was called off.

The 'funeral' was held two days later at Saint Theresa's Church on Devil's Tower Road. I remember going there with Big Gonzo, Master-Blaster and *el Follador,* the four of us clumsily dressed in black suits that we had bought specially for the occasion. It was a horribly emotional and draining affair. The church was packed with Manuel's relatives and we all took our places at the back of the building, silently and awkwardly, like gatecrashers sneaking into someone's party. I don't know how to put this logically, but it felt as if everything around us was part of a dream — the sight of Manuel's relatives all dressed in black, the empty mahogany coffin resting on the altar, the funeral wreaths tied with scarlet ribbons, the almost palpable sense of hurt floating in the air. Halfway through the homily, I remember, the priest read a passage from *Ecclesiastes:* 'For it is written that the dead shall rise again, as sure as the sun doth rise every morning.' Just as these words were uttered, Manuel's grandmother sighed aloud and fainted. It was terrible watching her being carried out, totally limp in the arms of a family friend — almost like a marionette whose strings had been cut. I don't know about the other guys, but I felt sick to the stomach.

Once the service ended, we followed the mourners to the cemetery just outside the church. I remember feeling a peculiarly empty sensation as the four of us trudged on in silence at the back of the queue, a kind of physical hollowness if that makes any sense, almost as if my insides had become detached and were floating freely within me. Meanwhile, at the head of the procession that stretched like a black serpent along the graveyard's twisting paths, the coffin could be seen bobbing up and down on the shoulders of the pallbearers. Manuel's body wasn't in there, of course. What was being interred was *the hope we all kept in our hearts of Manuel still being alive,* as the priest had said earlier. But to me it didn't seem to matter. For some reason I kept thinking he was actually inside, lying there outstretched in that shiny mahogany box. Inert, stiff, dead.

By the time we arrived at the graveside, a brisk easterly wind had picked up and was scattering leaves and twigs around the cemetery. Everyone around me was crying, but I was unable to shed any tears. I recall turning to one side and seeing *el Master* blow his nose, two trails of moisture slowly running down his cheeks. For a second I shook my head and looked up at the sky, a vast cerecloth of grey stretched over the cemetery and the rest of Gibraltar. 'Why can't I cry like *el Master?*' I suddenly thought. '*What is wrong with me?*' Manuel had been one of the best friends I'd ever had, we'd shared some of the finest years of our lives together — and yet there I stood, totally still and silent, unable to dredge up the tangle of raw emotion that lay like a hidden wound inside me. My callousness hurt me, it made me feel less human than everybody else. Guilt-ridden, I remembered the day that I had first met Manuel all those years ago. I could see him clearly within the eye of my imagination, standing there with his *Longboard* tucked under his arm. *Promise me that I'll always be your leader, that you'll always stand by me and be there for me whatever happens.* What exactly had he meant by those words? Could it be that he had glimpsed his own destiny all those years ago? That he'd somehow realised that one day he'd find himself all alone at sea, struggling with the waves, *with no one there for him when he needed them?*... Or was it all just a stream of puerile nonsense, a couple of random lines that a streetwise eight-year-old had once memorised after watching *The Godfather* or some other American gangster movie?

The coffin was lowered into the pit at ten minutes past two. Seeing it go down was a profoundly distressing experience. For a start, I don't think I have ever felt so alone — so alone despite the physical closeness of everyone standing around that grave. It seemed as if there were unbridgeable chasms between each mourner, with each chasm filled with each person's sense of their own mortality. It was lying there between us all, this sense of fleetingness, of life's fragility, of seeing how life can sometimes turn into dust without you even realising it. At that moment I realised that death is always there beside us. It stalks all our movements and thoughts, guiding us, accompanying us, beguiling us, the final destination that lies at the end of all the paths that we follow in life. It could come at any moment, when you least expected. It could be a heart attack, the sudden onset of cancer. You could be crossing the road when a car zooms out of nowhere and mows you down. You could be standing by a bus stop when a madman pulls out a gun and starts shooting everyone. You could catch a train one morning and it derails and kills every commuter in your carriage. One way or the other, I thought to myself, Death would entrap every single person standing in that cemetery — the mourners, the priest, the pallbearers, the other members of our gang, even the hundred-and-fifty-pound lump of flesh and blood that stood there thinking about these same things....

Coming out of the cemetery, I saw Manuel's Spanish girlfriend leaning against one of the funeral limousines. She was dressed in a tight black designer outfit and elbow-length gloves, her eyes hidden behind a pair of sleek wraparound shades. Two runny trails of mascara could be seen on her cheeks and the corners of her lips were smeared with splodges of rubbed-off lipstick. Beads of perspiration glistened on the side of her neck. Although I had never actually spoken to her before, I found myself walking in her direction and stopping by her side. I then leaned forward and gave her a consoling peck on the cheek.

'I'm sorry, Lydia,' I said, taking a step back. 'I really am.'

'Oh, don't worry,' the girl from La Línea replied, suppressing a hysterical giggle. 'Manuel's not dead. He's just hiding. He told me so himself. "If ever something bad happens," he said, "I'll just lie low for a while." That's what he said. *Eso fue lo que me dijo.* In a few days he'll come back. You'll see. In a few days he'll surprise us all.'

'Yes,' I said, 'I'm sure that he will.'

With those words I left the cemetery and walked back home. I then went straight to my room and fell asleep. When I woke up six hours later, I phoned Big Gonzo and told him that I would not be smuggling any more. 'Okay,' he said in a quiet, subdued voice on the other side of the line. 'I understand.' Then I hung up and went back to bed again.

**

Manuel died many years ago. For a long time I stopped talking or even thinking about him. I guess I wanted to forget everything about that black and fateful night, to bury it all under layers of denial. But, of course, the tactic never worked. Even to this day, I still have nightmares about what happened. I have them on average once or twice a month, sometimes even more often than that. Above all, there is *one nightmare* that keeps on coming back to haunt me. In this nightmare I am walking along a beach when I catch sight of a group of people gathered in a circle. As I move closer to them, I realise that there is a nailed-down coffin lying on the sand between them. Standing next to the coffin is a grey-headed priest delivering a funeral oration. Without knowing why,

I turn my back on them all and walk to the beginning of the beach. I sit down. Moments later, I am aware of a shadowy, spectral presence. As I look up, I see Manuel by my side. His hair is covered in seaweed and his skin is crawling with little marine insects. He looks like one of those anatomical figures you sometimes see in children's encyclopaedias, each and every fibre of his body raw and blood-red under his tattered clothes. 'I am dead, Peter,' he suddenly says to me. 'I am gone.' He says this tonelessly and matter-of-factly, as if it were the most normal thing in the world. I then begin to cry. I tell him that I miss him, that I wish that he was still alive and that we had never drifted apart during our teenage years. But at the same time I know that he is just a corpse and that none of these words will ever mean anything to him. So I close my eyes and turn away. And when I turn away like this, I always wake up. And when I do so, I always have tears in my eyes.

Suffice it to say that a lot of things have happened since I first had this dream. Three weeks after Manuel's funeral, I received a letter from my ex-girlfriend in Manchester asking me to stop pestering her with phone calls and letters and telling me that there was 'no fucking chance' of us getting back together again. I subsequently plunged into a massive depression which neither pills nor the finest remedies of modern psychiatry could pull me out of. At one point it even seemed like I would never snap out of it, that I was destined to spend the rest of my days as a socially crippled recluse. Somehow, though — to this very hour I don't know how — I clambered out of my depression and awkwardly pressed on with my life.... As for the other protagonists in this story, I should perhaps mention that they are all still alive and doing well. Fitoman spent two years in a high-security prison in El Puerto de Santa Maria before being released; he is now a successful businessman and sells interior furnishings through his own internet-based company. Big Gonzo went to college in England and became an accountant. *El Master-Blaster* opened his own hairdressing salon. As for *el Follador*, he married a Danish girl he met in Puerto Banus and now owns a bar in Fuengirola.

6. Strait Crossing

'Don't think I agree with all this,' the middle-aged woman said, standing on the passenger pier with her arms crossed. 'I may not be able to stop you from doing what you're doing, Steven, but don't think for one moment that I agree with it.'

Steven put his bag down and saw that there were tears welling in his mother's eyes. He saw that they were about to spill at any moment down her cheeks.

'Please, Ma,' he said, trying to look calm. 'Don't cry.'

'How can I not cry, Steven?' his mother whispered, the tears already streaming down her cheeks. 'How can I not cry when you're doing *this* to me?'

Steven sighed softly and looked down. 'Look, Ma, it's only Morocco I'm going to — not the frigging moon. Please don't get so worked up. I think you're being a bit unreasonable here.'

'Unreasonable?' the woman half-shouted back, her tears now dripping freely from her chin. 'You're calling me unreasonable? You who are abandoning your job and everyone who cares about you! You who are disowning the mother who gave birth to you and who's been cooking and cleaning for you for the last twenty-six years! Unreasonable? Is that all you have to say to me before you go away? Is this your way of saying goodbye?'

Steven shook his head and picked up his suitcase. 'Goodbye, Ma,' he said, leaning forward and awkwardly embracing his mother with one arm. 'I have to go now. Please don't make this even harder for me than it is. You know that I must do *what I must do*. I will write to you as soon as I get to Tangier.'

Then he turned around and began to walk up the *Mons Calpe's* gangplank, trying hard to block out the sound of his mother sobbing on the pier.

**

He was the only white passenger in the ship's lobby. The rest were all Moroccans and nearly all men. Some were drinking tea and smoking cigarettes. Others were hunched over their tables and conversing in low nasal tones. Others still were sitting cross-legged on the floor and reading the Koran. As he dragged his suitcase into the hall, a few of them stopped what they were doing and stared intently at him. Steven let them satisfy their curiosity for a couple of seconds, then sat down at the nearest table. Bringing out a paperback, he began to read:

> *... and then I arrived in Morocco, and nothing could have prepared me for the riot of colour, noise, visual and olfactory impressions that spread like an endless kaleidoscope, like a sumptuously-woven Berber carpet, wherever I looked or so much as turned my head to. Because that, my friend, is the spirit of Morocco, the spirit of a proud and free and enterprising people, resourceful in their ways, matchless in their generosity, peerless in their natural elegance, who for many years have withstood the innumerable pressures from outside their country to change.*

Steven stopped reading and put the paperback down on his lap. Its title was *Moroccan Joys: Memoirs of an American Missionary*. On the front cover there was a picture of a middle-aged Caucasian woman, very tanned and scrawny and with a wooden crucifix hanging from her neck, offering a bowl of food to a Maghrebi child. She looked a little bit like his mother, he thought, but older and thinner, with even more grey hair. Gazing at the book, Steven momentarily wondered whether the other passengers were still staring in his direction. The thought bothered him, gnawed away at his concentration. For a short while it made him think about Moroccans and how they must feel when walking through the streets of Gibraltar. Did they ever get the impression that all those Western European faces were staring at them? Were there times when they felt as lonely and vulnerable as he felt just now? Slightly intimidated though he was, Steven could not help feeling sorry for the poor geographically displaced buggers. Most Moroccans get a relatively raw deal in Gibraltar, being forced to do all the menial bartending and cleaning jobs that the locals are not interested in. To make things worse, a large percentage of Gibraltarians have the annoying habit of speaking to them in slow and broken-up phrases, as if by slowing down their sentences and syllabifying their words they somehow made themselves more easily understood: '*Mi-ra*, Mo-ham-med. You wan-to make-ee some money? Then you work *fue-rte*. *En-tien-de, a-mi-go?*' It was something that always pissed Steven off. Putting the book back into his bag, he recalled the summer he spent working at his grandad's garage as an adolescent and the kind of anti-Moroccan prejudice he witnessed there. In particular, he remembered how the Gibraltarian mechanics made fun of the young Moroccan guy who worked with them. His name had been Yunus Ibrahim Mohammed, but everyone in the garage knew him as 'Jesus'. Jesus 'no-bar-for-him' Mohammed: that's what they called him. Because he never said much, and because he was one of those good-natured individuals who take almost anything with equanimity, all the other mechanics would make him the target of their vulgar jibes and workingmen's raillery. The Koran, sex, alcohol, the prophet Mohammed — they would try to provoke the young Arab with anything they thought would get to him. One day, for example, the head mechanic caught Yunus gazing at one of the many posters of big-breasted women stuck on the garage's walls. 'What are you doing, Jesus?' the foreman immediately shouted. 'You're in the middle of Ramadan now! You can't go looking at women like that! Next thing we know you'll be locking yourself in the bog and having a wank!' It always shocked Steven to see how the others could be like this — so crude and outspoken, so cruelly indifferent to what the man must have been feeling inside. What right, after all, did those brainless idiots have to make fun of Jesus like that? What the hell made them so much better and greater than him? Was it because Jesus's skin was darker? Because he spoke with an accent? Because he did not believe in getting pissed up to his eyeballs whenever he could and behaving like an obnoxious pig?...

And yet, in spite of all this, Steven had never felt entirely comfortable in Jesus's presence. Although he hated what they did to the guy, there was always a barrier that he could not cross, a psychological divide that prevented him from going up to the poor bugger and telling him how ashamed he was of his fellow countrymen's behaviour. Perhaps it was because of what Steven had been taught all his life about Morocco and the dangers to be found there. Like most Gibraltarians, he had always found the idea of travelling to North Africa unnerving, unsettling. He was not exactly sure what had engendered this attitude among the Rock's native inhabitants, but he suspected that it was just a remnant of the old colonial mentality. For many years, after all, Gibraltarians had been told that their lot in life was to be found in Gibraltar and Gibraltar alone. *Get a job at the dockyard* was the subliminal message flashed at you from the moment you first entered school, *slug your guts out within its steel-lined bowels for half a century and then retire to spend your last ten or fifteen years living on your government pension.* That's how things had been until very recently. Gibraltarians were not like the English, in this respect. Told that the world is a prised-open oyster ready to be slurped out, that it was one's solemn duty to go out and experience as much of life as possible before settling down. How many times, for instance, did you hear of Gibraltarian kids travelling to India? Or hitchhiking their way through West Africa? Even youth exchanges with other countries were a new-fangled idea of the last two or three years, with hardly anyone packing their kids off to someone else's home like that. It was just not the done thing. Gibraltarians still lived their lives in the shadow of their colonial past, unwilling or perhaps unable to break the mould into which they had fitted for so long. That's why almost no one ever went to Morocco — even though the place was less than forty kilometres away. Steven himself had only been there once, back when he was eight years old and his parents were still together. They had stayed in a five-star complex about thirty kilometres from Tangier, one of those all-inclusive, self-contained hotels where tourists rarely have to set foot outside the property's barb-wired perimeter. *Hotel Mohammed II* was the name of the place. Together with six or seven coachloads of Germans, Britons and other Western Europeans, they had spent most of their time lazing around a pool and sipping drinks served by a young Moroccan in a dusty linen suit and a gimmicky red fez. *Two more Margaritas, Abdelbar. Plus a Coke for the kid here. All right, brother?* It had been like that almost throughout their entire stay there — three whole weeks of free cocktails, pool loungers, deferential waiters, rooms saturated with the smell of insecticide, and food that was served on plates of handpainted bone china but which nearly always unsettled your stomach.... Apart from their final day, that is.

It was no more than a casual whim, a last-minute impulse. The ferry was not due to leave till five in the afternoon and his dad decided to take a walk around the centre of Tangier to while away the hours until they embarked. 'I've always fancied a spot of haggling,' the brawny PWD plasterer joked as the three of them set off from the port terminal. 'Should be fun, don't you think?'

But there was nothing remotely amusing or entertaining about the next two and a half hours. Even now, almost two decades after the event, Steven could still remember all the excruciating little details of their hapless Tangerine odyssey. He could remember the limbless beggars sitting in doorways and the old women with trachomatous eyes. He could remember the leering policemen in white hats and the little boys who gawked at them in unsmiling silence. He could remember the open manholes in the streets and the constant clouds of flies. He could remember the three young men who followed them down a side alley, walking not more than three or four yards behind and whispering among themselves, always whispering — strange, lisping words that carried the imprint of some untranslatable obscenity and came punctuated with the murmur of occasional laughter. Most of all, though, he could remember the sense of relief that overwhelmed them when they finally got back to the port again. That is what Steven remembered above everything else from their two-and-a-half-hour stint in downtown Tangier: the wild, dizzying joy of knowing that they were out of there, that the nightmare had ended, *that he would never have to go back there again as long as he lived.*

Morocco, not surprisingly, turned into a 'no-go zone' after that, a place that you could easily see on a sunny day from Europa Point, but which for all intents and purposes remained as remote as Eastern Siberia. 'Tell you something about Morocco?' his father would say to his PWD mates whenever they asked him about their North African sojourn. 'I'd rather holiday in La Línea than go back to that fucking shithole, that's all I'll say about the place!' If anything, this perception was reinforced by the patchwork of rumours and wildly exaggerated facts that the Hernandezes, like most Gibraltarian families, often came to hear about the neighbouring Maghrebi kingdom. Take, for instance, the tale of the local couple murdered there on their honeymoon. That was a particularly crude and shocking little vignette. Guaranteed to whip up the most saintly of Gibraltarian minds into a rabidly anti-Moroccan frenzy. The couple had hired a car, so the story went, with the intention of driving around the country and doing some exploring. He was twenty-six and she was twenty-three — both of them members of the Gibraltar Charismatic Renewal Group for the last ten years. Your inseparable pair of lifelong Christian sweethearts, in other words. Unfortunately, somewhere near the southwestern edge of the Moroccan Sahara, they took a wrong turning and accidentally drove away from the beaten track. After that nothing was heard from them for a while. Then one day their bodies were found dumped in the middle of the desert, having been sexually assaulted and stripped of everything they had by Berber bandits.... Equally shocking was the story of the young English backpacker who alleged that the port authorities had planted drugs on her just before she left Morocco. It made all the headlines in Gibraltar after she came back on the Tangier ferry. Her name was Holly Thistlewick and she had been hitchhiking her way through North Africa. She maintained that she was detained for three days by Moroccan Customs, during which time she was locked in a cramped cell without lights or windows and fed scraps of stale bread and rotten fish. Even more sensationally, Ms. Thistlewick claimed that she had only been set free because she agreed to have sex with the officer in charge of her case. 'It was either that or spending the next ten years in jail,' she said in a tearful, middle-class voice while being interviewed on GBC television after her ordeal. 'I just couldn't say no.'

Steven's reaction to these stories was always the same: he would shake his head, clench his fists and count himself lucky that he lived in Gibraltar and not the bastion of uncivilised barbarity on the other side of the Straits. Nor could he understand, for that matter, why people in England and other northern European countries were always so keen to visit the bloody place. He simply could not see the attraction. What could possess any person in their right mind, after all, to visit a country where everything stank of shit and everyone was trying to con you out of every single dirham in your wallet? And yet — bizarrely, inexplicably, for some reason best known to them — people *did* want to go through all that. Steven only had to think about his English cousin Michaela (or Micky, as everybody called her). Michaela was the daughter of Angelina, Steven's aunt on his father's side. Never a big fan of the local menfolk, Angelina had married an English squaddie in the seventies and then flown back to England with him after his posting on the Rock with the Royal Greenjackets was over. Michaela, who had never been back to Gibraltar since she left at the age of five, and who had all but forgotten the most basic Spanish in the process, came inter-railing down to Gib with a female friend just after finishing college in Sussex. They had been studying International Business Marketing or something equally grandiose — two bright young things ready to take on the world after spending the last three years glued to their books. Steven had gone to meet them at the Algeciras Renfe terminal on a sun-baked August afternoon— only to discover that the 5.35pm from Bobadilla was delayed by over two hours. Tired and disgruntled, he went into the station café and ordered himself a *descafeinado de máquina*. Finally, at around eight o'clock, the train pulled into the station and they emerged out of one of its carriages. Two spindly, pretty-faced English girls with sunburnt arms and big red rucksacks on their backs.

'Hello, Steven,' Michaela said, putting down her rucksack and offering her cousin a hand. 'How nice to see you, cuz.'

'Hello, Michaela. How was your trip?'

'Uh, that's so funny, Steven,' his cousin said, highly amused. 'You pronounce my name just like my Mum. Mee-kah-ehla.'

'Do I? Must be our Gibraltarian accent…. Anyway, how was your trip down here? You been through a lot of adventures?'

'Our trip?' his cousin said, shooting a sidelong look at her mate. 'Not so bad, was it? We got our camera stolen as we got on the train at Lyon, but we also met some really cool Canadian guys on the sleeper train from Montpellier and hung out with them all the way down to Valencia…. By the way, I better introduce you two to each other — shouldn't I? Claire, this is my cousin Steven. Steven, this is my best mate Claire.'

'Pleased to meet you,' Steven said, shaking the girl's hand with a smile. 'God, I'm so glad that you're both here! I thought I was going to go mad sitting with all those drunken bums and gypsies in that horrible Spanish café.... Here, let me help you with your bags. I've got my car parked just outside.'

But the relationship between Steven and his cousin was not destined to remain cordial for long. That same evening, while they were enjoying a drink at a Gibraltarian bar, Michaela's friend let it slip that the two of them were planning on catching the Tangier ferry and going to Morocco. 'I've read in my *Lonely Planet Guide* that the Atlas Mountains are really beautiful at this time of the year,' Claire casually said, putting down her Martini and Coke. 'Perhaps we can do some trekking there when we go to Morocco in a few days — don't you think, Micky?' The words almost caused Steven to splutter out his beer. Trekking in the Atlas Mountains? What on earth was this Claire girl thinking? Did she believe that the Atlas were a parkland extension to a Butlin's holiday camp? That you could take a stroll through the mountains like you were power-walking through Hyde Park in London?

During the rest of the evening Steven could not stop worrying about what Michaela's friend had said. He could visualise the pair of them high up in the mountains, trudging along in their skimpy little vests with a dozen Muslim savages in tow. Jesus Christ, what was wrong with these two girls? Were they congenitally stupid or something? Didn't they realise how dangerous it could get for them up there? At last, just before last orders were rung at the *Admiral Collingwood*, all of Steven's apprehensions came gushing out of him:

'Listen, Michaela, I don't want to spoil your plans or anything, but you and Claire should be aware that the Atlas Mountains are full of bandits and that every year many Western tourists get raped and murdered there. I know because they're always going on about these things on Spanish television.... I just don't think it's safe for two young women to be going trekking there is what I'm trying to say.... Actually, I've got an idea: why don't you forget about Morocco and come up to the Costa del Sol with me instead? There are loads of great places I'd like to show you just past Banus. And if you really want to experience the whole Moorish "ethnic thing", we can always go inland and look at the old palace of Medina Azahara. I've never been there before, but I've been told it's a pretty amazing place, full of old-fashioned fountains and strange Islamic carvings.'

Michaela looked at Claire and then looked back at her cousin. 'Thanks for your advice, Steven,' she said, 'but Claire and I know what we're getting into.'

'I don't think you understand,' Steven went on, swallowing hard. 'Even at this time of the year, the Atlas can be really...'

'No, I don't think *you* understand,' Michaela interrupted him in a much more aggressive tone of voice. 'We've told you what our plan is and we're not prepared to change it for anyone or anybody. I'm sorry if I sound harsh, Steven, but who the hell are you to interfere in our lives, anyway? Just because you've been stranded all your life on this little Rock of yours doesn't mean that everyone else is as paranoid and scared of travelling as you lot are!'

Steven looked down at the plastic beer mat on the table and shook his head. 'You do not know anything about Morocco,' he thought sadly to himself. 'All you know is what you've seen in films like *Indiana Jones* — images clouded with Hollywood romance and spiced up by pretty-boy actors and beautiful actresses. But the reality is different. The reality is smeared with dirt, it is soiled with filth and ugliness. It is so ugly, in fact, that every year hundreds of Moroccan men and women drown in the Straits trying to escape their own country. Nevertheless, you people still go there thinking that you're *broadening your cultural horizons*. Can't you realise that you're only feeding the autocratic regime that keeps it all in place? That every dirham you spend is going straight into their coffers?'

But, of course, Steven never vocalised any of these thoughts. Instead he just sat there and endured the girls' accusatory looks. He sat there feeling crushed and deflated, emotionally defeated. Typical, wasn't it, really? Bloody typical! He had only voiced his concerns because he could not bear the idea of anything happening to two young, defenceless girls like them — and yet now Claire and Michaela looked at him as if *he* were the threat himself. At this point Steven realised a lesson that he would never forget — better to keep quiet than to offer advice to someone already intent on doing something. Unfortunately, as far as his cousin was concerned, it was a lesson that Steven learned a touch too late. After she left for Morocco the next morning, Michaela never got in contact with him again. Come to think of it, she didn't even bother to mail back the pocket camera that he had lent her just before she departed.

**

Around midday the Captain welcomed the passengers to the *Mons Calpe* and announced that the ship would be leaving Gibraltar soon. About ten minutes later, the mooring ropes were let loose and the ship slowly drifted away from the pier. Soon afterwards, everything began to be left behind — the luxury yachts anchored at the marina, the breakwater stones at the end of the airport runway, the fishermen who lined the coastal road opposite the landing strip. It was strange seeing all this glide by, silently and effortlessly, without any noise except the low hum of the ferry's engine in the background. It was almost like watching one of those old *cine film* home movies that play a touch too fast, the erratic speed of which always seems to add a slightly comical touch to your celluloid memories. As the images continued streaming past, Steven wondered whether his father would be out there with the other fishermen on the coastal road. He did this quite often now that he had taken early retirement. Only a few days ago, Steven had found him sitting there with his second-hand Chopper propped up against a rusty bollard nearby. 'So,' his father said, placing some bait on one of his fish hooks, 'I hear from Auntie Eileen you're going to work for a charity in Morocco. Are you sure that's what you want, son?' The old boy laid aside the hook at that point and looked up, his creased olive face and the grizzled tuft of hairs hanging from his chin revealing every single one of his fifty-five years. 'He looks just like an old seadog,' his son thought with amusement. Or at least that's what any tourist would have imagined had they been walking by — an old Spanish seadog, smoking his packet of Winston and listening to the *Cadena Dial* news on his transistor radio. An irony of ironies, considering that he hated the Spanish with every fibre in his being and had never shown an interest in fishing or anything to do with the sea until these last few years.

'Yes, Dad,' Steven finally said, raising a hand to shield his eyes from the light reflecting off the sea. 'That's what I want.'

'Then good luck to you, Steven,' his father said, picking up his hook again. 'I hope it all goes well for you and that God may bless you wherever you go.'

It was such a typical gesture on the part of his dad — so composed and taciturn, so detached from it all, as if his son had just told him that he was going to buy a pound of tomatoes from the fruit market across the border instead of giving up everything to go and work in Africa. Still, Steven did not mind. Some men are demonstrative in front of their sons, and some men aren't. Why cut yourself up about something you had no control over anyway? The important thing was that his father had smiled and wished him well, wasn't it?... Of course, in the old days things had been very different. Steven hated his father back then. Hated him with a passion. He hated the boozing and the swearing, the puking up and the hangovers from hell, the rowing with the neighbours and all those times that the old buffoon had to be carried back home *pissed as a fart* by his workmates. He hated always being made fun of by the other kids in the playground, always having to listen to all those jokes about *drunks* and *borrachos*, always having to keep quiet, to look away, to beg his friends not to tell the rest of the class how they had seen his father lying asleep on a park bench or swearing at tourists in Main Street. He hated the shallow looks of sympathy that he got from his mother's female friends, the meaningless pats on the head, the one or two coins they would sometimes place with a maternal smile on his palm — 'so that you can go and buy yourself a Coke and some crisps, *mi pobrecito'* — as if they somehow felt morally obliged to improve his quality of life because he had an on-and-off drunkard for a father. Didn't those stupid women ever realise how much he hated to be patronised in this way? Couldn't they see that it demeaned him to be constantly compared to his father, that it chipped away at both his individuality and his fragile sense of identity? Somewhere, someplace, it was true, there might have been a birth certificate which said that his name was Steven Hernandez — that much couldn't be denied. But what good was all that when everyone knew him as '*el hijo de Loni el borracho*,' the son of Loni the drunkard? What good was it to have your own name when everyone, from your schoolmates to your neighbours to your scoutmaster, knew you only in relation to a father who almost had nothing to do with you?

Dealing with all that had never been easy. Even now there were still moments when Steven had trouble separating the quiet, grey-haired fisherman sitting on the rocks from the memories the man triggered in him. Particularly hard to erase, in this sense, were the memories from just before his parents' last and final bust-up. *El Loni* had been such a prick then. Such a monumental and unthinking idiot. For some reason best known to himself, he had started going out and getting smashed every evening, drinking with a rage and a ferocity that bordered on the suicidal. Meanwhile, Steven and his mother would sit tensely in their Glacis living room, watching *Blind Date* or whatever piece-of-shit TV programme would help them forget about the maelstrom coming their way. At last, just before midnight, Steven would walk over to her side and ask if she was all right. 'Yes, yes, of course,' his mother would invariably say. 'You go upstairs and get some sleep, Steven. I'll remain down here a little bit longer. There is something I want to watch on the news at one.'

But she wasn't staying up to watch the news; she was staying up to wait for her drunken husband. On the nights he had trouble sleeping, Steven could hear her downstairs — putting the kettle on, noisily stirring her tea, heating up some apple pie in the microwave oven, shuffling up and down the living room, trying to occupy her time until one or two or whenever her husband decided to turn up and start banging on their front door. Once he even caught sight of the disgusting old sot as he came in. It must have been around half past two. Steven had got up to use the toilet and was about to return to his room when he heard the front door creak open. Cautiously, making as little noise as possible, he turned around and tiptoed his way to the top of the landing. Through a gap between balusters he saw his father stagger into the vestibule and his mother standing there beside the open door. The strange thing was that neither of them spoke or acknowledged each other's presence; they merely stood there without saying anything, eyes averted, doing their best to ignore each other. 'What a weirdo my mother is,' Steven thought to himself, quietly inching away from the railings. 'She hates my father's guts and yet she stands there without doing a thing.'

What Steven didn't know at the time was that his mother was already close to her breaking point. The first sign that something was seriously wrong came in September 1983, some five or six months after the crazy drinking started. Instead of staying up to wait for *el Loni* like she had always done, Marigloria now began to sleep on an inflatable mattress she kept in the utility room, leaving the front door key for him under the doormat outside. Then, a few months after that, she reduced all communication between them to the barest essentials. Finally, towards the end of the year, she went to see a lawyer and filed for a divorce. She decided to embark upon this course of action after her husband had turned up drunk to their son's fourteenth birthday party a few days earlier. He had come in staggering from side to side, weaving clumsily in and out of the toddlers playing in the corridor and smiling moronically at the mothers and grandmothers having tea and digestive biscuits in the living room. His breath stank of alcohol and a Z-shaped streak of vomit had dried along the front of his jacket; his eyes were reduced to two badly healed wounds. As he lumbered into the living room, he tried to kick a balloon that lay across his path but missed it completely and almost fell down in the process. 'Fuck,' he grumbled, clutching at a coatstand nearby to retain his balance. 'Fucking bastard balloon.' Meanwhile, standing on the other side of the room with his mates, Steven shook his head and looked down at the floor. His whole school, he was sure, would know all about this next morning. They'd be told about every single last detail: the swearing, the stumbling, the Z-shaped puke on his father's jacket, even his idiotic argument with the balloon. Closing his fingers around the Swiss Army penknife which his mother had given him a few hours earlier, the fourteen-year-old shut his eyes as tight as he could and wished for this: he wished that his father would go straight to bed and choke on his own vomit.

Events unfolded very quickly after that. By the end of the week, Steven's mother informed her husband about her wish to obtain a divorce. That same evening they had a massive row that continued all night and only ended when his father lugged his belongings to his brother's flat early next morning. 'I do not deserve this, Marigloria!' he shouted just before he slammed the door on his way out. 'You know that no one can love you the way I love you!' And then there was a tremendous bang: *Loni el borracho*, the whisky-soaked, puke-encrusted curse of Steven's youth, had finally walked out of their lives.

About ten months passed. *El Loni*, so the rumours went, had quit his job with the PWD and was living in La Línea now — frittering away the last of his savings on cheap Spanish brandy and *aguardiente*. The only verifiable piece of news about his whereabouts came from Uncle Toni, *el Loni's* elder brother. Steven and his mother had bumped into the quiet, slightly effeminate divorcee on their way back from Peralta's supermarket one evening. According to Uncle Toni, his brother had been working as a night watchman at a construction site somewhere near Los Junquillos. 'He told me he had fallen in with some really nice Dutch or Belgian contractors,' Uncle Toni said, hardly noticing the look of disgust on his sister-in-law's face, ' ... although that was some months ago now. Haven't heard anything from him since then, *pa decí la verdá.*' A few more weeks passed. Finally, just as everyone was beginning to forget about him, *el Loni* made a 'reappearance' of sorts. It happened on the tenth of December 1984 — exactly twelve months and two days after they had last seen him. Steven was in the kitchen, eating his dinner. The radio was on and his mother was mopping the floor. Clouds of peppery steam rose from the plate of *menestra* in front of him, blending sickeningly with the smell of diluted bleach. '*Dios bendito,*' the prematurely aged matron suddenly blurted out, pausing from her mopping with a pained expression on her face. 'You won't believe what I got told at Lipton's today, Steven? Your father's just come back from doing some alcoholics rehabilitation programme somewhere near Cordoba. Manuela, *la de la peluquería de Risso*, bumped into one of your father's cousins at the Piazza and he told her about it. Is the man desperate to stop our divorce or what?' And then she did what she always did whenever she was unnerved by something: she wiped the sweat from her forehead, kissed the medallion of Saint Jude dangling around her neck and mechanically made the sign of the cross.

At first Steven did not think much about what his mother had said. He dismissed the whole thing as a small-town rumour, one of those meaningless bits of *cotilleo* that Gibraltarians, following their natural Latin instincts, cannot stop themselves from spreading. A few days later, however, he met his father in Main Street and Steven immediately realised that it was no rumour. Yes, it was true — something about *el Loni* had changed. He only had to look at the guy standing there before him. He seemed older, more composed, the grey streaks in his hair making him look almost gentlemanly and dignified. Just before they had gone their different ways, he had even given Steven a hug and asked God to bless them both. That had shocked his son almost as much as the revelation that the old boy had now got a job as a warehouse supervisor with a local company down at New Harbours. Loni Hernandez — bringing up the good Lord's name without swearing, spitting, belching, farting or indulging in some other type of sacrilegious working-class crudeness? He decided to hurry back home and tell his mother about the news.

'You don't know how crafty that old dog is,' the ageing housewife said later that afternoon. 'If only you knew some of the things I know about him, you'd realise it's all just a plot to stop me from obtaining the divorce. A way of getting you on his side, of putting pressure on me to drop the case. But this time he's not going to get it his way, *te lo prometo*. That's something he knows full well,' she added, picking up a duster and moving towards the television. 'This time I'm going to stand my ground. Just you wait and see. *El tiempo lo dirá.*'

But Steven's mother was wrong — it was no plot. A few days later something happened that purged her son of any last remaining doubts. Coming home one evening, he saw his father jogging down Queensway in a bright yellow tracksuit. There he was, not more than thirty or forty yards away, running down the road like some twenty-year-old kid wearing the latest designer sports gear! For a second Steven had to rub his eyes to make sure he was not imagining things. 'My Dad jogging?' he thought, unable to decide whether to laugh or cover his face in embarrassment. 'I've got to be hallucinating, surely!'

From that night onwards Steven would often see his father running along Queensway, puffing his way through mile after mile in that infamous fluorescent yellow tracksuit. It was a sight that was always guaranteed to raise a few laughs. People would stop in their tracks and crack jokes about giant bananas. Old drinking partners of his father would shake their heads and wonder what had got into him: 'Hey, Loni, don't run so fast! *Qué el* London Bar doesn't close till twelve!' In short: from being a drunken good-for-nothing, his father had become a minor local celebrity, a man who had overcome his alcoholism and turned his life around — even if he seemed to have become something of an eccentric in the process.... Steven, for his part, was not sure how to deal with the transformation. For many years he had wanted a sportsman for a dad, someone who went jogging and worked out at the gym and who did all the other things that normal men did — and yet now, every time he saw his father running down the road, he felt acutely embarrassed, intensely pained by the sight, as if his dad was doing something that went against the very grain of things. Still, at least he was able to realise that his mother was mistaken: the man *had* changed. Not even Steven's sense of embarrassment prevented him from seeing this. Whenever he now met his dad on the street, the old boy was always sober and well-mannered, always impeccably dressed. Clad in a navy blue blazer and a brightly coloured silk tie, he looked more like a rich family patriarch out on his morning walkabout than the unkempt scruffbag he had always been. Even the conversational agenda of these five-minute encounters was different from anything they had ever shared before: they would talk about the weather and then about Spanish football, with a smattering of local sport usually thrown in, before finally turning to the topic that most interested his dad. 'So how's your mum?' the grey-haired divorcee would ask, pretending not to be too interested. 'Has she found anyone else?' 'No,' his son would awkwardly respond. 'I don't think she's really interested in looking.' It was only then, standing there and seeing *el Loni* fidgeting with his watch or anxiously rearranging his tie, that Steven realised that he was doing all this just to make himself worthy in his wife's eyes, just to show her that he had really changed. *Poor bastard. Doesn't he realise that she no longer wants him? That she'd rather hang herself than go back to him again?*

Sadly, the answer was 'no.' A year passed, two years, five years — and yet his father's eyes burned as bright as ever whenever his wife's name was mentioned in his presence. It did not matter that they had been divorced since the mid-eighties, or that they had not spoken for years. Instead of diminishing with time, his love seemed to have grown stronger, more intense, acquiring that ethereal and almost translucent quality that characterises a love when it passes from the realm of the physical to that of the purely spiritual. For his son it was difficult to comprehend. How could a person love another without any kind of reciprocity? How could they put themselves through such an ordeal for the sake of someone who spurned everything to do with them? He could not fathom it. He simply could not understand. More and more he wished he could turn around and say to his father, 'Let go. Let go once and for all. She will never come back to you.' But he also knew that his mother was the man's dream, what gave him the strength to carry on living, and that if he lost his dream, if it so much as started to erode in front of him, he could very well have turned to the bottle again or even worse. For this reason Steven never said much to Loni about his ex-wife. He never even showed him how concerned he was. Again and again he would find himself biting his lip, preferring to let his father believe in a dream that would never be fulfilled than smash the whole illusion to smithereens. It was only recently, now that he had retired from his job at Newall Holdings and turned to fishing, that the old man seemed to have found a measure of peace again. For the first time in years you could see that he was finally letting go, finally accepting that sometimes things are as they are and there is little point in trying to change them. You could sense it when you saw him riding towards the harbour on his old Raleigh with a Lipton's plastic bag slung over his shoulder, when you observed the gleam in his eye every time he landed a prize *sargo* or *pargo* down by the rocks: '*Mira, mira,* what a beautiful John Dory, *no?*' That wonderfully unrestrained smile, those whoops of adolescent-like delight — it was so great to witness all this after having seen the guy suffer for so long. Fishing had set his father on the road to salvation, Steven thought as he continued scouring the coastline in vain for the man and his Chopper, it had started cauterising his interior wounds. 'That was good,' he whispered to himself with a smile. '*Really, really good.*'

**

Soon the ferry was moving out of British territorial waters. Steven could see the last few Gibraltarian landmarks through the window — the pastel-coloured blocks of Varyl Begg Estate, the Moorish-style dome of the wine-bottling plant, the rows of parked duty-free cars waiting to be re-exported out of Gibraltar. Settling into his seat, he ordered a drink and was soon sipping a flat, tepid Coke that one of the white-jacketed Moroccan waiters had brought to him. The drink tasted slightly, although unmistakably, of washing-up liquid. For a short while Steven held the glass between his left thumb and forefinger and observed things around him. No one in the lobby was looking in his direction any more. The Moroccan passengers were all otherwise engaged — smoking, chatting, snoring over the sound of the ship's engines. The sight calmed him down a bit and made him refocus on his own predicament. Was he doing the right thing by going to Morocco, he wondered, putting the glass down on the table, or was he once again shirking his responsibilities (like his mother always claimed)? Even at this stage he was not one hundred per cent sure. For as long as he could remember he had drifted from one job to the other, leading a pretty vacant and directionless existence without bothering too much about it. Scaffold-erector with Charlie's Scaffolding, painter with Contreras and Co., porter at the Holiday Inn. He had done all these jobs *sin pena ni gloria*, as the Spanish saying goes, content just to earn enough money to fund his weekend trips to the Costa with his mates. That, at the end of the day, was all he cared about — having sufficient pesetas to go boozing with your buddies, to go crazy for a couple of days. Nothing else mattered beside this. Mortgages, girlfriends, college courses, home improvements — all that was for other people to worry about, not for Steven Hernandez.

For a couple of years Steven continued living in this hedonistic manner. Every Friday afternoon, at around ten to five, he would rush happily out of the Holiday Inn, catch a bus down to North Front, pick up his old Fiat Uno which he had parked on the Spanish side of the frontier the previous night to avoid the after-work border queue and then, surrounded by a motorcade of vehicles belonging to his mates, drive up the N-340 to Fuengirola. There, laughing and constantly switching between English and Spanish to confuse any Spaniards around them, they would book themselves into the first hostel they would find and then get up to the usual Costa mischief — popping Es, smoking joints, eating *calamares* and *gambas al pil-pil*, drinking ridiculously cheap bottles of San Miguel, dragging half-drunk women back to the hostel. In short: just the type of routine that was guaranteed to make you forget you were stuck in some dead-end job in a small provincial town for the rest of the week.

Of course, things couldn't carry on like this for long. Almost before anyone realised what was happening, outside pressures started to infiltrate into their lives and lure them away from the Costa. Business, girlfriends, marriages, work — the eternal set of bourgeois responsibilities began to loom over their heads, this time with the kind of heavy-handed insistence that could not be denied. First, it was Duncan, the bald-headed *Caleteño* whose trick was to down six successive B52s and then ignite a flurry of belches with his lighter. After that it was *el Cookie*, the curly-haired mechanic who took steroids and loved to pick fights with holidaying Englishmen. Then Mark *el mudo*, the Iron Maiden fan who never had any money and who was always leeching off the others. One by one, they all began to drop off. With a gradual yet inescapable sense of inevitability. *Como higos chumbos podridos cayendo de un árbol* (as one of the remaining diehards poetically described it.) Soon, out of the four cars that used to make up the original motorcade, it was only Steven's Fiat still doing the 200-kilometre round trip to Fuengirola. At this point the surviving *fiesteros* clung even closer together, became even more determined to enjoy themselves. 'Let those fools get married if they want,' they'd laugh, tilting back their glasses of cheap Spanish whisky. '*Ya se enterarán lo que es bueno.*'

But the sad truth was that it was never the same again. Unspoken though it was, there was a feeling among the remaining guys that something essential had changed — something that could not have been undone even if all the original lads had got back together again. This realisation weighed heavily upon them, removed the gloss from their coastal meanderings. It was only partially forgotten during those rare instances when one of their old comrades would fall out with his missus and return to the fold for a few weeks. When this happened there was always cause for celebration among the others. That is to say, they would forgo the usual round of bars and clubs and drive straight to some 'luxury' brothel, where they would spend most of the night buying overpriced drinks and talking to bare-breasted women before going upstairs and having sex with overworked, middle-aged Latin American prostitutes. But, alas, the bonds of friendship that were renewed during those alcohol-fuelled nights would never last long. Usually, after only a few weekends had elapsed, the prodigal son would either return to his missus or disappear into the beckoning arms of some new woman — without warning and usually without even saying goodbye, rather conveniently forgetting how a short time ago he had vowed never to get hooked up again. Hope will always triumph over experience — isn't that what they all say?

Under these circumstances it was only a matter of time before the group was whittled down to just two of them — Steven and his Spanish mate Pepín. Steven had met Pepín about three years ago, at the birthday party of some rich, snotty-nosed kid who lived in the Eurotowers block of luxury flats. He was from the border town of La Línea and used to cross the frontier twice a day on his way to and from the electronics shop in Main Street where he worked. Always dressed in black and with his hair firmly greased back, sporting a well-trimmed line of fuzz just under his lower lip, he could regularly be seen driving into Gibraltar on a shiny red Vespa with the flaps of his overcoat billowing out like a drogue parachute behind him. He was quite a character, a real attention-seeker. Customs officers would chuckle at the guy's jokes as he drove through the border. Pedestrians would point him out to each other, laughing at the display of wheeled nonconformity that sped noisily past them. *'Ten cuidao!'* they would shout, shaking their heads in mock disbelief. *'Qué vas a cojé vuelo con ese capote!'* ('Be careful, or you'll get blown away with that jacket!') In a small place like Gibraltar this was more than enough to stop people taking you seriously for the rest of your life. But the Spaniard had one great advantage in his favour — he was extremely good-looking. Tall and broad-shouldered, with a pair of emerald eyes that contrasted strikingly with his smooth olive skin, he was the sort of man whom women involuntarily adore and men secretly hate — the former thinking that those gigantic eyes of his were the windows to an uncommonly noble soul, the latter wishing that they too had been blessed with such a 'pussy magnet.' If that wasn't enough, Pepín had another considerable advantage going for him: the kid could speak English in the same moderately accented and slightly hesitant way that most Gibraltarians speak the language. This came about as a result of a year he spent in the UK as an eighteen-year-old, studying Tourism and Hotel Management at some obscure polytechnic in Tunbridge Wells. (About this period in England, Pepín would never say much. He would hint once or twice about 'some almighty fuck-up' that he had gone through, but never went further than that. It did not take great insight to realise that there were things embedded in his past that the Vespa-riding Spaniard did not want to talk about.) All his Gibraltarian friends knew him as *'el español'* or *'el sloppy'* or *'el rabúo* — but he did not seem to mind this much. What is more, if you questioned him about his nationality, he would always say that he considered himself an honorary Gibraltarian and that, as far as he was concerned, he would rather wipe his arse with the Spanish flag than lose his livelihood. (Always a cue for a pat on the back and a pint of lager on you.) Because of comments like these, everyone saw him as 'a good Spaniard,' *un español de los nuestros*, a kind of living, breathing, talking oxymoron. Not that Pepín really needed any of this to make himself popular with the Gibraltarians. Like most *Andaluces*, he was a born charmer, blessed with that blend of spontaneity and impish wit that for centuries has been associated with the people of Spain's southernmost province. You could see these qualities in action behind the sales counter at Rock Electronics in Main Street, as well as when he was chasing women up in the Costa del Sol. That was something else about the guy — he would stop at nothing to get the girls he wanted. Everyone in the group used to make fun of him because of this. Pe-*penis*, pe-*prick*, pe-*polla*, *pene*-pin — a whole range of puerile nicknames followed him around which Pepín took great delight in living up to. In a word, he was simply incorrigible when it came to the female of the species. As soon as they got to their hostel in Fuengirola, the normally affable and pleasant sales attendant would turn into a scheming, manipulative bastard who would do anything to make women open their legs and receive his member in their vaginas. It all reminded you of Doctor Jekyll and Mr. Hyde — the only difference being that this particular Jekyll metamorphosed at the sight of a short skirt and not upon the consumption of a vial of fluorescent green liquid. It was something that had to be seen. Brimming with self-assurance, without the slightest flicker of betrayal on his face, the La Línean shop assistant would tell his victims that he was a Swiss Duke on vacation, that he owned the biggest yacht anchored at Puerto Banus, that the Merc he had borrowed from his brother-in-law for the weekend was his — anything just to sleep with them. And the really funny thing was this: with one or two exceptions, they almost always believed him.

Bearing all this in mind, it is easy to understand how Steven felt when Pepín also decided to call it a day. The first sign of trouble came one hot and sultry summer night. They were somewhere along the motorway between Fuengirola and

Estepona, on their way back from yet another weekend of Costa del Sol debauchery. A thin and rather disfigured yellow moon hung in the sky. Puddles of yellow light glinted softly on the motorway tarmac. For the last ten minutes they had been talking about the DJ at Wily Salsa. Steven thought that his style was a touch too retro, more suited to the old Eurobeat than contemporary Spanish techno-funk. Pepín, in turn, said he did not mind one way or the other. 'So long as those stupid bitches carry on wearing next to nothing on the dance floor,' he added with a roguish smile. Then, all of a sudden, there was a lull in the conversation. A strangely awkward pause. From the corner of his eye Steven could see his friend's hands fidgeting on his lap, scuttling like a pair of spider crabs in the semi-darkness. Yawning hard, he asked Pepín if everything was all right.

'I've got something to tell you,' the Spaniard replied almost in a whisper.

'What's that, Pepinillo?'

'It's something that I've been meaning to tell you for some time, Stevie-man.'

'What is it, man? You don't half make things sound mysterious, you Spaniards do!'

'I don't know how to say this, man.'

'*Joder*, just say what you have to say, will you?'

'Well....'

'*Well, what?*'

'I'm getting engaged, man.'

So shocked was Steven to hear these words come out of Pepín's Spanish mouth that he immediately dropped down a couple of gears and pulled his Fiat on to the motorway's hard shoulder.

'You're joking, aren't you?'

With a look that signified that he wasn't, Pepín shook his head.

'Are you sure?' Steven insisted, momentarily frowning against the lights of a truck rattling down the other side of the motorway.

'Her name's Lucía,' the Spaniard sheepishly admitted. 'I met her about two months ago at the shop. It was a Saturday afternoon just after Corpus. I was just about to clock off for the day when in comes this beautiful little thing through the door. A real stunner, like you Gibbos say. Real classy and elegant. Very different from all those horrible *putillas* up the coast, if you know what I'm getting at. Anyway, in she walks through the door and, bang, *cómo te lo digo, tío* — it was like my whole existence had grinded — can you say "grinded" in English? — to a sudden halt ... like I had ... like I had ... *no sé qué ... cómo te lo explico?...* been hit on the head with *un martillo* or something. You know what I'm talking about, Steven? Does what I'm saying make any sense?'

The Gibraltarian hotel porter opened his mouth to say something, but found himself unable to vocalise any words.

'We've been seeing each other practically every day,' Pepín soon resumed with a nervous smile. 'She works at Barclays Bank, just up the road from our shop. She's such a great girl, Steven, I tell you. So funny. So kind. So spontaneous. Do you know that her uncle Oscar used to live in the same La Línea street — *Paseo de la Castellana* — where I was born? That's weird, don't you think?... Plus listen to this. Just listen to this: her sister Daphne's currently studying at the same college I attended in Tunbridge Wells. She's studying in the same fucking college that I went to all those years ago.... That's really strange too, *no crees?...* Anyway, I've told her about you and she says she's dying to meet you. That we all have to get together one of these days. "If this guy Steven is a real good friend of yours," she says, "then he is also a real good friend of mine." '

It is difficult to explain just how much all this affected Steven. Sometimes there are things that people say without much thought attached to them, discarding their words like paper streamers thrown against the wind. And yet, meaningless and inconsequential as these words are to those who speak them, they may at the same time be of the greatest consequence to those around them. That is the way it goes sometimes — little words, which were not supposed to be of any significance, which sometimes were not even meant to be heard by anyone, take root within the listener and change their perception of the world forever. For Steven that night was very much like this. Sitting in his Fiat Uno on the motorway's hard shoulder, he could only look at his friend and wonder whether everything he was hearing was part of some grotesque nightmare from which he had not woken up yet. How could Pepín have kept it all so secret, Pepín of all people, the kind of bloke who gave you a detailed description of a woman's genitalia the morning after having slept with her? However, the shock did not end there. Meeting the lady in question a few days later, Steven discovered that she was really tubby and plain-looking, nothing like the foxy, long-legged blondes that Pepín normally went for. She was decent and honest enough — that was clear from the unadorned silver crucifix around her neck. But that Pepín should end up with a woman like that — it just didn't make sense, it went against the grain of everything he knew about his friend. *What the hell was happening to the poor guy?*

But things were about to get worse — much, much worse. Just five or six days after the motorway bombshell, Pepín phoned Steven to say that he would not be going out any more. He claimed that he wanted to save money to buy a flat in Westside (plus that, in any case, Lucía did not like being left behind while he went up to the Costa). The news saddened Steven greatly, perhaps even more than the Spaniard's earlier revelation. For a while he carried on going up to the coast on his own, his hair gelled back and his shirt unbuttoned to his navel as always, using the same old chat-up lines he had been dishing out for so many years. But, of course, it was never the same as before. If things had been bad enough without *el Cookie*, Duncan and the others, they were even worse without Pepín. Everything — the laughs at the hostel, the drunken frolics in the bar, even the women whose mere sight had once stirred his blood so much — felt hollow, dreary, lustreless.

For a few weeks nothing happened. Steven's life continued as always, from Gibraltar to the Costa del Sol and back to Gibraltar again, with no major incidents to comment about — apart from Pepín's registry office marriage that Steven was not even invited to and the news a few weeks later that the Spaniard's wife was expecting a baby. Steven found out about the first of these developments as he was having a coffee in the hotel's staff room one day. It was about ten o'clock on a Monday morning and an intolerably dull ache had settled between his eyes — the direct result of having drunk ten pints of lager at Paddy's Irish Tavern in Torremolinos the previous day. 'Look,' one of the cleaners said, handing over the *Gibraltar Chronicle* to him and pointing at the classifieds section, 'isn't this your mate Pepín? Pepín Álvaro Gonzalez of Paseo de la Castellana 5, La Línea? It says here that he got married last week to someone called Lucía Jane Catherine Figueroa of Aquitania House, Varyl Begg Estate.... Why didn't you tell us he was getting married, Steven?'

News of the pregnancy came about two and a half weeks later. Steven had just finished at the hotel and was walking along Main Street on his way back to the Glacis maisonette he shared with his mother. It was just like any other evening after work: he felt tired and hungry after lugging suitcases around all day and could not wait to put up his feet for a brew. Coming up to Casemates Square, he saw Pepín walking out of BHS with two large shopping bags in his hands. The Spaniard was dressed in a green corduroy jacket with a matching green cravat around his neck. Absolutely faultless colour coordination. If Steven had seen him dressed like this only a few months ago, he would have thought that Pepín was consciously taking the piss, that he was trying to look 'middle-class' for a laugh. This time he was not so sure.

'Hello, Steven,' Pepín said, laughing heartily and patting his unmarried friend on the back. 'Guess what? You won't believe this! Lucía's going to have a baby! *Voy a ser padre, tío!*'

For the better part of a minute Steven stood in front of his old mate without saying a word. He had never seen Pepín so animated before, so lost within the bubble of excitement spewing out of his mouth. The sex of the baby, the little outfits that he had just bought, the different names that he and Lucía were considering: it was almost as if the guy had popped a mouthful of amphetamines and just wouldn't stop talking. Although Pepín himself was probably unaware of the fact, there was something highly unpalatable about such a state of self-absorption. It almost gave you the impression that, were you to turn around and walk away without saying anything, Pepín would still remain standing there, smiling contentedly and full of self-satisfaction, entirely oblivious of your departure. The thought made Steven dislike the Spaniard even further. As he gazed at the *Freeman's* catalogue cutout opposite him, it occurred to him that this was not the Pepín he knew. Not the one who used to go to the Costa with him, at any rate. He looked so settled down now, so sure of himself. Even the timbre of his voice appeared to have changed — lowering in pitch and adopting the vigorous, self-possessed tones of some well-heeled, middle-class patriarch. Absolutely frigging unbelievable! It was as if the face of respectability had been transposed on to the face of profligacy — without the slightest transitional hiccup. It was disconcerting, unsettling. Could this be the same Pepín who always said that women were there to be shagged like bitches, who enjoyed nothing better than having a twos-up with a couple of drunken whores? Anyone seeing him now would have found it hard to believe — but the memories were still there in Steven's head, still fresh and indelible, a mental photograph album that could not be closed just like that. Steven could even remember some of the things that Pepín and he used to say — how they had vowed never to get married, to remain wild and anarchic spirits for as long as they lived. Strange to think that now, less than a few months after they had last been to the Costa together, Pepín was married and with a kid on the way! What a fucked up life it is, Steven suddenly thought, watching the green-cravatted Spaniard slowly saunter away. Everything is so unstable, so fragile, so prone to break up in spite of the illusion of permanence that human beings give to everything.

That night Steven woke up at four o'clock in the throes of a major panic. To describe the experience that he went through during those moments of disorientated semi-consciousness remains an almost impossible undertaking. If you had asked Steven himself about it, he would have told you that it was like stepping outside his physical body and seeing his life from outside, seeing it as it really was, without any frills or adornments. He saw himself going to work every morning. He saw himself carrying suitcases around the hotel all day. He saw himself going to the Costa on his own every weekend. He saw himself getting drunk and trying to chat up women there. He saw himself doing all these things from an 'external' vantage point, almost as if he was a spectator to his own life. It was then that the sense of panic crept up on him, shooting into his system like a drug injected into his bloodstream. 'What the fuck am I doing with my life?' he suddenly thought, totally overcome with dread. *'What have I been doing with myself all these years?'* From Gibraltar to the coast and then back to Gibraltar again: that's what his life had become reduced to. The same routine week in, week out — unless we count the times he took a couple of weeks off during the summer and went to the Costa (where else?) for an extended holiday break. Was that what life was all about, he now wondered. Was that what it meant to be alive? To carry on living the same squalid and monotonous routine, grinding out your days in spite of your best intentions, blinding yourself to the sterile deadness of your existence? Surely there had to be something more than that! Surely! Emotionally distraught, he remembered how as a child he had always wanted to be a mountain climber, to conquer the still unclimbed peaks of Asia and Africa, to set foot where no man had yet been. With a red biro and a soaring heart, he had marked all the unclimbed mountains that he could find in his school atlas, totally convinced that he would be the first person to climb them one day, *actually seeing it within his mind's eye*, this picture of himself standing in explorer's garb at the top of some snow-covered peak, unable to imagine, to so much as contemplate for a second, that things could turn out any other way. Remembering all this brought tears to Steven's eyes. Had it all just eroded with the passing of time, he wondered. Was that the way with all childhood dreams? Did they always have to die a cruel death, bludgeoned by the cudgel of cynicism, trampled by the disillusion that accompanies the loss of innocence? Was it one of life's prerequisites that you always had to *abandon everything you once believed in?*

Early next morning Steven got out of bed and walked straight into the bathroom. For a while he observed his naked body in the mirror. He did not like what he saw — his hair was beginning to recede and his skin no longer had the tautness of youth, hanging from his armpits and his abdomen in ugly folds of sagging flesh. He had never felt so aware of the ageing process before, so conscious of its degenerative effects upon the body. For a few seconds he looked at his penis lying curled up between his legs. It looked so flaccid and inert, so devoid of life. Quickly averting his eyes, Steven turned on a tap and splashed some water on his face. After only a few seconds, however, he stopped and looked at his reflection again. He looked at it without moving a muscle. It was then that the reality of the situation came crashing down on him. He was twenty-six and he had never done anything with his life. That was what it came down to. He had been to the Costa loads of times, yes. He had spent three weeks in a heavily guarded Moroccan tourist resort as a kid. But that was it — no mountains, no explorer's garb and no sense of real achievement. As much as it pained him to admit it, that balding, slightly pot-bellied figure in the mirror was just a fuck-up, a loser in life. He had no woman, no flat of his own, he had never travelled anywhere, he had a job that one of the Rock apes themselves could do and he still lived with his mother. To be brutally honest, it didn't even matter whether he carried on living or not. Who would give a damn one way or the other? Even if he died the very next day, no one would miss him. Perhaps his parents would stand by his grave and shed a few solitary tears — yes, he could not deny that much. But why would these tears be shed? Not because he had been an exceptional human being or because he had ever done anything worthwhile with his life, but only because of the purely biological and emotional reason that they had lost their only son. Suddenly it dawned upon Steven that the person who stared back at him in the mirror was not the person he wanted to be. 'No, no, no,' he thought angrily, 'a million times no.' He would rather die than see the rest of his life waste away like this. He would rather sacrifice everything than cling to something that no longer had any meaning!

**

'Excuse me, sir,' a strongly accented voice said. 'We shall be arriving in twenty minutes. Have you finished with your glass?'

Steven looked up and saw a Moroccan waiter standing by his side. He was about six foot four and skeletally thin, with the bulging eyes and scooped-out cheeks of a lifelong ectomorph. He was also grinning widely, no doubt amused at having surprised his client in a state of reverie.

'Yes, yes,' the young man said, smiling uncomfortably. 'Take it away. Thank you very much.'

Steven handed the glass over to the man and thanked him again. He then leaned back and lit himself a cigarette. As the smoke slowly swirled down into his lungs, he remembered his night of panic and the episode in the bathroom the next morning. Yes, something had changed inside him that day. Something vital and essential, yet at the same time intangible and hard to define. Arriving at the Costa del Sol, for example, he would seek out quiet bars and read novels until sunset. Or else he would go for long strolls out of Fuengirola's town centre and down the N-340 highway, walking for miles and miles along the jagged, rocky coastline. Even more strangely, perhaps, Steven rarely attempted to chat up women during this time. He tried once or twice — and on each occasion the woman in question ran a mile as soon as he approached her, as if she could somehow sense the existential turmoil inside him: 'Sorry, darling, but I'm meeting some friends at the Red Lion in ten minutes. It's been nice talking to you. Ta-ra.' If this had happened only a few months ago, Steven would have wondered if he was losing his looks, if he no longer had the 'old magic touch.' Now, though, he was not even bothered.

It was on one of these last days at the coast that Steven finally severed the remaining ties holding him to the past. He had just returned to his hostel from the Swedish Arms in the centre of Fuengirola, one of his old haunts from some years ago. He had gone there earlier in the evening with the intention of killing some time, but had rapidly got bored after a couple of pints. Back in his room, there was nothing much that Steven could do. It was already ten o'clock and he did not really feel like going out again. For a while he lay on his bed and tried to read the novel that he had purchased just before crossing the border a day and a half earlier. It was about some European gunrunner who falls in love with a sheikh's daughter — *Codename: Broken Scimitar 77* was its rather grandiloquent title. Steven had reached the point in the book where the sheikh was telling his heavily moustachioed cronies to seek out the defiler of his daughter: 'Bring me the head of Mr. Quinn on a spike, comrades! Let the blond-haired infidel not escape with such an affront against our honour!' 'What a load of bollocks,' Steven thought, throwing the book angrily on the *pensión's* mildewed carpet. He then switched on the small transistor radio he kept on his bedside table. Straight away a self-assured Spanish voice could be heard coming from the radio's speakers. Sighing with irritation, Steven stretched out his arm with the intention of changing the frequency to a Spanish pop station. Then he heard the word 'self-transformation.' Rapidly, almost acting on instinct, he retracted his arm and sat upright against his pillow. He decided to carry on listening.

'It is generally believed that there are two types of drug addict undergoing rehab,' the voice on the radio said, '— those who want to quit their addiction and those who don't. At first it is very difficult to figure this one out, since both types outwardly profess the same desire to change. With tears of emotion, they both tell you that they want to change, that they will do anything to get out of the hellhole in which they are living. If you have no experience in these things, you accept their words blindly, you take them entirely at face value. But after a few days have passed and you get to know the patients better, you realise that there are those who really mean this and those who don't. Certain gestures make you see this, certain words, even certain bodily postures. It is not just a matter of saying things openly; it goes far beyond that. Sometimes drug addicts speak an unspoken language through their movements and their gestures. It is very difficult to explain, but it's almost as if they unconsciously externalise their innermost thoughts. Once you are able to understand this, you realise that what some of these people may be saying isn't necessarily true. More importantly, you realise that for a drug addict to turn his or her life around they must *really believe* that they can change. If this belief is not there, then the battle is lost even before the fighting has started. They may talk about changing, they may make all sorts of plans about what they intend to do after they leave the unit — but both you and they know that they are only kidding themselves.'

'Does this mean,' a female voice — middle-aged, deep-timbered, a touch mannish — asked at this point, 'that counsellors like yourself give up on certain people just because *you know*, in inverted commas, that they won't make it?'

'No, not at all.'

'What do you mean? Can you please elaborate for our listeners?'

'Like I've already said — some people want to change, others don't. But that doesn't mean to say that those who don't cannot wake up one day and decide that the time has come for them to turn their lives around. All it takes is one spark, one second of inspiration. I have seen it happen plenty of times before. There you are, thinking that so-and-so doesn't have a hope in hell, when all of a sudden there is a new light in his eye, a new sense of conviction. At our Casares unit, we call it "a moment of inner reconciliation." '

'That must be really beautiful — seeing that happen in front of you.'

'It is a very beautiful experience. And also a very humbling one. The kind of event that puts everything else into perspective. In this day and age, after all, many of us go through life without ever pausing to think about things, unable to find the time or the willingness to get out of the little ruts in which we find ourselves. "Life is shit," we constantly tell ourselves. "Nothing will ever change." But when you're there sharing someone's pain, when you're holding someone's hand while they vomit into a bucket and they still tell you that they want to change, when all this happens, you realise *that it is not at all like this*. There is always a choice open to us. Always. Whether we are fighting a coke addiction or merely sitting back and letting our life waste away. There is always hope, there is always the possibility of moving away from it all and starting anew. Because if there is one thing you learn through working with addicts, it is that life is a series of choices and that, even though it may not always appear so, we always have different options ahead of us. This applies to every single addict who has ever existed. To every single human being who finds himself caught in a rut. There is always a choice to get out of it. *Always*. It may be difficult, it may be hard, and the chances are that they will probably try and fail. But the choice is still there and that is something that should never be forgotten.'

'Nice words. But time is running out and we have to move on to our next guest. Briefly now, if there are any drug addicts out there listening to this programme, what would you say to them? What advice would you give? *Very briefly now.*'

'I would say this to them. In every single life, there will come a moment when bad things happen, when your faith in everything around you is shaken. The challenge is not to run away from these bad things or to wish that they had never happened, but to face them knowing that it is only by confronting life's obstacles that we can grow as human beings, that we can find out who we really are. Let me just finish by quoting some very beautiful lines by the Indian poet Rabindranath Tagore which express this in a wonderful way. "Let me not pray to be sheltered from dangers," he says, "but to be fearless in facing them. Let me not beg for the stilling of my pain, but for the heart to conquer it." Now that's what I call poetry, don't you think?'

Steven switched off the radio and lay still for some moments. Through the open window he could hear the sounds of the *Fuengirolan* night — beeping car horns, laughing teenage voices, the occasional shouted *piropo*. In an attempt to disconnect from the racket, he focused on the white foam tiles on the ceiling and the discoloured orange patches that decades of furtive cigarette smoking had left imprinted on them. Some of the tiles, he noticed, hung down a centimetre or two, exposing flattened lumps of dry adhesive and bits of the wooden ceiling. Others had large pieces missing. As he stared at the whole grisly ensemble, he began to remember what the man had been saying on the radio: 'Whether we are fighting a coke addiction or merely sitting back and wasting our life, we always have the choice to start again. Always. That is something that should not be forgotten.' For some reason the words unsettled him deeply. Somehow — he could not explain to himself why — he felt that he had been waiting all his life to hear these lines. No, even crazier than that: he felt that everything that he had experienced in life so far — his parents' divorce, his lonely childhood, his debauched excursions to the Costa, his estrangement from Pepín, even his recent self-doubts and insecurities — had been lived purely and exclusively to bring him up to this moment. The thought freaked Steven out, made him fumble for the packet of cigarettes on his bedside table. Like most people, he had heard how certain words or events can change the course of an individual's life. There was, for instance, what his father used to say about the day his wife had disowned him: 'It was my wake-up call, the instant I knew I had no option but to turn my life around.' Could something similar be happening to me now, Stephen wondered. Could I be going through some sort of life-changing experience too? Whether he was or he wasn't, one thing was certain: he could not carry on meandering through life any more. That was what it all came down to. He needed to find a new direction, to put some purpose back into his life, and, as no direction was available other than the one that had just been revealed to him on the radio, he decided that this would be the one to follow. It did not matter that he knew nothing about counselling or helping others. It did not even matter that he had no sense of vocation. All that would come in time. The important thing, for the moment at least, was to start *believing* that this was the path he was meant to follow. It was literally as simple as that. *As a man thinks, so shall he become.*

**

'Ladies and gentlemen,' the captain of the ship suddenly announced through the lobby's speakers. 'We will be arriving at Tangier in five minutes. Please have your passports and other travel documents ready.'

Steven looked out through the window and saw a row of moss-covered breakwaters protruding from the sea. A short distance beyond the breakwaters stood the port and city of Tangier — a crumbling array of whitewashed little buildings and rusting TV antennas. The sight brought a nervous smile to his face, made him recall what his mother had said the day he showed her the letter from the Moroccan orphanage: 'You will hate it there, Steven. The beggars, the kids hassling you, the filthy stench in the streets. You hated it when you were a kid and you will hate it again now. If you ask me, I can't see you lasting there more than a week.' It was the kind of remark that his mother excelled at — a real verbal slap on the face. He remembered how upset he was at the time, how much her words had cut into him. That sheet of paper had meant such a great deal to him, it had represented the culmination of so much effort and struggle. For the last six weeks he had been trying to find some new direction that would enable him to turn his life around. He had tried everyone and everything that he could think of — the Church, various government departments, different charities. But it was always the same: they all wanted qualifications, certificates, CVs with experience. Finally, one of the priests at the cathedral told him that there was a need for skilled and unskilled relief workers in Morocco. He even gave him the address of an orphanage he knew in Rabat called the Stirling Homes Foundation. That evening Steven sat down in his living room and wrote a short letter to the institution concerned, briefly outlining the reasons why he wanted to help others and asking if there was any voluntary work he could do for them. He then took the letter and dropped it into the red pillar-box just outside the Glacis Estate post office. Approximately three and a half weeks later, he received the following reply:

> *Dear Mr. Hernandez,*
> *We are pleased to acknowledge receipt of your recent letter and we would like to invite you to spend some time with our organisation in Rabat. We are a small charity that relies both on the generosity of our donors and the efforts of our volunteer workers. We have been operating in Morocco since 1966, the year that our founder Yannick Stirling decided to set up a small orphanage at his own expense near the port town of Kenitra. Although in recent years we have started getting a small amount of EU funding, we are still desperately short of monies to cover our growing needs and for this reason we are always interested in legitimate and properly*

accredited offers of help. At the moment, for example, we need extra assistance with the refurbishment of our orphanage in the Tidiquin district of Ketama. We are trying to get the building ready for winter and we are in desperate need of stonemasons, carpenters, welders, bricklayers, as well as anyone else wanting to 'give us a hand'. Once this building is ready, it will provide board and lodging for around thirty children who will otherwise have to spend winter in the streets of what is not the safest or most hospitable of areas. If you are still interested in seeing what our organisation is about, please call us on the number at the bottom of this letter and we will arrange for someone to meet you when you arrive in Morocco.

Yours,

Dr. Jacques Lavatte

(Institute Director, Stirling Homes Foundation)

Words alone cannot describe the rush of delight that overwhelmed Steven Hernandez when he first read these lines. For nearly a whole morning he wandered around the hotel clutching the letter, reading and rereading its words, showing it to everyone from Mr. Briars-Thompson, the duty manager, to the other porters. But when he got back home that evening all these feelings were rapidly quashed. 'Have you gone mad, Steven?' his mother said, unable to accept that any Gibraltarian in their right mind would want to work in a Moroccan orphanage. 'You haven't been brainwashed by some sect, have you?' Then she turned around and grimly carried on mopping the kitchen floor in silence.

It was more or less the same reaction that Steven got from everybody else. Colleagues would immediately stand back and narrow their eyes; friends of his would shake their heads and wonder what in God's name had possessed him. *Have you heard about el Loni's kid? He's giving everything up to go and work as a carpenter or something in Morocco! That family's something else, don't you think!* Although Steven hated being the object of such demeaning scrutiny, he could not exactly blame his detractors either. For many years, after all, he had been just like them. The moment that anyone had deviated from the norm, he had always felt puzzled and suspicious, unwilling to explain their behaviour in terms other than the deviant or the delusional. It may have been some hippy bloke who one day decided to set off on one of the merchant ships down at the harbour, some woman who was giving up her job as a lawyer to become a drug counsellor. As soon as he heard these things, Steven would always laugh to himself, unable to believe that people could go off the rails in this way. '*Valiente locura*,' he would say, rapidly dismissing whatever they did as the outcome of some mental imbalance or the other. It was only now — standing on the other side of the divide, as it were, and being the one whom everyone laughed at — that Steven realised how prejudiced he had been, how narrow-minded and judgmental. Who the hell was Steven Hernandez, after all, to judge other people in this way? How could he be so bloody sure that what he was doing was *so right* and what they were doing was *so wrong?*

Steven looked through the porthole again and saw that they were already approaching the first passenger pier. He could make out a few people through the heavily scratched Plexiglass — a middle-aged tourist with painfully sunburnt legs, two Scandinavian-looking girls with rucksacks on their backs, half a dozen young Moroccan men chatting them up, an ear-ringed woman in a *djellaba* trying to hawk a few packets of cigarettes, a coach driver looking stern and business-like next to his vehicle. 'People and more people,' Steven reflected, surrendering to a rare fit of emotion, 'each with their different concerns, each with their own worries and apprehensions.' The idea pleased him, brought a smile to his lips. 'Sometimes it is easy to dehumanise crowds into a simple swarm of bodies,' he told himself, 'but everyone carries a unique universe of experiences embedded within them, a hidden world of hopes and dreams that no one sees. Maybe the guy in shorts was thinking of the long sunless winters back home. Maybe the young Scandinavian girls were thinking about their boyfriends in Uppsala and how much they missed them. Maybe the coach driver was thinking about how he'd like his estranged son to get in touch again. Anything was possible, really, wasn't it?'

The pier was very close now and some of the Moroccan passengers were already gathering their belongings. For a second Steven looked at the battered plastic suitcase lying beside him and found himself wondering what his mother was doing at that particular moment. He wondered whether she was mopping the kitchen floor or polishing the bathroom tiles. No, more likely she was just sitting there worrying about him. Curled up on her living room sofa, with the TV remote nestled between her hands. Thinking what a fool her son was and wondering how long it would be before he was back in Gibraltar again. The thought made Steven feel sorry for her, but in a strange way it also reinforced his convictions. Let them all think he was mad. Let them think he was throwing his life away. What did he care? You only live once and if there is something you really want to do, you have to do it regardless of the consequences. *That is what it is all about, isn't it?* With this thought Steven stood up from his seat and exhaled aloud. Then he breathed in as hard as he could. He wanted to take in the dinginess, to absorb the stench of cigarette smoke and male sweat that hung in the lobby. As he did all this, the words of the radio broadcast suddenly came back to him: 'In every single life, there will come a time when bad things happen. The challenge is not to run away from these bad things or wish that they had never happened, but to face them knowing that it is only by confronting life's obstacles that we can grow as human beings, that we can find out who we really are.' The memory made Steven smile, killed off the little apprehension still left inside him. Yes, he thought: his mum was right — there was always a chance that he might return home in a week. That risk was definitely there. Would probably follow him very closely from now on. But even so he was not scared. For once in his life he knew that he was doing something that came from the heart, that felt right in every fibre of his being, and when you find yourself knowing this, Steven told himself, almost nothing can stop you from walking the path that you must follow. Emboldened by the thought, he picked up his suitcase and smiled at the Moroccans who had been staring at him earlier. Then he crossed the lobby and walked out on the deck. It was time to disembark....

7. Shrink

Peter Rodriguez is in a psychiatrist's waiting room. He is there with his cousin Richard, a twenty-nine-year-old mortgage advisor and the only member of the Rodriguez family who could drive him to his appointment in Algeciras that morning. For close to two hours he has sat in the tiny room with almost nothing to do — staring at the floor, clenching his fists, scratching his elbow, moistening his lips with his tongue, occasionally picking his nose, steadfastly refusing to look at the other waiting patients....

'I don't know why I'm putting up with this,' Peter says, turning to his cousin. 'I just don't know.'

Richard Rodriguez puts down the magazine that he is reading and looks up. 'You what?'

'I said I don't know why I'm putting up with this,' Peter repeats for his cousin's benefit. 'I mean, did you hear what her secretary told me just now? Did you actually hear? "The doctor's out having lunch right now," she said. "With a little bit of luck she'll be here before quarter past." "With a little bit of luck?" I felt like shouting in her face. "For Christ's sake, I was supposed to have my appointment at TWELVE and it's almost TWO already! Are you Spaniards slack or what?"'

'Slack is not the word I'd use,' Richard says, casually smoothing out a crease in his trousers. 'Fucking bloody useless is more like it.'

Peter sighs under his breath and then looks down at his hands. He shakes his head. He closes his eyes. Why must it always be like this, he thinks. Why? Is there some unwritten law that says that whenever you come asking for help they must invariably treat you like shit? Can the bastards sense your vulnerability? Can they smell your lack of self-esteem? Does it hang around you wherever you go? Like a substance one secretes? Doctors, lawyers, priests, nurses, dentists, doctors' receptionists, policemen — almost all of them recognise it when they see it in front of them. The moment they know they have power over you, they objectify you; they erase your humanity and stop regarding you as someone with feelings and aspirations of your own. Instead you become a name illegibly scrawled on a piece of letter-headed paper, a task that needs to be done before five, the latest object going by on the conveyor belt of their daily routine....

Peter looks up and sees that his cousin is reading his magazine again. On the front cover there is a picture of a young woman. She has very large eyes and her mouth is covered in a thick layer of glossy, cherry-coloured lipstick. For a few moments Peter tries to think what name would suit her best and eventually comes up with the name 'Adel.' He is not sure why he has chosen this name — he has never met anyone called Adel in his life — but it seems to fit her in a way that he cannot explain. Adel — shiny, happy, extrovert Adel. The kind of girl who rollerskates in the park and smiles at complete strangers. Faintly amused, Peter leans forward and looks at the other magazines scattered on the bottom tier of the reception's coffee table: *Hola, Semana, Diez Minutos, ¡Qué me dices!, Lecturas.* Acting on impulse, he reaches out and picks up the only magazine that doesn't seem like a *revista del corazón* — a rather battered and serious-looking medical journal. He opens it at random and comes across a page splattered with pictures of what appear to be fine-cut slices of Serrano ham. ('Photos of *pata negra* ham?' Peter thinks. 'Is this *el Boletín de la Asociación de Médicos Españoles* or a recipe book by Karlos Arguiñano?') Fascinated, he starts to read the accompanying text and discovers that the photographs are in fact cross-sectional images of a human cadaver that was cut into slices and then photographed by Dr. Michael J. Ackermann of the University of Colorado's Health Sciences Centre. The cadaver belonged to Joseph Paul Jernigan, a thirty-eight-year-old Texas murderer who spent twelve years in prison before being executed on August 5, 1993. According to Dr. Ackermann, it is 'the first time that transverse CT, MRI and cryosection images of a representative male cadaver have been obtained at an average of one millimetre intervals.'

'Richard?'

'Yes?'

'Can I ask you a question?'

'Yes?'

'Do you think the soul leaves the body immediately after death?'

'*You what?*'

'The soul. Do you think it leaves the body immediately after you kick the bucket? Or do you think it lingers around for a while — kind of letting you know what's happening around you?'

'Jesus Christ, Peter. You really come up with some belters at times!'

'You mean you've never thought about it?'

'Me — think about shit like that? What kind of a freak do you take me for?... No wonder you're depressed, man,' Richard says, shaking his head and picking up his magazine again. 'Thinking about stuff like that would send anyone totally *loco!*'

Peter sits back against the sofa and crosses his arms. He sinks his front teeth into his lower lip. The woman with the cherry-coloured lipstick, he thinks, looks similar to a girl he had once come across during his student days. She was a well-dressed and sophisticated type and he had met her at a concert given by the Manchester University Philharmonic Orchestra. In between the first and second concertos on the programme they had talked about Mozart and the 'Franciscan stillness' of his middle movements. Peter still remembers what it was like that night — the voices of the crowd, the glimmering lights, the feeling *of connectedness* between them. He remembers how the girl's eyes glistened under the chandeliers, how her pupils kept contracting and dilating as she talked. For a second he even thought about reaching forward and kissing her on the lips — but in the end he decided that he could not be unfaithful to his girlfriend at the time. 'God, how could I have been so stupid?' Peter now thinks to himself, unable to understand why he had carried on talking all through the interval about Mozart and other banalities. 'How could I have just sat there and let it all slip by?' She was a really beautiful woman too, possibly the most beautiful he had ever met. She would have been a good screw, he thinks. *A long, slow, deliciously drawn-out screw.* The thought saddens him, spreads like poison inside him. But it also fills him with surprise — the jarring, slightly unpleasant sense of surprise that suddenly descends upon you when you find yourself reflecting on what you were thinking just moments ago. 'How can I even be thinking of women at this time?' he ponders for an instant. 'A deadbeat like me, sitting in a psychiatrist's waiting room with a chronic case of anxiety?' Strange, he thinks. Awfully strange. Could it be because he hasn't been with a woman for so long? Because he knows he will probably never be able to chat up a girl again? It is a macabre and twisted thought, but Peter finds himself wondering whether men actually think about these things during their final dying moments. Stretched out on the roadside, blood and guts spilling out of their stomachs. *God, why didn't I fuck more? Why didn't I take all those opportunities I fumbled?*

'This is getting ridiculous, Richard, don't you think?'

'What is?'

'Us waiting here like this.'

'Mmm.'

'I mean, what sort of psychiatrist leaves her patients hanging around like this? *Qué clase de cachondeo es éste?*'

'Mmm.'

'Is there no sense of professionalism in this bloody country or what?'

'Mmm.'

'I mean, do you think I would have waited so long to see a psychiatrist in Gib?'

Peter is thinking about Spain now. Like most Gibraltarians, he is not too sure what to make of the country and its inhabitants. Some five or six months ago, he had even written an essay on English attitudes to Spain, trying to prove how Englishmen's dislike of bullfighting and donkey-beating could be traced back to the Armada and the fear of all things Spanish which the failed invasion provoked within the Anglo-Saxon psyche. He had written the piece in response to an essay competition advertised in the local press, secretly hoping to take the first prize and the one hundred and fifty pounds that accompanied it. But in the end Peter did not win anything. Worse than that: he wasn't even on the list of ten runners-up. That had pissed him off almost as much as learning that the top prize had gone to a piece entitled 'Memoir of a Girl Guide Girlhood'. 'Fancy that,' Peter thought, opening the *Gibraltar Chronicle* and seeing the winning essay printed there before him. 'Just fancy that!' It had been a personal watershed, one of those things that shape and define an individual's life from then onwards. There he was trying to be an apologist for the Latin race (and that included the majority of Gibraltarians themselves) and the jury goes and gives the prize to a treatise on the virtues of drinking tea and singing Abba songs around a well-tended campfire! 'That just about sums up the Latin character,' Peter now thinks, staring glumly at his cousin Richard. 'Don't know why I even bother defending the buggers in the first place!' With a mounting sense of resentment, he recalls the time when three Spaniards laughed in his face at a student party in Manchester. The party had been held in the loft of a rented house and was organised by a group of young guys from Madrid. Although it was pitch black and it took a while before your eyes became acclimatised to the darkness, you were immediately aware of a great number of bodies in the surrounding gloom. You could catch their odours rushing at you in separate, individually distinguishable wafts — the scent of newly shampooed hair, the acrid spirals of cigarette smoke, the smell of alcohol on people's breath. Before long three Spaniards had approached Peter and asked him where he was from. '*Soy de Gibraltar*,' he replied, extending his hand. '*Habéis escuchado?*' one of the three young men immediately said. 'A British gentleman *con acento Andaluz?!*' Then they began to laugh, all three of them — a cruel, heartless laugh that pierced right through Peter's adolescent soul and brought him to the verge of tears. Is this what it means to be Gibraltarian, he briefly wondered as their laughter continued ringing in his ears. To be pissed on by the English and spat upon by the Spanish? Or was there something else? Something that Gibraltarians could claim as their own, some unique sense of *Gibraltarianness* that came with being born on the most famous rock in the world? He thought about this last question for some moments, thought deeply and searchingly, but, much to his regret, realised that he could not come up with anything other than tobacco smuggling, cars with tinted windows, and big, fuck-off medallions on tanned and hairy chests. That's what it all amounted to, really. Everything else was borrowed — the history, the statues, the monuments, the fortresses. All that belonged to the Moors, to the Spaniards, to the British — to all those who fought over the three and a half square mile peninsula in the name of lucre, territory or whatever other imperialistic aims they had on their agenda....

'Cheer up, Petie,' Richard suddenly says. 'It's not as if you're going to the gallows.'

'What's that?'

'Cheer up, *hombre*. You know it ain't that bad.'

Peter nods and tries to smile. He smiles as if to say, 'Yes, you're right — it isn't that bad. I'm just indulging in self-pity and I should just snap out of it like everyone tells me.' But his performance, he knows, is not particularly credible. Within only a few seconds he can feel his artificial smile slipping away from him — rather like a mask sliding down his face. 'I should not be here,' he subsequently thinks. 'I don't deserve this.' A: he has never done anything bad in his life. B: he has never consciously hurt anyone. Maybe he has never done anything good, that much is also true. No acts of selfless courage, no monumental feats of altruism for the benefit of mankind. But he has certainly never done anything that could be remotely classed as bad. Why, then, did it all have to come to this? What had he done to deserve such a disastrous run of bad luck? Could it be that Providence was so fickle that it did not matter whether you were good or not? That was what cynics and misanthropes said, wasn't it? Or was it because of something that he had done in a past life, perhaps? He had heard that innocent people sometimes suffer for this reason. Once, while attending a Freshers coffee evening in Manchester, a Pakistani student called Wajid had read Peter's palm and told him that he had been a Spanish soldier in a past life. Seriously, with the utmost candour, Wajid had informed his sceptical listener that he could visualise him standing on some kind of ship, sailing towards a foreign land. 'I can see you scared and lonely,' he said. 'I can see you holding your sword by your side with a heavy heart.' What exactly had he done when he had reached that foreign land, Peter now wonders. Had he murdered and raped? Had he desecrated some holy place? Had he taken his own life and cursed himself to spend a second lifetime paying the price for squandering life itself? *What the fuck had he been guilty of?*

'Do you think human beings can change, Richard?' Peter all of a sudden asks, his face cupped despondently between his palms.

'What do you mean?'

'People — do you think they can alter what's inside them, change the essence of who they are?'

'Of course,' Richard answers his cousin with an awkward attempt at a smile. 'That's what being human is all about — isn't it?'

Peter smiles at Richard and looks down. For some reason he is now thinking about his ex-girlfriend and the events that led to their break-up over a year ago. Her name was Marsha and he had met her shortly after moving into his student hall of residence in Manchester. To this day, Peter still struggles to understand how it all went wrong between them. Unlike most of the other guys in the residence, he had never been unfaithful or messed about behind his girlfriend's back. Marsha had always been his beacon of light, the one unfailing refuge to which he could always turn when everything else was going against him. People always commented on how suited they were for each other, how they seemed destined to be together for the rest of their lives. Unfortunately, the exact opposite had come to pass: whereas all the other guys were still together with their girlfriends, he had been abandoned by the woman he loved, extirpated from her life like a cataract removed from a diseased eye and then thrown into a nearby slop bucket. What is the moral to be learned from all this, Peter wonders. That in real life the good guys never win? That the dirtier one plays, the less chance there is of getting dirt thrown back at you? Peter still remembers the day it all came to an end. He remembers it every night before going to bed. He remembers standing in a room with the lights switched off. He remembers holding the phone to his ear and listening to isolated phrases that seemed to have no direct connection with each other — 'You're too cynical,' 'I'm sorry that I'm hurting you,' 'We're just not compatible,' 'You deserve something more than what I can give you.' He remembers banging the receiver against the wall one moment and then crying the next. He remembers feeling powerless, emotionally numbed, consumed by the terrible frustration of wanting to reach out to someone whose voice he could hear with total clarity but who in reality was thousands of miles away. He remembers going to bed and crying himself to sleep. He remembers waking up at ten o'clock the next day and lying within the warm folds of his bed for a few minutes, the memory of the previous night drowned in a haze. He remembers how everything suddenly came back to him, abruptly and without warning, like an ulcer that has been accidentally rubbed and starts bleeding again. He remembers getting out of bed and opening the curtains. He remembers seeing a cloudy grey sky before him. He remembers looking at the swaying masts of the yachts anchored in the nearby marina. He remembers seeing a lone gull perched on the tallest of them. He remembers thinking 'She has left me' as the bird struggled against the wind. He remembers moving away from the window, feeling *utterly defeated*.

'People *can* change, Peter,' Richard now says in a much more enthusiastic tone, as if feeling guilty that he had not put up a better show earlier. 'It's possible *as long as you believe that you can.*'

Peter smiles sadly and looks down at the palms of his hands. Thirteen months have passed since the day that Marsha left him, yet he still finds himself continually thinking about her. Thirteen months that seemed to have collapsed and imploded into a few days, as if it was only last Wednesday that she had phoned and said that things were through between them. Time and again he has wondered if time has shrunk for her in a similar manner — or whether she has just continued with her life as if nothing were the matter: getting up early every morning to catch the 96A into uni, doing her shopping at Tescos every Thursday afternoon, going out with her friends to the same pubs and wine bars. That's the most tragic thing about the end of a relationship, Peter suddenly thinks — *what takes a second to unbind on one side, often takes an age to heal on the other*. He remembers how much Marsha used to mean to him, how he once imagined that their lives until they met were like two separate rivers, flowing in parallel directions for a while before merging together for the rest of their joint course to the ocean. He liked to imagine her growing up in England, going to school, studying for her A-levels, starting university — and then he liked to remember what he was doing at these different times, trying to determine if there had been some kind of augury along the way that pointed to the subsequent intertwining of their destinies. Two separate lives, he used to think, moving in totally different circles yet fated to meet all the same, spinning uncontrollably towards each other, drawn into each other's orbit. 'How could I have been such a sucker?' he now sighs, wondering what had possessed a cynic like him to be seduced by the greatest of all romantic lies. 'How could I have imposed a sense of sacredness where patently there was none?' Yes, it might have been true that two lives had come together and met — he could not deny that much; but it was also true that both of these lives had since moved on and would never come into contact with each other again, drifting apart like two planets whose orbits bring them close to one another for a brief moment before separating again for the rest of eternity, a meaningless, astrological coincidence that happened once and would never ever happen again.

A short while later, the psychiatrist arrives at the clinic. Because he is sitting with his face cradled between his hands, Peter does not see her come in. Richard, however, nudges him lightly on the shoulder and tells him that he has seen her walk into her office. 'What does she look like?' Peter asks. 'I don't know,' Richard replies. 'Like a doctor, I guess.'

Peter rests his head against the sofa and tries to relax. He tries very hard, but it does not work. He can almost taste the dryness in his mouth, that rough, frothy sensation that builds up at the back of your palate and then slowly seeps down to your tongue and the inside of your lips. He knows that he is very nervous. He also knows that this nervousness stems from the fact that she is already there, sitting behind her desk and preparing her files, this unknown woman who walked in a few minutes ago, this mysterious stranger who will soon be asking him to lie down on a couch and tell her all the most intimate details of his directionless existence.

'Richard?'

'Yes?'

'Can I ask you a question?'

'Go on, then.'

'Have you ever been to a psychiatrist before?'

'Me? No, never.... Why do you ask?'

'I was just wondering if you had any idea what kind of questions she'll ask.'

'You mean the shrink?'

'Yes, of course.'

'I don't know, Peter,' Richard replies. 'She'll probably ask you about how you feel, *yo diría*. You know, whether you have bad dreams, at what times you feel worse. That sort of stuff.'

'You think so?'

'Yeah, I'd say so. I mean, what else could she ask?'

**

Less than ten minutes later, Peter is standing outside the psychiatrist's door. He is very, very, very nervous by this stage. His legs ache after having been still for so long and his lips keep sticking together because of the extreme dryness of his mouth. He can also smell his own sweat: a harsh and pungent odour, partly enfolded in the aroma of deodorant but still lingering heavily in the air. Turning around for a moment, he catches sight of Richard reading the magazine. He is scratching his nose as he reads, totally engrossed in the page before him. The sight sickens Peter and makes him turn back towards the door again. 'Okay,' he thinks as his heart pounds anxiously within his ribcage, 'this *is it.*' He knows that the moment has come — the moment when he loses all his inhibitions and strides manfully into the future. All he has to do is reach out for the doorknob, turn it purposefully and enter her office. No big deal, right? But when the moment of truth arrives, Peter cannot move; it is almost as if his feet had been riveted to the floor. 'What good will this do, anyway?' he tells himself. 'What good will come out of all this rubbish?' He thinks like this for a few seconds, ready to give in and walk away, ready to walk out of the building and never come back again — but then he tells himself not to be so negative. 'If this is your attitude,' he thinks, grabbing the doorknob again, 'you might as well shoot yourself....'

It is a big room. It is lined with bookcases on all sides. It has a musty, *museumy* sort of smell. It is the kind of room you see when priests or politicians or writers are being interviewed on Spanish television, Peter thinks. A large, sophisticated, expensively decorated, rather inhibiting room — with a hand-woven Persian rug laid on the floor and a Zulu shield and spear propped up in one corner. He cannot see any of the tomes on the shelves, but he is sure that they are big and intellectually demanding titles. Tolstoy's *War and Peace*, Homer's *Odyssey* — the sort of books, in other words, that doctors, lawyers and other upright gentlemen and gentlewomen read.

'You are Mr. Rodriguez, I expect?' a voice says in English.

Peter looks ahead and sees the face that pertains to the voice. It is a very common face, he immediately decides. Pale and thin and framed on each side by clumps of rusty, scouring-pad hair. It belongs to a small, red-eyed middle-aged woman who is sitting behind a bulky mahogany desk. She is wearing a black cardigan and a pair of large, old-fashioned glasses. She is not pretty, but she is not ugly either. On the table next to her there is an elaborate silver crucifix that could almost pass for a church monstrance. Although the lower half of her face is partly hidden by the crucifix, he can see that there are two shiny patches of red on each side of her nose, as if she were suffering from a cold.

'I am Dr. Esperanza del Río Montes,' the woman says, gesticulating towards a chair next to her desk. 'Please take a seat.'

'I can speak Spanish,' Peter replies, still standing by the door.

The woman smiles with a hint of condescension. 'It's all right. I like practising my English with my Gibraltarian patients. Please take a seat.'

He nods and sits down. He does not like this woman. He does not like her one bit. She has not apologised for the lateness of the appointment. She has not come up with some cock-and-bull story about how her car had broken down that morning, or how she had just missed her bus. This is *serious stuff* we're talking about.

'Can you tell me what emotions you associate with each of the pictures on this card?' the psychiatrist says, handing him a laminated sheet of paper.

'Sure,' Peter replies.

A girl about to be run over by a car — futility.
A dog sitting with its tail between its legs while being scolded by its master — payback time.
A princess about to kiss a frog — folly.
A father and his son fishing by a brook — cordiality.
A climber reaching the summit of a mountain — elation.
A little boy sitting beside a grandfather clock — innocence.

'Now turn the paper around and write down whatever comes into your head,' Dr. Esperanza del Río Montes says.

'Whatever comes into my head?' Peter asks, somewhat mystified by the request.

'Yes, whatever comes into your head.'

'Okay, then.'

> *i remember your eyes*
> *glistening like shells.*
> *i remember your eyes*
> *giving me hell*

'Why have you written that?' the psychiatrist asks moments later.

'I don't know,' Peter truthfully replies. 'You asked me to write whatever came into my head and that's what came into it.'

'Does it have any specific meaning? Have you seen it anywhere, for example? Was it a poem you wrote out for a girlfriend?'

'I've never had a girlfriend,' Peter lies.

'You mean you just invented it on the spot?'

'Yes.'

'Are you serious?'

'Yes.'

She looks annoyed, Peter thinks. You can tell from the way her reddened nostrils have dilated. This is going to be one big major fuck-up, he thinks to himself.

'Tell me, Mr. Rodriguez, are you scared of death?' the psychiatrist suddenly asks, removing her glasses and holding them by one of the ear stems.

'Should you fear what is inevitable?'

'No, not at all. You shouldn't. Tell me, has someone dear to you ever died?'

'No,' he lies yet again.

'Are you sure about this?'

'Yes.'

'Are you scared you may lose someone who is dear to you one day?'

'No.'

'Are you totally sure about that? I get the impression you're keeping things from me.'

'No, that is not what I'm doing.'

'What about sex?' she casually asks, still holding her glasses by the stem. 'Do you think a lot about sex?'

'No, I don't think a lot about sex.'

'Are you sure?'

'Yes, I'm sure.'

She shakes her head at this point and puts her glasses back on. 'Describe to me how you're feeling right now.'

'Right now?'

'Yes.'

Peter looks down at his hands. 'I'm not sure.'

'What do you mean — you're not sure? How were you feeling this morning, for example? Or yesterday? Or last week? *Es decir*,' she says, momentarily lapsing back into Spanish, 'have there been any days when you've felt worse than others?'

'I suppose there have.'

'Can you describe them for me?' the psychiatrist asks.

'Well,' Peter says, scratching the side of his neck, 'last week was particularly hard.'

'In what way?'

'I felt bad.'

'Bad?'

'You know, just uninterested in anything.'

'Any particular incident that triggered this feeling?'

'No, not really.'

'Are you sure?'

'Yeah.... Although now that I think of it....'

'Now that you think of it — what?'

'Well,' he begins apprehensively, 'earlier during the week I was walking past a construction site when something ... well ... something very strange happened.'

'What was that?'

'I thought that nothing around me had any real purpose. The labourers, the cranes, the houses under construction. It was all one big horrendous joke.'

'Can you tell me more about this?'

'I don't know. It was like I had suddenly lost the filter through which ordinary people see life and I found myself staring at the world in all its chaotic, meaningless reality. Everything seemed pointless. The workers, the houses they were constructing. It was all drained of colour.'

'Is that all?'

Peter nods timidly and looks down at his interlaced hands. He cannot understand why she doesn't want to know more about his 'construction site' experience. He cannot understand how she could have dismissed it all with such a peremptory shake of the head. Meanwhile, the psychiatrist is doing what psychiatrists do best: she is lecturing him on how to conduct his life. Basically, she is telling him that life is like a river and that you have to sail with care in order not to crash against the banks or get grounded on the shallows. A cross between Kahlil Gibran and Auntie Deirdre's page thirteen column, with one or two bits of medical jargon thrown in for good measure. ('You must try to relax, Mr. Rodriguez, to focus outside yourself in a way that will increase your serotonin levels and help you harmonise your thoughts with the world around you.') The whole performance, not surprisingly, pisses Peter off. If he had wanted to learn about any of this rubbish he could have dug out his battered second-hand copy of *The Prophet* from his bedroom cupboard. He could have gone to the 'Mind, Body and Spirit' shelves at the John Mackintosh Library. He could have popped into Sacarello's Newsagents and quickly flicked through the letters section in *Cosmopolitan* or any other woman's magazine. Any of these options would have been better than *this*.

'Remember, Mr. Rodriguez,' the doctor says, starting to write out a prescription, 'even though I'm going to prescribe some tablets for you, you have to try and make an especial effort to get well.'

'Yes, doctor.'

'You have to force yourself to go out, to mix with friends, to do the things you used to do before you started feeling unwell.'

'Yes, doctor.'

'If you just take the tablets without doing these things, you'll never get better again.'

'Yes, doctor.'

'Okay, Mr. Rodriguez,' Dr. Esperanza del Río Montes says, handing the prescription over. 'I want you to take three different drugs for the time being. Make sure you take them as *indicado*, as otherwise there is no point in me prescribing them for you. The first thing I'm going to give you is something called Tryptizol. This is what is known as a tricyclic drug. It works by blocking the reuptake of the neurotransmitters norepinephrine and serotonin in the central nervous system. You have to take one every morning. At first you may feel a bit unsettled when you take this tablet. You may experience muscular cramps or what some patients describe as "transient moments of vertigo." These side effects only last two or three minutes and then they are gone. Make sure that you continue taking the pills, as after two weeks your body should acclimatise to the drug and you shouldn't get any side effects at all.... The second thing I'm prescribing for you is Dicepin B6. This is just something to calm you down. It is similar to Valium, but *más absorbible*. I want you to take three of these a day, one after every meal.... The third and final thing I'm giving you is an anti-depressant called Tofranil. This is a tricyclic similar to

Tryptizol, but tends to help people with anxiety also. I want you to take two of these every night before going to bed. Is that understood, Mr Rodriguez?'

'Yes, doctor. Thank you, doctor.'

'Okay, then,' Dr. Esperanza del Río Montes says, rising from her desk. 'You can go now.'

'Yes, doctor. Thank you, doctor.'

'*No hay de que*,' she replies, quickly sitting down again. 'Just don't forget to come and see me every four weeks so that we can monitor your progress. It's very important that you don't forget, Mr. Rodriguez. You are mentally ill and need to be regularly monitored — that's how things stand at the moment. My secretary will make an appointment for you when you pay her for today's session. Please ask her to give you a slot in four weeks' time. If for some reason you can't make it to your next appointment, please let us know at least three days in advance. Otherwise we will have to charge you for your missed appointment. Is that all right?'

'Yes, doctor. Thank you, doctor.'

'Remember, Mr. Rodriguez, you *must* come and see me every four weeks. I can't stress this enough. Although Tryptizol and Tofranil are largely safe drugs, they are still very potent forms of medication and their use has to be closely monitored at all times. That's why you *must* come and see me every four weeks. You understand what I'm saying, Mr. Rodriguez, don't you? You understand that you are mentally ill and need regular medical supervision? '

The way she stresses those last words removes any doubts from Peter's head. The bitch is doing this purely for the money, not because she cares one iota for the faceless saddos that regularly parade in front of her. What a fucking bitch, he thinks. What a fucking callous, pitiless, money-grabbing bitch. For a split second he is filled with the desire to pick up the crucifix on her desk and wallop her with it on the head, to grab her by the throat and tell her that he is not easy pickings like the other half-brained morons she keeps in tow. But does he do any of that? Does he hell! 'No, I won't forget, doctor,' is all that he says, nodding and smiling like a congenital half-wit. 'I will see you in four weeks' time. Thank you for seeing me today.' Then he turns around and scurries out of her room.

So it is official now, he thinks. *I am mentally ill.*

8. Dream Sequence

At the lunatic asylum, the lunatic said, 'Many years ago I loved a woman, but she did not love me in return.'

Come, come, Mister Lunatick. That's a bit poor for someone who lost his head after a romantic entanglement. Surely you can do better than that!

'She might have *thought* she loved me,' the lunatic calmly admitted. 'I will not dispute that. But, as Pascal said, tell yourself a lie often enough and you will end up believing it.'

Fair enough, Lunatick. But would not the lie then transmute into a truth? Is a lie still a lie when the prism of perception transforms it into a reality?

The lunatic twitched uncomfortably within his straitjacket. 'If you open that ivory casket resting on the mantelpiece behind you (something which I, at present, find myself unable to do), you will come across three letters in which she claimed to have loved me. Very pretty letters, too. Written on the finest vellum and scented with the perfume of violets and Indian frangipani. But, alas,' the lunatic sighed with regret, 'they are not to be taken as reliable evidence of her love for me.'

Not to be taken as reliable evidence? My dear Lunatick, you wouldn't be suggesting that the female half of our species is by nature inconstant, would you? That would be rather naughty of you — especially seeing that you are not so mentally constant yourself. Do not play the Socrates with me, sir. We are living in the 1990s and not in ancient Athens, let me remind you. Try to be a little bit more politically correct.

'You can tell by the thread-like connections between her letters,' the lunatic quickly replied, 'the tightness of her loops.'

Listen, Lunatick, you know that you shouldn't believe in such superstitious rubbish. Reason, that is the only God that we bow down to in this age. Pure, cold, clear, unmitigated reason.

The lunatic smiled sadly. 'She would often tell her friends that I wasn't good-looking,' he said. 'Balding, pot-bellied and slightly bow-legged, that is how she would describe me.'

Well, maybe she considered you ugly. Women have been known to love ugly creatures before. It is a very common trait — especially among the more pretty members of the fair sex. Look at the case of the Beauty and the Beast. A love affair of the most exquisite kind, unrivalled for either passion or tenderness. Are you going to tell me, Lunatick, that Beauty was not in love with the Beast?

The lunatic started quite noticeably. 'And do you know what the ending of that particular story was, sir? Beauty remained twiddling her thumbs in their forest mansion for three years (while the Beast attended to his business concerns in New York, Paris and London) until one day a handsome young cyclist who was lost in the vicinity chanced upon the mansion and, after being offered a cup of tea and a cucumber sandwich, fucked her senseless.'

You are being extremely crude, Lunatick, and crudity is not permitted within this establishment. I understand that the maggot of bitterness is still eating away at your insides, but that is no excuse for indulging in degrading obscenities of this nature. If you persist in this behaviour, I shall have no option but to contact Androcles the security guard immediately.

The lunatic looked down for some seconds. 'Do you want to hear a little story?' he finally said in a much quieter tone. 'Once upon a time she went to see a masseur because of a problem with her back. The masseur, a hunky Styrian by the name of Siegfried Heinrich Von Eisenstein, gave her an all-body massage every day for the next two weeks, paying special attention to the buttocks and the lumbar region. Once the treatment was finished, he asked her whether he could have four photographs of her in the nude — one from the front, one from behind and one from each side. He claimed he needed them for a Powerpoint presentation on musculoskeletal problems that he was giving before the National Society of Masseurs — or whatever it was he called it.'

What's wrong with that?

'Nothing,' the lunatic replied. 'Except I don't think that most women who go to see an Austrian masseur called Siegfried are requested that kind of thing — and even less of them actually agree to it.'

You are just being paranoid, Lunatick.

'Perhaps,' the lunatic conceded with growing sadness. 'Although I should maybe point out that (a) seven out of ten masseurs admit to having sexual feelings for their female patients; (b) that in the year 1987 alone 733 masseurs in the USA raped or sexually assaulted their female patients; (c) that it is estimated that every year over 3000 additional cases go unreported; and (d) that also in the same year 1987, Dan Friar Hurst, a well-known masseur from Philadelphia, admitted to having secretly installed a video camera in his clinic with the object of filming his female patients while he was massaging them and later, when asked whether he considered this to be an immoral act, allegedly claimed, "Why pick on me? Everyone's doing it. Doctors, dentists, gym owners, restaurateurs. Everyone's got hidden cameras installed somewhere." '

You are just being paranoid, Lunatick.

The lunatic tried shrugging his shoulders within his straitjacket. 'What do you expect? Vulnerability of that sort pisses you off, it irritates you, it plants the seeds of doubt within your head. If that masseur could have got away with such flagrant abuse, then any other fellow could have come along and tried his hand, so to speak.'

I'm afraid your insecurities don't flatter you, Mister Lunatick.

The lunatic looked down again. 'No, maybe not.'

Self-pity is the refuge of the weak, Lunatick, the sanctuary of the mediocre. I'm sure your mentors must have already told you that on countless occasions.

'They have, they have.'

Hmmm.

And then the lunatic said: 'In the end, she claimed that she was forced to leave me.'

Did she give you any reasons?

'I was too intense.'

Too intense?

'Plus, of course, her family would have never approved of a romantic liaison with someone of my background. That much could be read between the lines.'

A disapproval that is perfectly understandable, Lunatick — considering your rather prominent gonial angles, your barely noticeable zygomatic arches and the distinctly mesocephalic measurements of your Western Mediterranean cranium. Miscegenation, although in theory quite a productive exercise, is not everyone's cup of tea.

'I know,' the lunatic replied coldly. 'I have already gone through it all with Drill Sergeant Orestes.'

That's it, Lunatick. Sit there and sulk over the way Nature has made you. Cry your eyes out over the fact you weren't born a W.A.S.P. like the rest of us. Colonial little shits like you never learn, do they? Always trying to subvert the order of things, always moaning and complaining about the lot that life has handed out to them. Can't you see that everything has been pre-programmed? That there is no such thing as individual volition? Freedom is an overflowing pisspot only emptied whenever Dame Chaos decides to shit in it.

The lunatic's lips twisted into a smile.

Go on, laugh. Laugh, if you must. You know what your problem is, sirrah? I'll tell you what your problem is. You have this idealised conception of love that holds no currency — it's as simple as that. You are a dreamer, Lunatick, an idealist, a dealer in the spiritual-metaphysical. So once a woman loved you for your mind rather than for your body — what's the big deal? Wouldn't it have been far worse if she loved you for your money instead? Can't you be satisfied with the fact that you spent some happy days by her side before she left you for someone who — temperamentally, spiritually, as well as physically — was more suited to her than you.

'You're implacable, sir,' the lunatic said icily.

And I'll tell you something else. You think you're so cool, don't you — sitting there in those white overalls, with those leather straps wrapped around you and your hair flopping down wildly over your forehead. A straitjacketed Marlon Brando, a cigarette-less Marlboro man. But do you know what you are? You're just a lunatic conversing with the sound of your own voice — that is all you are, no more, no less. Sorry to dispel the illusion, matey — but that's just the way it is. If you don't wake up to this fact now, you never will. Do you hear what I'm saying, Mister Lunatick?

The lunatic did not answer after that.

9. Novalis the Magician

It was Daniel García's last chance. He knew it the moment he opened the *Gibraltar Chronicle* and saw the ad in front of him — a small, insignificant text box squeezed between a polar bear drinking a bottle of Coca-Cola and a half-page spread for Rock Reliant second-hand car dealers: 'Need a Rock Runner? Come to Reliant and grab yourself a real stunner!' Putting the newspaper down, working up some saliva to moisten his lips, Daniel Garcia reached into his jacket pocket and brought out a cheap black biro. Then he picked up the newspaper again and rapidly and forcefully circled the ad several times with the pen:

Father Eugenio Sánchez Cuevas
We are pleased to announce the arrival of Father Eugenio Sánchez Cuevas, Colombian priest and internationally renowned healer. Father Sánchez Cuevas will be at the Cathedral of Saint Mary the Crowned for tonight's eight o'clock Mass, during which he will be laying hands on the faithful. Everyone is welcome to attend.

**

It was so ironic, Daniel thought as he gazed at the newspaper ad. So incredibly ironic. He had never really believed in priests. He had not even allowed his children to be baptised by them. He had always considered them fakes, imposters, spiritual mercenaries who cashed in on mankind's perennial need to believe in something higher than itself. And yet now he found himself in a position where everything — the prospect of seeing his wife and kids again, his ability to get a new job, even his existence itself — depended on one of these guys....

**

Handwritten note left on Daniel García's coffee table: 'If you get to read this, it will mean that the inevitable has come to pass. I am sorry that things went wrong. I really did change, but you never gave me the chance to prove it. I love you and the kids more than words can say. Please forgive me.'

**

He arrived at Saint Mary the Crowned at five to eight. It was already starting to get dark. The cathedral bells had just stopped ringing and a pair of old women were walking arm-in-arm towards the entrance. Typical mid-week churchgoers, judging by the black shawls on their shoulders and the rosaries wound around their bony hands. Not far from the entrance gates, a street entertainer stood on a plinth trying to win a few final coins before retiring for the evening. Daniel had seen him last time he had been in town — holding a cane and wearing a top hat on his head, each and every part of his motionless body painted in silver. A cardboard sign at his feet had announced the man to a largely indifferent Gibraltarian public: 'Novalis the magician. Juggler, street entertainer and poet of the wondrous soul.' As the women reached the entertainer's plinth, they disengaged from each other and the taller of the two began to arrange her shawl. She did this slowly and laboriously, in that drawn-out, premeditated way that old people have of doing things. 'Do you think it's better now?' she said, twisting her shoulders from side to side so that her friend got a better view. 'Yes, yes,' her companion replied. 'Much better. Shall we go in now?'

Daniel entered the building and sat down on one of the back pews. The smell of melted wax lingered heavily in the air, a dense and sickly-sweet odour that was made even more oppressive by the scorching electrical lights attached to every pillar. A reasonable crowd had gathered to see the Colombian healer. Forty to forty-five people, Daniel thought, turning his head from side to side. Maybe fifty if you included those obscured from his line of vision on either side of the transept. Before he had time to settle on a figure, though, a bell was rung and everyone rose. Coughs, clearing of throats, old bones cracking into position. Moments later, a priest and two altar boys walked out of a doorway behind the altar. The priest was dressed in bright green vestments and looked mightily pleased with himself. The two altar boys plodded on beside him with mischievous grins on their faces. A few paces behind the trio came an elfin man in a black soutane. Heavy, square-rimmed glasses masked the top of his face, giving him a sober, scholarly, somewhat reactionary look. Wisps of grey hair clung tenaciously to his largely bald pate. It did not take much guesswork to figure out that this was none other than the internationally renowned Father Eugenio Sánchez Cuevas himself.

Daniel's participation in the Mass that followed was rather limited. He stood up when the others stood up and he knelt down when they knelt down, but none of the words spoken either by the local priest or the congregation registered properly in his mind. Instead he thought about his wife and two kids. He wondered how they were doing, whether they were missing him, whether his eldest daughter Ayesha had enjoyed her recent birthday. She had turned six only two days ago and Daniel had sent her a card with a twenty-pound note taped inside. It was posted to his wife's parents' address in north Surrey. He wondered if his wife had given the card to Ayesha, if she had used the money to get her a gift, if the card had even been received at all....

It was only when the Colombian priest stood up to deliver the homily that Daniel's attention momentarily returned to what was going on around him. For a few seconds he sat up straight and watched the man adjust the microphone clipped to the lectern. 'The old codger looks anxious,' Daniel García thought, placing his feet on the padded kneeler. 'Visibly irritated.' From a speaker fastened to a nearby pillar, he could hear the swish of the priest's sleeves as he struggled with the retractable microphone, the jangle of the different crucifixes hanging around his neck. 'Does this guy have a clue?' Daniel wondered. Then, all of a sudden, a high-pitched screech blasted out of the speakers. Grimaces, hunched shoulders, looks of general vexation among the congregation. Presently one of the altar boys left his seat behind the altar and rushed to the priest's aid. He tinkered with the microphone for some moments until the screeching stopped and a low, crackling buzz could be heard in its place.

'I have not come here to preach or to tell you what to do,' the visiting priest began in a breathless South American accent. 'I have come to tell you simply that you have within you all possibilities. That is the promise that the Lord has made to you and which is revealed by John in today's Gospel. All you need to do is turn within to Him, and let Him direct your thinking and your desires. Then will your desires come true, your life become one grand harmony, your world a heaven and yourself one with the light of God inside you....'

Daniel raised a hand to his mouth and stifled a yawn....

**

The Mass finished at ten past nine. As soon as the last person had left the building, Daniel got up and started to make his way down the central aisle. He walked resolutely, with his chin held high, trying not to let the marbled splendour of the surroundings overawe him. But when he reached the nail-studded door of the sacristy a wave of last-minutes scruples assailed him. 'How can I go ahead with this when I don't even believe in God?' he thought, shaking his head. 'How can I act like such a hypocrite?' He even began to remember what one of his old RE teachers at school used to say: 'To go to church you must be ready to commune with the Holy Spirit itself. To go there in any less state than this is to commit sacrilege against God and his blessed saints.' He wondered if the same principle applied to what he was about to do now. Was it sacrilegious to seek the help of a faith healer without believing in God? Or did his secret, last-chance longing for redemption at the healer's hands somehow absolve him from that charge? Fortunately for Daniel, his moment of indecision did not last long. Noticing a flicker of movement through the half-open door, he shook his head and told himself not to be so ridiculously impractical. 'So what if I'm committing an act of sacrilege?' he thought, annoyed with the way his conscience tried to sabotage his actions. 'So bloody what? I'm not even supposed to believe in God, *remember?*' Drawing a peculiar sense of comfort from the thought, he took a deep breath and knocked twice on the door. About twenty seconds later, an old man with dark, Coke-bottle glasses appeared framed against the doorway.

'Is it possible for me to see Father Sánchez Cuevas in private?' Daniel asked.

The verger nodded silently and Daniel rapidly found himself walking down a corridor crammed with a series of tall bookcases. Hundreds of ancient, leather-bound tomes could be seen on each side, heaped randomly on top of each other and speckled with silvery cobwebs here and there. Soon the corridor wound its way down some steps and into a small interior courtyard with a stone fountain and a palm tree. It was very dark out there and you could see the night sky through a large, star-shaped aperture in the roof — a gaping black chasm bereft of clouds or stars. To his great surprise, Daniel discovered that he was not the only person waiting to see the Colombian priest. A young couple with a pram were already there.

'Please wait here for a few minutes,' the verger said in a sombre whisper. 'I will take you to *el Padre's* room as soon as he deals with the others.'

**

She said, 'I'm worried.'
He said, 'It's okay, sweetie.'
She said, 'I'm scared.'
He said, 'It's okay, darling.'
She said, 'I'm feeling a bit sick.'
He said, 'It's okay, sugar.'
She said, 'I don't think this is going to work.'
He said nothing.

**

Father Eugenio Sánchez Cuevas was attending to some paperwork. He was sitting behind a large and cumbersome wooden desk, still dressed in the same black soutane. The square glasses he had worn earlier had been ditched and he was now wearing a pair of delicate, rather old-fashioned wire-framed spectacles. A very strong smell, sweet and pungent like ammonia, combined with the reek of mould hanging in the air.

'Excuse me for a second,' the South American priest said, pausing for an instant from his writing. 'Would you care to take a seat while I finish what I am doing? I will only be a few moments.'

Daniel sat down and watched the priest write some lines in a shaky old man's hand. He wondered where the smell of ammonia could be coming from. It was so intense. So overpowering.

'Well,' the priest eventually said, pushing his papers to one side, 'what can I do for you?'

'I'm not sure,' Daniel replied.

'What do you mean, my son?'

'I'm not sure if you can help me. I mean, I don't even know why I'm here.'

'Well,' the ageing priest said, slowly removing his glasses, 'if you have come here, it means that there is a part of you that thinks that maybe I can help. So why not tell me what's wrong and we'll take it from there?'

Daniel looked down at his interwoven hands. 'My wife left me some time ago,' he forced himself to say. 'She took my two daughters with her to her parents' in England and I haven't heard from her since. I've tried to get in touch with her several times, but she is not answering any of my letters or telephone calls. I feel like my whole life has fallen apart. I don't want to carry on living.'

'Have you told anyone else about this? Your desire not to carry on living, I mean?'

'No.'

Eugenio Sánchez Cuevas put his glasses back on. 'Why did she leave you, my son? There must have been a reason.'

'We were not getting along well,' Daniel responded, still looking down. 'We were quarrelling all the time. You know what it is like with couples sometimes.'

'Is that all?'

Daniel shook his head. 'There is something else. I hit her. We had an argument the week before her birthday and she was annoying me so much that I lost control and hit her across the face. I don't know what possessed me. I can't find the words to explain what went through my head. I had never so much as raised a hand to my wife or any other woman until then and I immediately regretted what I had done. I told her that I was so sorry, that I would never do it again — but she would have none of it. "That's it," she said. "I've had enough of this farce. I'm leaving you and you'll never see me or the kids again." ' All of a sudden Daniel looked down, pained by the memory of what he was relating. 'I didn't even get the chance to give her the gold bracelet I had bought for her birthday. It's still lying at home in its case.'

'How long ago was this now?' the Colombian priest asked.

'Six months ago, Father. Six months and three weeks. I've been trying to get in touch with her ever since. I've sent her letters, cards, flowers. I've tried to call her. I've even asked a mutual friend of ours in England to speak to her. I've done everything a man can do, but she's just cut herself off from me as if I never even existed.'

'That's not good,' Eugenio Sánchez Cuevas answered with a solemn look. 'You should at least talk about it. People say and do stupid things in the heat of the moment, but that doesn't mean to say that they can't reflect on things later and change their views. It's part and parcel of us growing up as human beings. By the way,' he continued in a less serious tone, 'what did you write in those letters you sent her? Do you mind if I ask?'

Daniel carried on looking down. 'I told her that I love her and that I'm sorry. That I've realised how much she means to me and how I want to spend the rest of my life together with her and our children.'

Eugenio Sánchez Cuevas looked at him warmly, a touch of paternal affection glinting in his *mestizo* eyes. 'If she loves you,' he said, 'she will come back. She will take the risk to see if what you're saying is true. Even if you hit her like you say you did, she will do so. I've seen women who've been beaten black and blue by their husbands and yet they still ended up going back to them. That's the nature of real love. It repeatedly extends its hand to the beloved. It forgives and carries on forgiving — even when reason and logic are screaming at it not to do so.'

'But what if she doesn't come back?' Daniel asked.

The priest picked up a marble paperweight from his desk and stared at it for some seconds. 'Things happen for a reason, my son,' he said in a calm, matter-of-fact voice. 'You may not be aware of it when they occur, but there's always a reason that becomes clear in time, either in this life or in the life to come. Maybe, if she doesn't come back, it is because you're meant to learn some kind of lesson from it all. Or maybe you had to split up because you were never meant to be together in the first place. There could be an infinity of reasons that we're not aware of. The important thing is to accept that what you're going through is happening for a specific reason. Once you can accept this, then you can start to heal again.'

'But what about my children?' Daniel asked with tears in his eyes. 'What if she doesn't come back? What if she meets someone else and decides I am not good enough for her? What am I supposed to do then? How can I accept I won't ever see my children again? I'm prepared to lose my wife if she finds someone else, Father — that is a pain I'm ready to assume. But my children — how can I accept that I'll never be able to be with them again, to take them to the Alameda Gardens, to drive them to the beach in Spain, to play video games with them at home? How can a man relinquish his own flesh and blood like that?'

'If you take the matter to court,' the priest said, putting the paperweight back on the desk, 'I'm sure that you will be granted regular access to them.'

Daniel looked down at his clasped hands. 'I've already lost my job at the Met office because of my depression, Father. I don't have enough money to fly to England, let alone to fight a court case.'

'There are more mysteries in this world than the human mind can comprehend,' the priest replied, lifting his shoulders in the slightest of shrugs. 'In my own country, homeless children are shot for no reason other than for being out in the street begging for loose change. People get murdered for expressing political views. It would be hard for either of us to see any justification for this. Yet, make no mistake, it is all part of the plan that the Lord has put in place for us all.' He picked up the marble paperweight once again and grasped it tightly. 'It is important to believe this, my son, to accept that there are things in life that go beyond our comprehension. Once you're able to do this, you can carry on living with joy in your heart and peace in your soul, knowing that events are unfolding in the way they are meant to unfold.'

'I don't know if I can accept that, Father,' Daniel replied, suddenly embarrassed that he had burst into tears a few moments ago. 'I think I'd rather kill myself than live with the knowledge that I'll never see my children again.'

The priest looked at him for some seconds and then sighed gently. 'Come here, my son,' he said. 'I will pray for you. I will pray that the Lord may come into your heart and light up this period of darkness that you're going through.... *God is our refuge and strength, an ever-present help in trouble. Therefore, we will not fear, though the earth give way and the mountains fall into the heart of the sea, though its waters roar and foam and the mountains quake with their surging. There is a river whose streams make glad the city of God, the holy place where the Most High dwells. God is within her, she will not fall; God will help her at break of day. Nations are in uproar, kingdoms fall; he lifts his voice, the earth melts. The Lord Almighty is with us; the God of Jacob is our fortress. Come and see the works of the Lord, the desolations he has brought on the earth. He makes wars cease to the ends of the earth; he breaks the bow and shatters the spear, he burns the shields with fire. Be still, and know that I am God; I will be exalted among the nations, I will be exalted in the earth. The Lord Almighty is with us; the God of Jacob is our fortress. In Nomine Patris, et Filii, et Spiritus Sancti. Amen.'*

Daniel thanked the priest and hastily walked out into the courtyard. It was almost totally dark by then and a cold evening breeze was making the palm tree's leaves rustle softly in the pitch-black gloom. Seeing that the verger was nowhere to be seen, he decided to sit down on the edge of the stone fountain. Tears of disappointment quickly gathered in his eyes. 'How could I have been so stupid?' he thought, staring at the outline of the tree beside him. What could a priest know about losing your own children, about never ever seeing the woman who you love again? What could he know about these things, he who was committed to a vow of celibacy and would never experience what it was to see his own children spring out of his loins and blossom with the passing of the years? For a short second Daniel remembered how his hands had trembled while holding the newspaper that morning. He remembered how his heart had suddenly skipped a beat. How could he have been so pathetic, he now thought. So goddamned bloody pathetic! His wife was gone and she would never come back again — that was what it all amounted to. How on earth could a priest have possibly remedied the situation? The bitch had taken flight at the first sign of serious trouble between them and obviously had neither the courage nor the willpower to try to reclaim everything that had once been good and sacred about their relationship. *Why bloody deny it any longer?*

**

'Well,' the verger said, stopping by Daniel's side with a bright torch. 'How did it go?'

'Fine,' Daniel said, forcing out a smile. 'Just fine.'

He stood up and followed the old man back into the vestry. The lights had already been switched off in the building and only the glow from the verger's torch illuminated their way. Daniel watched the beam as it jittered across the marble flagstones, a single shaft of light slicing through the all-engulfing darkness. As they entered the nave a few moments later, he thought he could hear laughter ringing out from somewhere. It was no more than a distant echo, a fleeting blur of sound. But to Daniel it seemed real enough. An absurd idea then crept into his head. He thought that God was laughing at his faithlessness, ridiculing the pathetic, last-minute glimmer of hope that had momentarily led him to abandon his unbelief and come running to the cathedral. 'Yes,' Daniel whispered under his breath. 'Laugh at me. Laugh at the fuck-up I've become. Laugh while you can. You won't be laughing when I put an end to it all.'

**

He had not been imagining things. He realised as much the moment the cathedral doors swung shut behind him and he could hear laughter again, this time coming loud and clear from just down the street. All at once he remembered the entertainer. 'He's probably at it again,' Daniel thought, surprised at how late the man stayed out performing. But his first impressions quickly changed. This was not appreciative laughter that he was hearing; this was vicious and mocking, the echoing, high-pitched cackle produced by a group of aggressive drunks. Nervously, Daniel García stepped forward and peered around the cathedral's entrance archway.

What he saw across the street made Daniel sick to his stomach. The entertainer was still standing on his plinth like he normally did — only this time he was surrounded by a group of pissed-up English sailors. They were all laughing and staggering around him, completely and utterly off their heads with drink. After a few seconds, one of them came forward and kicked the entertainer's cane out of his hand. Then another mooned him. Finally, one of them unzipped his trousers and did something that just about encapsulated their collective intelligence: he began pissing against the entertainer's plinth.

'What is this guy made of?' Daniel thought, staring apprehensively at the sailors from his sheltered position under the archway. 'If he doesn't react now, they're going to slaughter him!'

But Daniel García was wrong. Seeing that the entertainer did not react to their lavatorial provocations, the sailors rapidly got bored. For an instant or two they stood around the plinth, looking dumbly and uncertainly at each other. Then one of them yawned and asked what time it was. 'Time to go find some local bitches,' the guy next to him replied. And then, without further ado, they all walked off — five idiots in Man United and Liverpool shirts who were probably destined to return to their ship later that night in a Royal Navy police van. With a sigh of relief, Daniel crossed the street and picked up the man's cane for him.

'Thank you, my fine fellow,' the entertainer answered in a polished English voice that straight away threw Daniel off guard. 'You are most kind.'

'What is your name?' Daniel said.

'Novalis,' he replied, breaking into a smile that caused the silver paint to crack around the edge of his lips. 'Juggler, magician, street entertainer and poet of the wondrous soul.... And yours, my dear sir?'

'Daniel. Daniel García.'

'Nice to meet you, Mr. Daniel García,' the entertainer said, extending a hand in the same mechanical way that he sometimes used during his act.

Daniel shook his hand and then smiled uneasily, not quite certain what to say next. In the end he blurted out the first thing that came into his head:

'Doesn't it make you sick?'

The entertainer frowned rather quizzically. 'What is that, my fine fellow?'

'The way those people treat you,' Daniel replied, a little quieter.

The man called Novalis shrugged his shoulders. 'It is not the most exemplary behaviour, I must admit, but I can cope with it.'

'But doesn't it really irritate you?' Daniel continued regardless. 'The way those thugs go around? Drinking like pigs? Picking on people they've never even met? I mean, who do they think they are? Have they got no shame or what?... Every time we get the navy in town it's the same, you know. Broken shop windows, scratched cars, overturned rubbish bins, street corners stinking of piss. It really annoys me, you know. Really, really annoys me. People here keep on going on about *free association* with the UK and the rest of it, but what's all that worth, I ask you, what's it all worth when to your Leading Seaman Smith and Petty Officer Brown we will always be a little colony where they can take the piss and do all the things they wouldn't dare do back home?'

The Englishman looked at him pensively for a few seconds. 'Let me tell you a little story, Mr. Daniel García. Some time at the beginning of the eighteenth century there was an English soldier based in Gibraltar. Nothing much is known about him except that he was a drummer and he was a member of Colonel Egerton's regiment. Between 1713 and 1728 this unfortunate soul received 30, 000 lashes, 4000 of these during the space of a single year. If there had been a *Guinness Book of Records* back then, he would have had an entry under the category "Most-flogged soldier in the British Army."'

'What's that go to do with what happened just now?'

'Nothing much, I suppose — except that it shows that *soldiers will always be soldiers* and that today's problems can always be traced back to some hidden psycho-genealogical imbalance or the other.' He then smiled again, suddenly and theatrically. 'Do you know where I can clean my box and wipe off my make-up, by any chance? A respectable family public house, perhaps, or some other similar establishment?'

He decided to take the entertainer to the Castle and Key — a cheap, rundown bar in City Mill Lane that was only frequented by locals. Daniel used to go there some years ago to play pool with his mates, back in the days when his marriage had been free from complications. It was always quiet and relaxed, the kind of place where you could just as easily stuff yourself with tapas as get sloshed on cheap Tequilas and Coke. He was pretty sure that none of its Gibraltarian patrons would take offence to a hybrid between Abraham Lincoln and Metal Mickey.

'I'm a bit confused about something,' Daniel said after they had been walking for a few minutes. 'How come you know so much about local history?'

'I don't,' the entertainer replied, smiling calmly. 'I'm just naturally curious about what's around me.... How about you, my good man?' he asked Daniel. 'Do you have an interest in Gibraltese ... sorry, I mean Gibraltarian history?'

'No, not really. I have enough on my plate without having to worry about the problems of the past.'

'That, my dear sir, is a most reprehensible attitude to have,' Novalis said, pausing by the bar's entrance to let Daniel walk in first. 'You should always make it a point to find out about your past. I know it sounds like one of those insufferable axioms that people love to spout when they have nothing better to do, but, believe you me — and I am living proof of this — if you don't know what has moulded you, quite literally, into who you are, then *how are you going to be ready for what the future has in store for you?'*

Daniel smiled awkwardly and then walked in through the door. The bar was just as he had predicted: empty but for a couple of teenagers playing pool. Behind the counter there was a young guy with a wispy goatee and a pair of large hoop earrings. He was drinking a small glass of beer and watching Real Madrid against Atlético Madrid (or was it Sevilla against Atletico Bilbao?) on a portable television. As the two men came in through the doors, the bartender glanced briefly in their direction and then focused back on the screen again.

'Would you like a drink?' Daniel asked the entertainer. 'I think I can just about manage to treat you.'

'A coffee would be absolutely heavenly,' Novalis answered, already walking in the direction of the bar's toilets. 'I will return as quickly as I have washed my plinth and divested myself of my apparel.'

He appeared about five minutes later dressed in a faded pair of jeans and an old woollen jumper. Apart from a few specks of silver that still clung to his face, the paint had been almost entirely scrubbed off. Without it he looked quite young. About thirty, possibly thirty-five. He also looked very English.

'You are very kind, Mr. Daniel García,' Novalis said, nodding towards the coffee waiting for him on the table. 'Very kind.'

The entertainer brought out a packet of Marlboros from his jeans and offered Daniel a cigarette. The unemployed office clerk accepted it and let the Englishman light it for him. The entertainer then put the packet into his pocket again, without taking a cigarette himself.

'By God, this is a charming place,' Novalis said, looking around him. 'Wonderfully high ceilings. Exceptionally fine cornices. First-class plasterwork.'

Daniel took a puff from his cigarette. 'May I ask you a question?'

'Certainly, my dear fellow.'

'Is your name really Novalis?'

The entertainer smiled. 'My real name is James McAllister. Novalis is just my stage name, so to speak.'

'Why did you take it on?'

'Novalis was a German poet of the late eighteenth century. He wrote poems chiefly about love and death. I suppose you could say that he is one of my main sources of inspiration.'

'May I ask you in what way?'

He paused thoughtfully for a second. 'Apart from being a poet, Novalis was a naturalist and an amateur alchemist. A kind of periwigged flower-power child of the Enlightenment, if you catch my drift. If you read his poems, you will find that there are various recurring themes running through them — love, death, the sacredness of life, the poet's closeness to nature. But, above all, there is one theme that stands above all others — it is the theme of personal growth, of spiritual awakening, of mental and emotional transfiguration. He believed that the most important thing in life was to grow as an individual, to transform oneself spiritually and physically so as to achieve oneness with God.'

Daniel took a sip of his coffee and looked down at the chequered tablecloth in front of him. For a fleeting instant he remembered Father Sánchez Cuevas' face staring at him from the other side of his mahogany desk. The entertainer, he suddenly realised, spoke in the same slow and measured tones as the South American priest, infusing each and every word with a similar sense of importance. He wondered whether this meant that both men shared the same naive attitude to life. It was a real enough possibility. If Daniel had learned something from seeing so many 'New Agers' and other assorted travellers pass through a major crossroads like Gibraltar, it was that a large percentage of them are crackpots, drug-crazed eccentrics — sadly deluding themselves into believing some fantastic lie or the other. Could this guy be the same as the rest of them? Certainly that was the impression that anyone else would have got. And yet there was something about him — a certain dignity, an essential truthfulness behind his words — that seemed to belie the idea.

'Can I ask you another question?' Daniel said.

'Of course, my dear sir. Feel free to ask whatever you wish.'

'Have you always done this for a living?'

'Not always, my friend,' the entertainer replied theatrically. 'Not always. To quote the great Lao Tzu, many paths must be trod before the true path is reached. A very useful axiom — especially for those of us who suffer from permanent, inextinguishable wanderlust.'

'What did you do before, then?'

'Nothing very important, I'm afraid. I was your conventional nine to fiver, your suited and booted reader of the *FT*. Extremely rich, completely stuck-up and about as sensitive to the plight of my fellow brethren as a street lamppost.'

'You mean you were a lawyer?'

'Not I, sir: none of that parasitical foraging into other people's finances for me. I was a PR consultant, a stinging, stabbing, jabbing doctor of spin. A maker and breaker of companies, a restorer of corporate reputations. In brief, I was the very reincarnation of Machiavelli himself.'

Daniel looked at the man for a few seconds and then raised his cigarette to his lips. 'Why did you decide to leave your job and become a street entertainer if you were doing so well?'

The Englishman called Novalis smiled at this point, amiably and kindly, the folds around his mouth contracting into a series of pleasant wrinkles. 'That, my dear fellow, is a complex question — one that would take many hours to answer properly.'

'You mean you don't want to tell me about it?'

Novalis smiled and put his coffee down. 'About five years ago I was a very different person to the one I am now,' he said quietly.

'What do you mean?'

'Have you ever gone through a phase in life where everything you wished for seemed to occur, where all you wanted simply materialised in front of you, just as you had previously imagined it in your dreams?'

Daniel shook his head.

'No,' Novalis replied, looking down, 'I suspected not.'

With those words began one of the saddest and strangest tales that Daniel had ever heard. It all started in the village of Appletreewick, a small, middle-class sanctuary of leafy lanes and landscaped gardens in North Yorkshire. James Herbert Randolph McAllister, eldest son of Thomas Herbert McAllister and Margaret Rachel Fenton, was born there on Sunday the twenty-fourth of April 1954. According to *Moore's 1954 Astrological Almanac*, Saturn, Jupiter and Mars were positioned in the House of Aquarius that day — a triple alignment of the planets believed to be an augury of upheaval and subsequent transformation. Not that any of this manifested itself during the course of James McAllister's childhood and early manhood. Actually, things could not have gone better for him. He was brought up in a loving family; he went to a famous public school in Northamptonshire; he met his future bride-to-be at a party in his parents' house at the age of twelve; he attended Oxford University and obtained a 'first' in Economics. It was all going according to plan — and it only seemed to improve with the passing of each year. After graduating from university, he married his sweetheart and got a high-powered job as a PR consultant in the city of Leeds. He then began to ascend through the corporate ranks — district manager after six months, head of operational planning after nine, director of the Midlands and the North after two years.... Meanwhile, his wife was not doing that badly either. A graduate of Leeds University Law School, she got a job with a leading legal firm and was soon gaining a reputation as one of the best barristers in the county.... Then, at the beginning of 1979, they were blessed with the birth of a baby boy. Named Thomas after his paternal grandfather, he was the most beautiful child anyone could have hoped for, always smiling and laughing, with big blue eyes that exactly mirrored those of his mother. Just three weeks after he was born, his father got promoted again — this time to the vice-presidency of his company. With their joint income, the McAllisters could now afford anything they wanted — regular trips to Paris and New York, dining out at the most expensive restaurants, the very latest designer clothes, a nine-bedroom house on the outskirts of Appletreewick and a *pied-à-terre* in the West End of London....

'Life was like a dream,' Novalis said at this point, picking up his coffee cup and looking at Daniel with a smile. 'Everything I wished for seemed to occur. It is very difficult to describe, but all I had to do was dream it for it to happen, picture it there in my mind and then just wish for it to take place, as if I had been put on this earth with no other purpose than to take everything I wanted out of life.' He stopped smiling and looked down. 'But even dreams have to come to an end — and so it proved with this one.'

It happened on the sixth of January 1981, two weeks before his son's second birthday. On that day James McAllister, flamboyant PR executive and twenty-six-year-old director of one of the country's fastest-growing companies, returned home after work to find that neither his wife nor his son was in the house. 'Strange,' he thought, pouring himself a glass of whisky — *his wife was always home early now that she had cut down her working hours to look after Tommy*. Then he remembered something: he had asked his wife the previous night if she could buy some wine after work. The thought reassured him, made him loosen his grip on the glass. *Obviously she must have returned from work, dismissed the nanny and taken Tommy with her to the shops.* It was quite an important errand, actually. In a few days' time they were having a reunion with some old friends from college, and, as one of them was something of a port freak, he had asked her to drive into Leeds and supplement their regular supply of Ruby with a couple of bottles of the late-vintage stuff. 'Mustn't let that prat Gary think he's the only one with any taste round here,' he had said, laughing.

The hours passed and still there was no sign of them. Eight o'clock came, then nine o'clock, then ten o'clock. By this stage he was quite frantic with worry, biting his fingernails and pacing up the living room when he wasn't sitting down and flicking nervously through the different TV channels. He had already phoned his in-laws twice to see if his wife had decided to pay them an impromptu visit, but each time her father had said that he had not heard anything from his daughter. 'Are you sure everything's all right, James?' the old man asked him in a worried tone at the end of the second call. 'Lucy and you haven't had an argument, have you?' 'No, no,' he quickly replied, trying his best to sound unconcerned. 'She's probably just gone to visit one of her friends. I'm sure she'll be back soon.' Finally, at around half past eleven, the phone rang. Putting down his tenth or eleventh glass of whisky, he got up from the sofa and picked up the receiver. 'Is this Mr. McAllister?' a tired voice said on the other side of the line. 'I'm calling from Leeds General Infirmary. It's about your wife and child. There's been a terrible accident....'

Dropping the receiver, he ran out of the house and started up his car. For the next twenty or thirty minutes he drove without lifting his foot off the accelerator — swerving from lane to lane, beeping his horn at anything in front of him, almost crashing into another car as he went through a set of red traffic lights. At last he got to the hospital. There, in a waiting room with pastel-coloured walls and bright fluorescent lights, they told him the grim reality of what had happened: his wife and child had died in a car accident. She had been on her way into Leeds on the A667. A lorry had veered into her lane on the outskirts of Ilkley and collided with her car. Thomas and Lucy had died instantly, crushed to death in the smashed-up wreckage.

And then the dream suddenly died, it withered away just like that. All those years of happiness, of living without worry — they all faded, disintegrated, slowly went under the darkening horizon. Instead all that remained was guilt, a terrible sense of loss, a feeling that he had indirectly killed his loved ones by asking Lucy to buy that damned wine. To try to escape these thoughts, he would sometimes buy a bottle of whisky and sit with it in his living room, drinking glass after glass of the golden liquid until he would pass out on the sofa. Finally, one morning he could not stand it any longer. With tears in his eyes, he finished what was left of the whisky from the night before and then drove down to the local cemetery where both of them were buried. He did not know what he was going to do there, but he knew that he had to be as near to them as possible. Just before leaving the house, he thrust a flask of brandy and a bottle of Valium in his pocket. 'Maybe these will come in handy later,' he told himself.

'It was, without doubt, the worst day of my life,' Novalis said, lighting himself a cigarette. 'There is a song by the Rolling Stones that talks about how the death of love hurts like a knife. "Love is like a knife," it goes, "a knife that cuts you up and makes you bleed inside." I had never really known what this meant before, but as I walked through the cemetery that windswept morning I knew exactly what Mick Jagger had been talking about when he sang those words. Every step that I took, every second of consciousness — it was all weighed down by pain, by sorrow, by the memory of a love that I had felt for two human beings who had come and gone and were no more. It is difficult to explain this to someone who has never felt it, but I could actually feel it *physically* inside me, twisting and turning continually, this red-hot knife that love can sometimes be, hurting me in a way I had never previously imagined. Because love, my friend, *can* be like a knife — it can be every bit as violent and dangerous as a blade stuck right into your heart. It can also be a beautiful thing, there is no denying it. A beautiful, brilliant light that ignites two hearts and fuses them together in an explosion of the most marvellous colour. But it can also be something much darker and more frightening. Once this is understood, then it becomes clear that, as the great Knut Hamsun once said, love is two things at the same time — *the marguerite that opens wide as night draws on, and the anemone that closes at a breath and dies.'*

He stopped talking at this point and focused his eyes directly on Daniel's. A slight smile could be detected on his lips, his pupils seemed to have dilated under the subdued bar light. Was it mockery flitting across his eyes, Daniel wondered. Was it madness? Or was it just the slow-burning glaze left behind by years of untold suffering?

'Are you acquainted with the legend of the Holy Grail?' Novalis abruptly asked, still gazing straight into Daniel's eyes.

'What?'

'I don't mean the Monty Python film,' he continued in the same breathless, rapid-fire tone. 'Although I must admit I am quite partial to the scene with the coconut shells and the galloping horsemen. I mean the actual medieval romance of the Grail. Told in different versions by Chrétien de Troyes, Robert de Boron and Wolfram von Eschenbach among others.'

'Yes, I'm aware of the story. Why?'

'The Grail saved me that day at the cemetery.'

'What do you mean?'

'I mean, my friend, exactly what I've just said — the Grail changed the course of my life, it brought me back from the edge of the abyss.'

'*Really?*'

Novalis smiled and took a puff from his cigarette. 'You think I'm mad, don't you? You think I'm cracked in the head.... Okay, then. Try this. Imagine you're sitting next to a gravestone. Imagine you've been crying for hours. And now imagine this: imagine that as you rub your eyes and look down, you see a cup lying on the ground. A dirty, broken coffee mug. It is made of white earthenware and has tiny floral motifs inscribed along the rim. It looks cheap and nasty, the type of thing you could buy for less than a pound at a market. You can almost imagine some burly guy with a beer gut and a Cockney accent having once flogged it from his stall. *Get your brand-new coffee mugs here, my luvs! Three for a pound, my darlings! Three for a pound!'*

'Okay. I get the picture. So what happens then?'

'*Voilà!*' Novalis replied, picking up his coffee spoon and brandishing it in the air like a magic wand. 'Sparks fly, splinters of invisible electricity collide, the imagination awakens from its slumber!'

'I don't think I understand.'

Novalis smiled again. 'It's very simple, my friend. That cheap mug made me remember the story of the Grail. More specifically, it reminded me of the moral behind the Grail story. In most versions of the Grail myth, you see, there comes a time when the hero's world is turned upside down, when everything that he has believed in so far has crumbled and he is forced to re-evaluate his life until that point. In particular, there is this moment in the legend when the Grail knight stumbles for the first time into the Grail Castle. In the Castle lives a king who is very unhappy and dejected. He is, to put it bluntly, massively depressed.... Anyway, to save the king — and claim the Holy Grail as his prize — the Grail knight must ask the king the question that no one has dared ask yet. He must ask the question that will make him worthy of the Grail itself. When the wounded king is brought before him, the Grail knight wants to ask, "What ails thee, brother of mine? How can I share your pain?" But, because he is convinced that such a simple question cannot possibly be the one that he is looking for, he decides to ask him something else. Something like: *Pardon me, your highness, but don't you think that this dark and rather lugubrious wainscoting may be affecting your mental well-being?* Or: *With all due respect, sire, wouldn't it be better if you dismissed these quack apothecaries around you and booked yourself into a spa run by some decent, godly German matrons?* You know — the usual patronising rubbish handed out to anyone suffering from a simple humoral imbalance.... So, of course, the inevitable happens: the castle disappears in a puff of smoke and the Grail knight is left standing alone in the middle of a dark forest.... *Alone and weighted down by the knowledge of his failure....* "What have I done?" he thinks, holding his head in his hands, unable to forgive himself for the terrible mistake that he has committed. "Why didn't I follow my heart and ask the king the question I wanted to ask?" '

Novalis put his cigarette out and looked seriously at Daniel. 'At some point in life,' he said, 'we are all a bit like the Grail knight. We look upon the past and we see the mistakes we have made — and the weight of those mistakes crushes us, it takes away our desire to carry on living. But we must go on living all the same. It is like that for everyone. There comes a point when bad things happen. They burn a hole in you and a part of you seems to die. But in the hollow that is left behind something else can grow, something more beautiful than what was there originally. Like Parsifal, we must go out into the world and search for the castle again, ready this time to ask the right questions. It is either that or rotting inside the shell of an empty past.'

'What happened after that?' Daniel asked, somewhat unsettled at how the entertainer's last words related to his own personal circumstances. 'After you found that cup, I mean?'

'I'll tell you what happened,' Novalis responded, lighting himself another cigarette. 'When I returned home that afternoon, I put the bottle of Valium away and went straight to bed. When I woke up later in the day, most of the pain had gone. For the first time I could think about the accident and not feel crushed by the thought. Could even understand that what had happened hadn't been part of some terrible conspiracy against James Herbert Randolph McAllister.'

'Is that when you decided to ... well ... to do what you're doing now?'

'Not exactly, but near enough.' He put his cigarette on the metal ashtray and looked up with a kind smile. 'I know that you have gone through a rough time too. I can see it in your eyes. But whatever it is, Daniel, you can leave it all behind. It is easier than you think.'

What happened next took Daniel entirely by surprise. Suddenly and without warning, he began telling the entertainer everything about himself. He told him how he had slapped his wife and how she had taken their kids away with her; how he had realised the mistakes that he had made, but how he had never been given the chance to put them right again; how he had gone to see the priest that same night, but how nothing that the old man said had made him feel any better; how he would have done anything, *absolutely anything*, to get back together with Andrea and the kids again.

'Let me tell you one of Novalis's most famous stories,' the entertainer said shortly afterwards. 'Once upon a time there was a middle-aged alchemist. He was the most famous alchemist of his day. An erudite and softly spoken gentleman, well known throughout the length and breadth of his province for the profundity of his learning and the incomparable sweetness of his Christian humanist disposition. This fine gentleman didn't drink, didn't gamble, didn't even indulge in any of the pleasures of the flesh. Instead he went to church every morning, prayed to God to guide his hand for the rest of the day and then returned home to spend the next fourteen to sixteen hours engaged in the wholehearted pursuit of his alchemical dreams.... A most worthy and commendable routine, I'm sure you will agree.... Anyway, one day a burst of smoke and fire suddenly leapt out from his furnace and the dream became a reality! Yes, the miracle had finally occurred! He had managed to transform a chunk of lead into a nugget of the purest, shiniest gold! "Jesus, Mary and Joseph!" our friend thought, removing his goggles and picking up the gleaming nugget with a pair of rusty iron tongs. "I've done it! I've actually done it! God's sweet and infinite grace has at last shone down on me!" '

The entertainer looked up and smiled. 'The story should have ended at this point,' he said, exhaling some cigarette smoke as he spoke, 'but it didn't. You see, even though the discovery of the gold represented the realisation of a lifelong dream, it also brought with it a number of unexpected changes, a whole set of brand-new complications. All of a sudden, for example, he became worried that someone would steal his secret, that it would fall into the wrong hands. To stop this from happening, the alchemist destroyed all the copies of his formula except the one safely stowed under his bed. He also stopped going to church and leading the life that he was used to, thinking that the formula could be stolen while he was away from his house. Unfortunately, what he didn't realise was that, rather than keep his secret hidden away like he intended, his behaviour actually started making people suspicious. That is the way life sometimes goes, I'm afraid — *the more you cling to something, the more it slides away from your possession.* And so, alas, it proved in this case. Seeing that he no longer attended church like he used to, some local crooks began to suspect that the alchemist had finally discovered a method of turning lead into gold. "That old dodderer hardly comes into the village any more," their leader remarked one night to his followers. "Bet you the old fool has discovered something." The next morning the crooks rode to the alchemist's house and positioned themselves strategically behind the surrounding bushes. For two days and two nights they waited, hoping that the alchemist would pop out of his house for a while, laughing at the man every time they caught sight of his bald head through the cottage's windows. Finally, on the third day, while the alchemist was away on a short trip to buy some much-needed provisions, they broke into his house and took the formula with them. When the alchemist returned later that afternoon and saw that it had been stolen, he was absolutely distraught. Totally and utterly gutted. He had only one copy of the formula and now it was gone! His life's work, which had taken him years and years to gather, had been cruelly snatched away!

'That same evening the alchemist walked to a nearby cliff and stood there staring at the sea below. For a moment he closed his eyes and thought about jumping into the void ... but then he felt faint and decided to lie down for a while. Finally, exhaustion overtook him and he fell asleep. And then he had a dream. And this is what he saw in the dream: he saw himself working in his laboratory, surrounded by his test tubes and Bunsen burners; he saw himself going to church every morning, praying to God to steer his efforts, thanking Him for giving him the strength to carry on searching for his dream; he saw himself reading through his books at night, annotating key passages in them, trying to draw the connections between them that would unlock the secret he was searching for. He saw himself doing all these things and then he heard a booming voice say, "You crazy, crazy, crazy old fool. It is not the loss of the formula you should be mourning, but the sense of sacredness that once resided in your heart." '

Daniel, however, did not look convinced. 'Is it fair that he lost his formula, though?' he said. 'Is it fair that he should have had it stolen like that?'

'Life is neither fair nor unfair, Daniel,' Novalis replied, rapidly offering him another Marlboro. 'It is just life. *Comprendes, señor?* Look at Parsifal. A nobler and purer soul did not exist at Arthur's court. And yet because he made one mistake, one simple, silly mistake that under normal circumstances would have had absolutely no significance, he was condemned to spend the next five years roaming the land until he found the castle again and this time asked the right question. There was nothing fair or unfair about this. It was just the way life was. The only important thing for him was to learn from his mistake, to use the experience to recreate himself into an even better knight. That's what it's all about, my good Gibraltese man. To carry on believing in yourself, to continue walking through life with faith and self-belief in your heart. That, my friend, *is* the alembic, the distilling apparatus that can turn a frightened, cowering heart of lead into a pure, shiny soul of gold. "The greatest of sorcerers," my dear pal Novalis once wrote, "would be the one who would cast a spell on himself to the degree of taking his own phantasmagoria for autonomous apparition." Or, in other words, *if you want to achieve, you really have to believe.* There is nothing remotely mystical or esoteric about this; it is just the way life is. You see, Daniel, at the end of the day, life is neither a bed of roses nor a blood-soaked minefield; it is just life, a vast ocean of experiences and sensations, neither intrinsically positive nor intrinsically negative. But if you tell yourself often that life is positive, then that is precisely what it will become for you. "Tell yourself the same lie every morning and it will end up turning into a truth" — have you never heard that expression before? No truer words than these — and I use the adjective in its loosest possible sense — have ever been spoken. The man who is positive and has self-belief in his heart tells himself that the world is a place full of opportunities — and this is what it becomes for him;

whereas the man who is negative and has little faith in his abilities tells himself the opposite — and finds himself enmeshed in a world of darkness and despair. It is as simple as this, my friend. That is why I urge you to forget your sadness and start believing in yourself again. I urge you to discard your past and change for the better.'

'She said I cannot change,' Daniel responded sadly, suddenly remembering what his wife had said just before her departure, 'that that is the way I am.'

'She is wrong, Daniel,' the entertainer replied, now visibly trembling with emotion. 'You can change! *You can!* She only says that you can't because she sees you in a certain way and she has told herself that you will never change. It is even quite understandable. You argued and you hit her and now she feels that she can never trust you again — perfectly understandable. But she is wrong — everyone can change. Let me give you an example of what I'm saying. Cynics say that nothing ever changes, that the world will always be a terrible and harrowing place, that mankind's lot will always be entwined with suffering and pain. But they are wrong, Daniel, they are so wrong. Proof of this lies in their cynicism itself — for no one was born cynical and their current outlook in life can only have come about as a result of great personal change. Think about it, Daniel. Please listen to what I'm saying. Babies don't come out of their mother's wombs complaining, "I'm sorry, missus. I'm going back in. Don't want to be part of this miserable life. Too much pain. Too much sorrow. Too much abject suffering. Goodbye." No, sir, of course not. Babies are the uncharted territory of our expectations, the virginal blank folio lying on the escritoire of the human imagination. Do you understand what I'm getting at, Mr. Daniel García?'

Daniel nodded a little warily. 'You mean that we create our own reality or something like that?'

'Yes, yes, yes!' the entertainer said, seizing Daniel's hand and shaking it with manic energy. 'That's exactly and precisely what I mean! Couldn't have put it better myself! You see, Daniel, even if your wife leaves you and takes away your children, even if there seems to be nothing going in your favour, you are always changing — if only to become more disillusioned and cynical about your lot in life. Change is always there, it is an ever-present feature of our lives — and it is up to each and every one of us to grasp this fact, my dear friend, and *change for the better*. All that is needed is belief in oneself, that is all. With this key everything — and I mean *everything* — is possible. It is the key that led David to defeat Goliath — just as it is the key that helps some of us find strength when we are on our last legs. In whatever situation you may find yourself in, Daniel, in whatever psychological, emotional or physical rut life may have placed you, the odds against you diminish a hundredfold when you start believing in yourself! That is why you must forget your sadness and carry on living! Be like the Grail knight and find the hero within you. Search again for the castle and this time ask the right question. Do not waste your life focusing on old memories. She chose to leave you and you must now forget her in turn. Life is too beautiful to be constantly thinking about the ghosts of the past.'

He got up and picked up his plinth. All of a sudden he looked like a totally different man: dark bags had swelled under his eyes and his skin had acquired the sickly grey tone of someone about to collapse with exhaustion.... Unable to understand what was happening, Daniel could only stare at him in open-mouthed surprise.

'I'm going now,' the entertainer said.

'You're going?'

'Yes,' he replied, slowly but insistently inching away from their table. 'I have talked enough already.'

'Are you sure? We can have another coffee if you want.'

'No, thank you,' Novalis responded with a quick shake of his head. 'That would be awfully kind of you, but my caffeine levels have been sufficiently elevated already. Besides,' he added with an apologetic shrug, 'I've remembered I am meeting someone else tonight.'

'Do you want me to give you a lift somewhere then?' Daniel said. 'I've got my car parked about ten minutes from here.'

'No, no — it's okay,' Novalis said, smiling uneasily. 'I prefer to walk. I've got this thing about cars. Sort of like a phobia. I'm sure you understand.'

'What about your platform? Shall I give you a hand with it?'

'No, no, no. I can manage perfectly all right on my own. In fact, I much prefer it that way. Nothing like a bit of good old exercise, after all, is there?'

'Are you sure?'

'Yes. Positive.'

'Really?'

'Yes, of course.... By the way,' he said with a slight bow of the head, a flicker of the old mischievousness resurfacing in his eye, 'thanks for the coffee and the company. It was much appreciated. Novalis the magician — juggler, street entertainer and poet of the wondrous soul — bids farewell to a fellow seeker of Herr Von Eschenbach's Grail.'

He turned around after that and started to walk off. Daniel watched him for some moments as he weaved his way in and out of the tables, surprised as much by the suddenness of Novalis's departure as by the number of people who had come in through the pub's doors without him realising. It was just the kind of eclectic mix you could not escape from on a Gibraltarian Friday night: young lovebirds holding hands over untouched plates of tapas, middle-aged couples slurping down bowls of homemade *callos*, spotty-faced teenagers drinking bottles of Heineken and loudly declaiming their sexual experiences to everyone within earshot. Daniel studied the jumble of new faces for a second, then turned away from them and looked at where the entertainer had just been sitting. He looked at the empty coffee cup speckled with traces of silver. He looked at the spoon lying in a puddle of coffee to the cup's side. He looked at the steel ashtray and the four or five cigarette butts that lay curled like spongy little foetuses on its shiny concave surface. He looked at all these things and then turned his attention to the bar's entrance, just in time to catch Novalis on his way out of the building. 'The poor devil's right,' he thought, watching the entertainer dissolve into the night with his plinth tucked under his arm, 'life *is* neither fair nor unfair.' The thought made Daniel smile. He decided it was time to get up and pay the bill.

10. In the Territory of the Last Things

2nd of November, 199_. Earnings over the last two weeks: 1x£1, 1x50p, 2x20p, 4x10p, 1x5p, 7x2p, 16x1p. Thirty-two coins heaped together on the bottom of a foam cup, with bits of grease and sand and dried moss still stuck on most of them. Why the hell I have got back into this game again is anyone's guess!

3rd of November, 199_. Got up this morning and packed the metal detector into my bag, but bottled it just as I was about to go through the door. End result: remained all day on the sofa smoking cigarettes.

4th of November, 199_. I went to the beach today. The machine beeped quite a few times, but all I managed to uncover was two or three rusty Coke cans and an assortment of aluminium ring-pulls. Pretty much the same kind of shit as always. You would have thought that my experiences over the last few months would have put me off this game for life, but no — pathetic as it may sound — I am still clinging to the hope of pulling off 'the big one' one day.

5th of November, 199_. Couldn't sleep last night. A tumult of thoughts raced through my head. The beach, the pills in my bathroom cabinet, memories of my old friend Manuel, the foam cup on the shelf, the heaviness of my limbs, the voice of my mother begging me not to leave home and, above all, Marsha, always Marsha, her eyes and her lips, her smile and her laughter, her hair and her hips ... like an invisible presence permeating the entirety of my consciousness, like a cancerous growth that has taken root inside me. I think I still love her, as foolish and impractical as that idea might seem.

6th of November, 199_. Another bad panic attack. Occurred as I came back from Safeways with some much-needed cigarettes and bread. Overwhelming sensations of dizziness, of extreme sensory disconnection, as if the soul had become detached from the body and only a lump of flesh and bones remained. To counteract these feelings, I clenched my fists and tightly gritted my teeth, desperately trying to maintain control over my thoughts. Not that this tactic helped much. Within minutes my panic was so great that I was forced to break into a run that did not come to an end until I was safe back in the flat. Lesson to be learned: from now on I will go everywhere on my bicycle.

7th of November, 199_. Cycling down to Eastern Beach this morning, I was almost hit by a car. Great big gold Mercedes, gleaming alloys, tinted windows all around. 'Be careful, *coño!*' I shouted on the spur of the moment, struggling to retain my balance on the bike. As I reached the entrance to the beach four or five minutes later, the same Mercedes suddenly appears from nowhere, blocking my way and almost making me crash to the ground. Out of the car comes this humongous guy, about six foot three and very tanned, with a massive tattoo of a lion peeping out of his Joe Weider muscle vest. A real, 100% authentic Gibraltarian Winston boy.

The Tobacco Smuggler (in a menacing rasp): What did you say back there?

Me: *Qué?*

The Tobacco Smuggler (in an even more menacing tone, with fists clenched): What was that you said earlier, *hijoputa mamón?*

Me (looking down): Nothing. I said nothing.

The Tobacco Smuggler (still angry, but now somewhat placated): Okay. Because next time you say something to me, next time I'm going to get that gayboy bicycle of yours and shove it up your fucking ass, do you hear me, *maricón de mierda?*

(I look down. Pause.)

The Tobacco Smuggler (losing patience again): I said have you heard me?

Me: Yes, yes. I've heard.

At that point the smuggler got back into his car, revved his engine three or four times and then rapidly sped away. As for me, I climbed back on my bike, cycled slowly back home and spent the rest of the afternoon throwing up in my bathroom.

8th of November, 199_. I stayed in today.

9th of November, 199_. Same as yesterday.

10th of November, 199_.

Summary of a typical day.
6.53 Wake up.

6.54 Smoke a Marlboro Light.

6.58 Take one tablet of Dicepin and one of Tryptizol; check tongue for any suspicious signs of discoloration.

7.01 Lie in bed for two hours (staring at the patches of damp on the ceiling and/or thinking about the state of my bank balance, previously fumbled sexual encounters, etc. etc.)

11.12 Eat three slices of bread (unbuttered) and drink a glass of heavily diluted orange squash; take another Dicepin.

11.16 Either (a) consider the mechanics of my failed relationship with Marsha (b) check all the plugs in the flat to make sure they are properly wired.

15.00 Watch *The Jerry Springer Show*.

16.06 Eat six Rich Tea biscuits and drink a glass of heavily diluted orange squash.

17.45 Entertain feelings of little self-worth.

19.11 Eat a Pot Noodle. Take another Dicepin.

21.09 Consider 'Cyclone Betty' and other similarly distressing items on the news.

21.11 Go to bed.

21.12 Repeat what I did at 7.01 this morning.

11th of November, 199_. Tomorrow they disconnect the electricity. I got a letter ten days ago saying that I hadn't paid my arrears for 5 months and that they regretted it very much but they had no option except to switch it off. I guess that my mother was right: it was madness moving out of home without a steady income. I suppose I could always go and tell the pertinent authorities that I am currently a patient of Dr. Esperanza del Río Montes of Algeciras, couldn't I? That would surely force them to give me a few days' reprieve. 'Listen here, Pili,' some fat woman with a perm and lacquered fingernails would probably shout to her superior across the crowded customer service area at the Electricity Department, 'this guy here says he can't pay because he's suffering from clinical anxiety. *Tú sabes* if there's anything in the special cases rule-book about *that?*'

12th of November, 199_. Can't sleep. Feeling very restless.

13th of November, 199_. Spent all morning thinking about my ex-girlfriend. Wondered what sort of job she has now and whether she is still happy with her Irish fancy man.

15th of November, 199_. I went to Catalan Bay today instead of Eastern Beach. I did not find anything apart from a ten-penny piece and two one-penny coins. The ten-penny piece was covered with bits of dried chewing gum.

16th of November, 199_. I do not like detecting at Catalan Bay. There are always *Caleteños* painting/ sandpapering/ inspecting their fishing boats around you and, in addition, you get the impression you are continuously being watched from the houses lining the crescent-shaped cove. If only I wasn't so worried about meeting up with Mr. Winston-Boy again at Eastern Beach!

17th of November, 199_. Searched Catalan Bay for three hours today, but only found a rusty can of sardines. The words *Sardinas* *la Sirena* were engraved on the half-open lid, along with a faded picture of a mermaid. 'For God's sake!' I thought, sitting on the sand and shaking my head in disgust. 'Will I ever get a lucky break?' Seconds later, an old man who was walking his dog on the beach stopped by and asked me if something was wrong. 'Nothing,' I replied, suddenly getting up and slinging the detector over my shoulder. 'Nothing at all.'

And then something very strange happened: I remembered a story that my late grandfather had once told me as a kid. I couldn't remember it in its entirety, but I knew that it featured a beautiful, long-haired mermaid with blue eyes and an exquisite fin and all the other charming attributes that such legendary creatures are supposed to possess. I remembered that the story had been related in the lobby of the Bristol Hotel (my grandfather's regular haunt and the scene of many a frenzied game of backgammon between him and his old cronies) — in the company of a hardened old drunk by the name of Cacciato. I remembered this last part quite distinctly because, until that day, Cacciato had always sat alone and never so much as looked at me or my grandfather. The story itself revolved around a mermaid they had once seen while out fishing on a boat. Isolated fragments remained in my head — Cacciato and my grandfather lost somewhere out in the Straits, a swirling sea-mist suddenly descending upon them, a loud splash to the boat's stern. 'Don't ever breathe a word of this to anyone,' my grandfather added in a whisper at the end of the story, 'for if you do, others will go and capture her and sell her to a scientific organisation, where they will cut her up into little pieces or perform macabre experiments on her.'

Then I remembered something else: Cacciato was a *Caleteño* from Catalan Bay. I remembered this from a phrase that my grandfather had repeatedly used that day at the Bristol Hotel: 'Fancy getting lost in the Bay with *un Caleteño!*' Intrigued by the thought, I shuffled up the slipway leading out of the beach and made my way towards Paqui's Shop, the only grocery store in the village.

'Excuse me,' I asked a plump teenager with red cheeks who was standing behind the counter. 'Could you tell me if someone called Frank Cacciato lives near here?'

'Frank Cacciato?' she said, chewing on some gum. 'Nah, don't think so.' Then, turning around: 'Ma, *tú sabes* if anyone called Frank Cacciato lives round here?'

'What's that?' a tired, asthmatic voice shouted from inside the shop's storeroom.

'Do you know someone called Frank Cacciato?' the young woman hollered back, still chewing gum.

A short while later, the mother appeared by the storeroom door. She was small and pale and her hands had the gnarled look of someone who's been working hard all her life. An original *Caleteña*, if ever there was one.

'What was that you said?' she asked her daughter.

'Frank Cacciato,' the girl repeated for the third time, by now doodling idly on a sheet of greaseproof paper on the counter. 'Do you know if he lives round here?'

'Frank Cacciato?' the woman muttered with her hands on her hips. 'Yeah, he used to live here some years ago.'

'Is he dead?' I asked.

The woman shrugged her shoulders. 'Don't know,' she said, picking up an empty cigarette packet that her daughter had left on the counter. 'They took him to the Golden Twilight Home when he lost his marbles a few years ago. Why do you want to find out?' she asked.

'I'm writing an article on old Gibraltarian fishermen,' I lied for no particular reason, 'and I just wanted to see if I could interview him.'

'Well,' she said, walking back into the storeroom, 'even if he is still alive, I doubt whether you'll get much sense out of him. That guy was never quite right in the head.'

**

It is now over three hours since I got back home from the beach and I can't stop thinking about Cacciato and what the woman at the shop told me. The thought of him losing his head, I must confess, feels really strange. I can still visualise him all these years later — the square boxer's chin, the grey stubble, the matted locks of black hair streaked with greasy threads of silver. Could such a guy really have broken down like that? Could he really have lost his marbles? He seemed so tough and so hard, a man who no longer cared what life threw at him. I find it all difficult to comprehend.

18th of November, 199_. Cycled to the Golden Twilight Retirement Home this morning after doubling my dose of Tryptizol and throwing in an extra Dicepin for good measure. Arrived there dripping in sweat and cursing the place for having been built so high up and so far away from the town centre (First rule of architectural topography: nothing's a coincidence). From the outside, the building looked exceptionally grim and uninviting, built in that ghoulish shade of greyish-brown brick you see in most English inner-cities: a monument to the functionalism of the sixties as much as a reminder of our copy-cat colonial mentality. For a second or two I wondered whether going in was such a good idea — but in the end my breathlessness, not to mention the dull ache in my legs, forced me off the bike and I soon found myself entering a poorly lit lobby that reeked of cheap floor polish.

'Excuse me,' I asked a middle-aged woman who was typing away behind the reception desk. 'Do you know where I could find Frank Cacciato, please?'

'Go upstairs,' the woman replied without looking up from her typewriter. 'He should be in the TV lounge.'

'Do you think my bike will be okay outside?'

'You what?'

'My bike,' I repeated, swallowing hard. 'I've chained it to a lamppost outside. Did you think it will be okay?'

'Yes, of course. Why wouldn't it be okay?'

I thanked the woman for her time and made my way to the upstairs lounge. A dozen octogenarians were sitting in a semicircle around an old television. Tired yellow eyes, glinting white stubble, lingering hints of ammonia. Trying to make as little noise as possible, I approached an old woman on a wheelchair and asked her if she knew where I could find Cacciato.

'He's over there,' the old lady said in a squeaky voice. 'No use in talking to him, though. Won't say a word. He's a stuck-up snob who has nothing to say to anyone. Why don't you stay here and talk to me instead?'

I gazed at where the woman had pointed and saw an old guy with a denim baseball cap and a tartan shawl spread across his lap. Thanking the old lady for her help, I walked over in Cacciato's direction.

'Hello, Mr. Cacciato,' I said, slowly extending my hand towards the old geezer. 'My name's Peter Rodriguez.'

I waited for a few seconds, but Cacciato didn't respond. He didn't even stop looking at the TV. It was only now, standing less than a foot away from him and seeing the paper-thin texture of his skin, that I realised how old the bugger was.

'My name's Peter Rodriguez,' I began again after a few moments. 'Alfred Mahoney was my grandfather. Do you remember him?'

'He won't talk to you,' the old woman croaked from the other side of the hall. 'He doesn't talk to anyone. *Es un verdadero malaje, ya te lo dije.* Why don't you come here and talk to me instead? I'm a very good conversationalist, you know.'

The old woman laughed coquettishly; someone else in the hall sniggered. I could feel the situation slowly slipping out of my hands.

'Mr. Cacciato,' I pressed on, by now quite flustered. 'My name's Peter Rodriguez. Alfred Mahoney was my grandfather. Do you remember him? He used to go to the Bristol Hotel to play backgammon. He used to take me with him sometimes. Once you and my grandfather told me this story about a mermaid. I was just a little kid, but I still remember it. Do *you* remember it, Mr. Cacciato?'

I looked at him with a pleading expression, but there was still no reaction. In the meantime, the old woman had pushed her wheelchair across the lounge and was now trying to take hold of my arm. ('Let's get married,' she said to the sound of general laughter. 'I'll cook and I'll do the washing for you and I'll even suck your dick every now and then!') As if this wasn't enough, one of the old men across the room suddenly got up and began to tell me about his chances of success at the next Olympic weightlifting contest — rolling up his sleeve and showing me his atrophied biceps just to prove the point. 'This is getting ridiculous,' I thought. Gently disengaging the old woman from my sleeves, I prepared to leave.

And then: 'What do you want from me?'

I turned around immediately. 'Did you speak?'

'You heard,' Cacciato snarled back.

'I just wanted to talk to you,' I replied, not knowing what else to come up with. 'About my grandfather, the Bristol Hotel, the story you told me.'

Cacciato looked at me wearily for a few seconds and then looked away. 'I'm too tired to talk today,' he said in a rather less irritated tone. 'Come back tomorrow.'

19th of November, 199_. Stayed at home all day smoking cigarettes next to the living room window. Two thoughts occurred to me: (a) that everyone who walked past the window — a long-haired postman, a belching drunk, several children on their way to school, a pregnant woman pushing a pram — all of them carried their moment of death engraved somewhere inside them (b) that life was like the solitary candle flickering on my coffee table — a sliver of light between two eternities of darkness.

20th of November, 199_. Went to the Golden Twilight Retirement again this afternoon. Made my way to the TV lounge without telling the woman on reception. Found Cacciato sitting in a corner with an old copy of *Hola*. He looked much more alert — and much healthier — than two days ago.

'It's true,' he said as soon as he saw me walk into the room.

'What's true, Mr. Cacciato?'

'The story about the mermaid,' he replied calmly, almost measuring my reaction to his words.

It was not exactly what I wanted to hear. Either the old boy's taking the mickey, I thought, or senile beyond the point of redemption. For a moment I wondered whether coming to see him again had been a wise move.

'You don't believe me, do you?' Cacciato said, a wry smile forming on his lips. 'Not that I expect you to. That's the problem with you young people nowadays. You have no faith in anything.' He pointed to an empty chair across the hall. 'Bring that chair over here, will you? Take advantage of our five-star fittings.'

'Did you know my grandfather well?' I asked, still standing.

'Did I know your grandfather well?' he said, considering the question. 'Yes, I suppose that I did.'

'Where did you know him from?'

Cacciato smiled evasively. 'I have a picture of the mermaid, you know. Your grandfather had this old monstrosity of a Kodak. Cost a bomb back then. If you look hard enough, you can just about see the mermaid's tail.'

'That's very interesting,' I muttered rapidly. 'Do you remember when you first met Alfred Mahoney?'

He looked down and sighed resignedly. 'Do you see that old gal over there?' he asked.

I looked at where he pointed and nodded.

'Do you know that she shits herself every hour?' he said without any discernible emotion. 'But that's not all. Sometimes she likes to spread her shit across her hands and face.' He paused. 'Like a soggy old chocolate éclair.'

I shook my head and looked down. Cacciato removed his cap and flattened a few strands of hair against his scalp. Moments later, he told me four things that I never knew about him and my grandfather.

1) that they had been best friends at school.
2) that when the Second World War broke out my grandfather's family paid their way to Jamaica, whereas Cacciato and his family, having no money to go anywhere, were forcibly evacuated to London like the majority of working-class Gibraltarians.
3) that, while in Jamaica, my grandfather accosted Cacciato's girlfriend and future wife (who, coming from a

rich family herself, was also there) and made all sorts of lewd suggestions to her.

4) that, when the war ended and they all returned to Gibraltar, she told Cacciato about my grandfather's romantic sallies and that, apart from that day at the Bristol Hotel (when my sweet cherub's smile had brought them fleetingly together), Cacciato and my grandfather never spoke to each other again.

'Impressive story, isn't it?' he said sarcastically. 'Could be made into a fine film, wouldn't you agree? Olivia de Havilland and Errol Flynn roaming through the Jamaican plantations, while the faithful Trevor Howard dodges the V1s and the V2s in London. Quite a lot of potential there, don't you think?'

'Is that why you always used to sit there drinking without saying a word?' I asked.

'That wasn't because of your grandfather,' Cacciato said, staring at the magazine on his lap. 'That was because our only son had died of cancer a couple of months earlier.... By the way, you'll come to visit me another day, won't you?'

It was mainly small talk after that. The state of the weather, the kind of food they ate at the home, the latest results in the Spanish football league, the sexual escapades of some of the residence's randier octogenarians, the political vagaries of the current government. It continued like this until about quarter to seven — at which time Cacciato fell asleep and I, having nothing better to do, cycled down to my unlit and unheated council flat in Queensway.

21st of November, 199_. Didn't feel like going to the Retirement Home today. Stayed at home instead and smoked cigarettes by the living room window.

22nd of November, 199_. Spent about two hours with Cacciato today. We talked about his time in London during the war and the different jobs he'd had there. He told me that his first job had been at the Lyons factory in Richmond, loading and unloading sacks of sugar for two pounds and three shillings a week. He then moved to the Rolls-Royce factory in White City, where he cleaned aircraft parts with diesel oil before packing them in boxes. He said that he really liked this job, but in the end was forced to quit because of the constant taunts (which, even though he could hardly speak English at the time, he understood well enough) of his fellow workers. He also told me that his nickname at both factories was 'the refugee' — quite ironic, I thought, considering that the British had removed him from a relatively safe Gibraltar and deposited him in London at the height of the Blitz. Again and again I found myself wishing I had been carrying a tape recorder with me.

23rd of November, 199_. I told Cacciato many things today. I told him about Marsha and my university debacle. I told him about my short time smuggling and about Manuel's disappearance at sea. I told him about my 'big argument' with my parents and how I moved out of their flat shortly afterwards. I told him about my electricity being switched off and my having no money in my bank account. I told him about my depression and my metal detecting at the beach. I told him about all these things and he listened with an air of genuine interest — although he still couldn't understand why it was I didn't have a job.

24th of November, 199_. Cacciato told me that I shouldn't be so depressed today. He said that I was just a kid and that I should know better than to get so depressed.

25th of November, 199_. We had an argument this afternoon. He told me that I should stop thinking about Marsha (like it was clear to him that I was still doing) and that I should get on with the rest of my life. 'If that bitch had really loved you,' he said, 'she wouldn't have abandoned you just like that. She would have moved heaven and earth just to be with you. You're simply wasting your time thinking about some broad who isn't worth it.' He then told me to forget about her and to start looking for the love of my life who was out there somewhere waiting for me. He told me to be positive and to have faith and to feel glad that I was alive and healthy and had the whole world at my feet. 'Life is such a gift,' he said. 'You can't imagine what a crime it is to let it slip you by.'

This was too close to the bone to be left unheeded. 'What about you, then?' I immediately snapped back. 'You tell me to be so positive and yet you sit there looking like the most miserable bastard in existence. Tell me, where's the sense in that?'

Following a short silence, Cacciato looked up at me and said these words: 'As you think in your heart, so shall you be.'

26th of November, 199_. He told me the same thing again. That life was a gift, that it is sacrilegious to waste it, etc. etc.

27th of November, 199_. Went to visit Cacciato this afternoon, but a nurse told me that he was transferred last night to the sick ward with a pulmonary complaint. I hung around for a while in the hope that I would be allowed to see him, but in the end I got tired of waiting and cycled back home.

28th of November, 199_. Was allowed to see Cacciato for ten minutes today. He had several tubes connected to his body and a drip attached to his left arm, but he still seemed happy to see me. He told me that he was feeling much better and that one day he'd come with me and show me where he had seen the mermaid. 'As soon as they get rid of all these tubes,' he said, wheezing noisily, 'I'll slip out of here one night and use my mate Freddie Tarano's boat to sail us there. It's something I've been meaning to do for many years now.' He then wanted to tell me all about Freddie's boat, but a nurse came in and said that I could not stay any longer.

29th of November, 199_. He is worse again. One of the nurses told me there's a chance he may not live for more than twenty-four hours. She also said it was a shame that Cacciato had no living relatives.

30th of November, 199_. 'The old boy's still hanging on in there,' the nurse said today. I don't know why, but I thought I detected a faint tone of mockery in her voice.

1st of December, 199_. Got told at seven this evening that Cacciato had died three hours earlier. The news made me feel dizzy and weak. The nurse who I thought yesterday was being sarcastic gave me a glass of water and said there was something that Cacciato had left for me just before he died. She then brought out a plain yellow envelope with the word 'Peter' written on it in a shaky hand. I thanked her for it and quickly left the building. Once out in the street, I walked over to the lamppost propping up my bike and opened the envelope, pulling out a very old black and white photograph from inside. I studied the photograph for a few seconds, but could distinguish nothing except a mass of foam and bubbles on a dark black background. 'So this is your mermaid,' I thought, sadly shaking my head. Then I turned the photograph over and saw the following words inscribed on the back: 'Faith and imagination are one and the same thing. Never forget that, my boy.' The words froze my blood, made me feel as if Cacciato himself was standing there beside me. *The cheeky old devil*, I thought with a smile. Putting the photograph back into the envelope, I turned around and started walking down the hill. Who needs an old Raleigh bicycle in a small place like Gibraltar, after all?

THE END

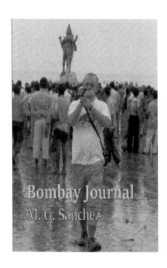

Imagine that you come from one of the world's smallest micro-territories. And that you have a lifelong dislike of crowds.

Now imagine that you wake up one day and find yourself in a mega-city with eighteen million residents and a population density thirty-three times higher than central London.

Imagine the sounds, the crowds, the smells, the endless traffic, the mixture of exhilaration and panic coursing through your veins....

"M. G. Sanchez chronicles the highs and lows of his three-year residency in India with unflinching honesty, opening a novelistic window on India's 'maximum city.'"

Dr Esterino Adami, Department of Oriental Studies, University of Turin.

In July 2013, just as a full-blown diplomatic row was erupting between Britain and Spain over the Rock of Gibraltar, Joseph Sanchez collapsed and died while cycling in Taraguilla, a Spanish village twenty miles north of the border. In this honest and sensitively written memoir Gibraltarian author M. G. Sanchez relates the hardships his family endured while trying to repatriate his father's remains during one of the most acrimonious phases in recent Gibraltarian history. Part-family memoir, part-act of remembrance, *Past: A Memoir* mixes personal reminiscences with political and historical commentary in a shifting, multi-layered narrative which explores – and vigorously upholds – what it means to be Gibraltarian.

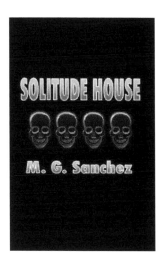

Meet Dr John Seracino, predatory ladies' man and born misanthrope. All he wants in life is a property free of any annoying neighbours. But Seracino has a problem: he resides in Gibraltar, where almost everybody lives in flats and where detached properties come at a premium. For the last few years he has been attending property auctions in the hope of bagging himself one of the old colonial bungalows that intermittently come up for sale. So far, though, he keeps getting outbid by lawyers and bankers, men for whom the annual £90,000 that Seracino earns as a GP are no more than small change. Then one day Seracino's luck changes and he manages to land himself an old colonial property in the Upper Rock area, the aptly named Solitude House. For the first couple of weeks the misanthropic doctor sits every evening on his newly refurbished veranda, looking out over the Bay of Gibraltar with a glass of his favourite alcoholic tipple. But events are about to take an unexpectedly nasty and frightening turn....

Jonathan is a member of the Bishop Audley Children's Home. He has been an orphan since the age of three. He is a strange kid – quiet and self-absorbed in some ways, but violent and ill-tempered in others. One day he slips halfway through a street fight and is repeatedly kicked in the head. From this time on he is beset by the strangest of conditions: he can hear voices near places where crimes and misdeeds have been committed in the historical past.... *Jonathan Gallardo*, M. G. Sanchez's third novel, is one of those books that defy generic classification. On one level it is the story of a working-class Gibraltarian kid striving to improve his lot in life . . . but at the same time it is an exploration of Gibraltar's largely forgotten colonial history – or what the narrator of the novel at one point describes as 'an unrecorded history of division and conflict that wasn't supposed to exist but which nonetheless oozes like spectral mould out of Gibraltar's crumbling ancient walls.'

"So this, more or less, was how things stood for me at the end of 1981. I was twenty-nine years old and I was still on the lowest rung of the civil service pay scale and I lived alone in a three-bedroom government flat with twenty-four different sized statues of the Sacred Heart of Jesus...."

Spanning over ten years and moving between locations as different as Cambridge, Venice and Gibraltar, *The Escape Artist* (2013) is a novel about loneliness and broken friendship and what it means to be Gibraltarian in a rapidly changing world...

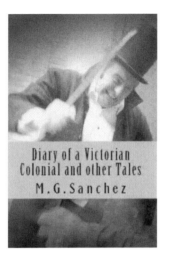

Diary of a Victorian Colonial and other Tales consists of three pieces centred on the themes of emotional and geographical displacement. The first and longest of these is set in late nineteenth-century Gibraltar, a British outpost known throughout Christendom for the intemperance of its military men and the contrabanding conducted by its civilian classes. Into this fin-de-siècle world enters Charles Bestman, an Anglo-Gibraltarian returning home after twenty-five years of exile in mainland Britain. What is the infamous criminal stain that follows Bestman's name and why is he so reluctant to let anyone know about his past? The exilic connection continues in 'Intermission' and 'Roman Ruins', two modern-day tales which explore the problems faced by individuals when trying to recreate themselves outside their home environment.

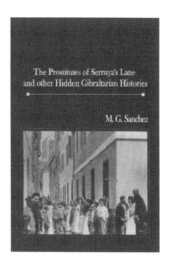

'Smugglers and swindlers, pimps and prostitutes, grog-sellers and generals, soldiers, sailors and ship chandlers, all lived cheek by jowl ... within Victorian Gibraltar.' So wrote the British historian Ernle Bradford in his 1971 study *Gibraltar: the History of a Fortress*. Nearly forty years later, Gibraltarian scholar and writer Dr. M. G. Sanchez uncovers part of this lost world in *The Prostitutes of Serruya's Lane and other Hidden Histories* (2007), a groundbreaking new book of essays on smuggling, prostitution, racism and other little-known aspects of Gibraltar's Victorian history. If you want to know what life in a nineteenth-century British military fortress was really like, then make sure to pick up this book. You will never view the Rock again in the same light....

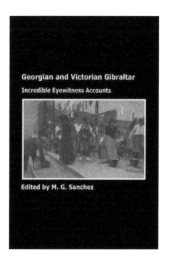

Georgian and Victorian Gibraltar
Incredible Eyewitness Accounts

Edited by M. G. Sanchez

Drunken sailors, dandified English officers, hard-bitten Gibraltarian boatmen, polyglot Jewish rabbis, winsome Moroccan traders, moustachioed Spanish smugglers, cigar-smoking American adventurers, irascible Catholic priests, hoity-toity British military Governors – these and other emblematically colonial figures are to be found in *Georgian and Victorian Gibraltar: Incredible Eyewitness Accounts* (2012), a large collection of curious and surprising writings about eighteenth- and nineteenth-century Gibraltar compiled by M. G. Sanchez and published by Rock Scorpion Books.

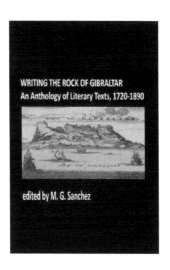

WRITING THE ROCK OF GIBRALTAR
An Anthology of Literary Texts, 1720-1890

edited by M. G. Sanchez

Byron described it as 'the dirtiest and most detestable spot in existence'; Coleridge complained that the onset of the Levanter Cloud made him ill with 'a sense of suffocation' that caused his tongue 'to go furry white and his pulse quick and low'; the Scottish writer John Galt thought that the same was 'oppressive to the functions of life, and to an invalid denying all exercise'; Thackeray was entranced by the mixture of 'swarthy Moors, dark Spanish smugglers in tufted hats, and fuddled seamen from men-of-war' sauntering through Gibraltar's Main Street; Benjamin Disraeli thought that the Rock was 'a wonderful place, with a population infinitely diversified'. These and other comments about Gibraltar are to be found in *Writing the Rock of Gibraltar: an Anthology of Literary Texts, 1720-1890* (2006), a new volume compiled by M. G. Sanchez.

Printed in Great Britain
by Amazon

79938771R00141